WHO KILLED FRANK?

THE HARRY STARKE NOVELS
BOOK 26

BLAIR HOWARD

Print PaperbackISBN: 979-8-9988024-7-8

Cleveland, TN, USA

This book is for the thousands of Harry Starke fans who've stuck with me throughout the twenty-five previous novels, and made it possible for me to do what I do. Thank you one and all.

PROLOGUE
CHATTANOOGA RIVERWALK

Ten years ago

JENNIFER MORRISON NEVER SAW IT COMING.

She'd been jogging the same route along the Riverwalk for three years, ever since she'd started her senior year at the University of Tennessee at Chattanooga. The path was well lit, well-traveled during daylight hours, and seemed safe enough. She always carried pepper spray and ran with her cell phone, and she'd never had so much as a close call.

But tonight was different.

The October air was crisp, and full of the scent of fallen leaves and the muddy smell of the river. Streetlamps cast pools of yellow light along the riverside path, with deep shadows in between. Jennifer had started late—her statistics study group had run longer than expected—but she needed the run to clear her head before tomorrow's exam.

She'd just passed the old boat ramp near Coolidge Park when she heard footsteps behind her. Not unusual—other joggers often used the path, even at night. She glanced over her shoulder and saw a figure about fifty yards back, keeping pace with her steady rhythm.

She frowned. Something felt wrong.

The footsteps were too measured, too deliberate. When she sped up, they sped up. When she slowed to check her phone at a streetlamp, they slowed too. The hair on the back of her neck stood up, and she felt that primal warning that had kept humans alive for millennia.

Jennifer reached for her pepper spray, fumbling in the small pocket of her running jacket. Her fingers found the canister just as the footsteps suddenly accelerated behind her.

She spun around, raising the spray, but her attacker was already too close. A gloved hand knocked the pepper spray from her grip, sending it clattering into the darkness beyond the path. She opened her mouth to scream, but another hand clamped over her face, cutting off the sound.

"Don't fight," a voice whispered in her ear. "It'll be easier if you don't fight."

But Jennifer Morrison was a fighter. She'd been captain of her high school volleyball team, had taken self-defense classes in college, and wasn't about to go quietly. She bit down hard on the hand covering her mouth and drove her elbow back into her attacker's ribs.

The grip loosened for just a moment—long enough for her to break free and run. She made it maybe twenty yards before strong hands grabbed her from behind, tackling her to the ground beside a cluster of trees that blocked the view from the main road.

"You shouldn't have done that," the voice said, no longer whispering. There was something familiar about it, something that made her stomach clench with a different kind of fear.

She tried to roll over, to see her attacker's face, but firm hands held her down. She felt something tighten around her throat—not hands, but something else. Something that cut into her skin and made it impossible to breathe.

"Please," she gasped, the word barely audible. "Please, I won't tell anyone. I won't—"

The pressure increased. Her vision began to tunnel, dark spots dancing at the edges. She clawed at whatever was around her neck, her fingernails breaking as she fought for air that wouldn't come.

In her final moments, as consciousness slipped away, Jennifer Morrison thought about her little sister Lisa, who was supposed to graduate from the police academy next month. Lisa was going to be so proud, finally following in their father's footsteps into law enforcement.

Lisa would find her killer, Jennifer thought. Lisa would make sure justice was served.

THE JOGGER WHO FOUND JENNIFER MORRISON'S BODY AT SIX-thirty the next morning would later tell the police that she looked almost peaceful, lying among the fallen leaves beside the riverside path. Her running clothes were neat, her hair arranged carefully around her shoulders. If not for the ligature marks around her throat and the purple tinge to her lips, she might have been sleeping.

Detective Frank Callahan was the first investigator on the scene. He stood over the body, his weathered face grim as he studied the positioning, the careful arrangement of the victim's limbs. *This wasn't random violence*, he thought. *This was something else entirely.*

"What do you think, Frank?" his partner, Detective Mike Rodriguez, asked, crouching beside the body. "Looks like our boy has himself a signature."

Frank nodded slowly, his gray eyes taking in every detail. Twenty-six years on the force had taught him to read crime scenes like books, and this one was telling him a story he didn't like.

"Get the area cordoned off," he said. "Double the usual perimeter. And call in the photographer. I want every angle documented before we move her."

An hour later, as the crime scene team began their work, Frank walked the perimeter of the scene, looking for anything the killer might have left behind. The October morning was still and quiet, with early commuters beginning to fill the nearby streets. Normal people were going about their normal lives, unaware that something evil had walked among them the night before.

Frank found the pepper spray about fifteen yards from the body, partially hidden under a pile of leaves. He marked it with an evidence flag and continued his search. Near the tree line, he discovered signs of a struggle: disturbed earth, broken branches, drag marks leading toward where the body was found.

"Frank?" Rodriguez called. "Come take a look at this."

Frank walked back to where his partner was examining the victim's neck with a magnifying glass.

"See these marks?" Rodriguez pointed to the ligature impressions. "They're too uniform for a rope or cord. My guess is we're looking at some kind of wire or thin cable."

Frank leaned in for a closer look. The marks were indeed precise, the kind that would be made by something designed to cut through material—or flesh—efficiently.

As the morning progressed and the crime scene team worked, Frank interviewed the jogger, Sarah Grant, who'd found the body. Sarah was in her forties, a regular runner who used the path every morning before work.

"I noticed her right away," Grant said, wrapping her arms around herself despite the warming morning air. "She was just lying there so still. At first I thought maybe she'd fallen and hurt herself, but when I got closer..." She shuddered. "I called 911 immediately."

"Did you see anyone else on the path this morning?" Frank asked. "Anyone who seemed out of place?"

Grant shook her head. "It was quiet. Sometimes I see other early runners, but not today. Just her."

Frank thanked her and sent her on her way, then returned to the body. The medical examiner had arrived and was conducting his preliminary examination.

"What do you think, Doc?" Frank asked.

Dr. Richard Sheddon looked up from his work. "Strangulation, obviously. But look at this." He pointed to the victim's fingernails. "She fought back. We might have some DNA under here."

Frank felt a spark of hope. DNA evidence was the holy grail. It had already helped solve several cases in Chattanooga. If they could get a profile from the killer...

"How long has she been dead?" he asked.

"Based on rigor and liver temperature, I'd say between ten and twelve hours. So between seven and nine last night."

Frank scribbled it down in his notebook, already forming a timeline in his mind. Evening jogger, isolated location, signs of struggle followed by careful positioning of the body. This killer had taken time with his work, which suggested either supreme confidence or local knowledge of the area.

As the body was loaded into the medical examiner's van, Frank stood looking out over the Tennessee River. The morning sun was reflecting off the water, and in a few hours, this would be a pleasant place again, filled with joggers and dog walkers and families enjoying the riverside park.

But right now, it was a crime scene. And Frank Callahan had a killer to catch.

He had no way of knowing this was just the beginning, and that over the next eighteen months, nine more women would die along this same stretch of river. Or that the case would consume his career and ultimately cost him his life.

All he knew was that Jennifer Morrison deserved justice, and he was going to make sure she got it.

Even if it killed him.

1

OLD WOUNDS

Present Day

FRIDAY AUGUST 12

"DADDY, CAN WE GO FISHING TOMORROW?"

I looked down at my six-year-old daughter, Jade, as she snuggled against me on the sofa. Her jade-green eyes, so much like her mother's, stared up at me with a hope that was almost palpable. She'd been asking me the same question every day for a week.

"It's supposed to be a beautiful day," Amanda said. She was sitting in the armchair opposite us, a glass of red wine in her hand.

"Sure, sweetheart," I replied. "First thing after breakfast."

"Promise?"

"I promise."

Promises to a six-year-old are sacred things, not to be

broken lightly, if at all. Jade's smile was worth all the gold in Fort Knox.

Amanda gave me a small smile over the rim of her glass. She knew how much I valued these quiet evenings at home with my family. After all we'd been through, the normal and mundane had become precious, a treasure to be hoarded and savored.

The call came at nine-fifteen, just as we were tucking Jade into bed. I felt the vibration in my pocket but ignored it until we'd finished the nightly ritual of a story, a kiss, and turning on the night light shaped like a mermaid that threw shadows of sea creatures across the ceiling.

"Sleep tight, princess," I said as I pulled her door almost closed.

Amanda was waiting for me in the hallway, leaning against the doorframe, her arms crossed. "Your phone. It's still vibrating."

I sighed and pulled my iPhone from my pocket. The caller ID showed Kate Gazzara. This late, it couldn't be good news.

"Kate, what's up?"

"Harry." Just one word, and I knew. Something bad had happened. Really bad. Her voice was tight, controlled, with an edge I'd learned to recognize over the twenty-four years I'd known her.

"What is it?"

"It's Frank," she said. "Frank Callahan."

Frank had been my mentor when I joined the force back in '97. A legend in the department. One of the old-school detectives who'd taught me more about policing than all my training combined.

"What about him?"

"He's dead, Harry. Murdered."

The world tilted slightly on its axis. Frank had retired three years ago after thirty-three years on the force. He'd been looking forward to fishing, traveling, and doing all those things cops promise themselves they'll do someday.

"When? How?" I asked.

"About two hours ago, in his home. I need you to come, Harry. Now."

"Kate, I'm not a cop anymore_"

"This isn't official. This is..." She paused, and I heard the strain in her voice. "He was my friend, too. This is personal. Frank would want you here."

Amanda was watching my face, her expression shifting from curiosity to concern.

"I'll be there in twenty," I said, ending the call.

"What's happened?" Amanda asked.

"Frank Callahan's been murdered."

"Oh my God." Her hand went to her mouth. She'd met Frank several times, even interviewed him once for Channel 7 when he retired. "Was it a robbery?"

"I don't know yet. Kate wants me at the scene."

"Go," Amanda said, placing her hand on my arm. "We'll be fine."

I kissed her quickly, grabbed my jacket from the hall closet, and headed for the garage. As I backed my Range Rover out of the driveway, a heaviness settled in my chest. Frank Callahan had been one of the good ones. One of the best.

Frank's house was a modest single-story ranch in East Brainerd, a quiet middle-class neighborhood where most of the residents had lived for decades. As I pulled up to the curb, I counted three police cruisers, Kate's unmarked Charger, the medical examiner's black SUV and an ambulance. The area was cordoned off with yellow crime scene tape, and a couple of uniforms stood at the perimeter, keeping the small gathering of neighbors at bay.

Kate met me at the tape. She looked exhausted, her tawny blonde hair pulled back in a ponytail, her hazel eyes shadowed. She was wearing lightweight black pants, black shoes with flat heels, and a white tee under a tan buckskin vest. The Glock 26 on her right hip completed the ensemble.

"Thanks for coming," she said, lifting the tape for me to duck under.

"What happened?"

She gestured toward the house. "Let's go inside."

I followed her up the narrow concrete path to the front door. Two crime scene techs were dusting the frame and doorknob for prints. Kate nodded to them as we passed.

The living room was neat, almost obsessively so. Nothing seemed out of place. No signs of a struggle. A single lamp burned on an end table next to a recliner where a book lay open, face down, a pair of reading glasses resting on top.

"Who found him?" I asked.

"A neighbor," Kate replied. "Mrs. Packard from next door. They had a standing dinner date every Sunday. When he didn't show up and didn't answer his phone, she came over. The door was unlocked, which she said was unusual. She called it in when she found him."

Kate led me down a short hallway to what had apparently been Frank's home office. The sight that greeted me turned my stomach, and I've seen a lot over the years.

Frank Callahan lay on his back in the center of the room, his arms spread wide, his legs straight. He was wearing khaki pants and a blue button-down shirt, now soaked with blood from the multiple stab wounds that punctured his chest and abdomen. His eyes were open, staring lifelessly at the ceiling.

But it was the arrangement around him that made my blood run cold. Photographs had been placed in a perfect circle around his body, each one positioned with meticulous care. I knelt down to look at them without touching anything. They were crime scene photos. Young women, all strangled, all posed by the Tennessee River.

"The Riverside Strangler," I said softly.

Kate nodded. "Frank's obsession. Even after he retired, he couldn't let it go."

The Riverside Strangler had terrorized Chattanooga for eighteen months a little more than ten years ago. Ten victims, all women in their twenties, all strangled, all left in similar poses along the banks of the Tennessee River. The case went cold, and despite Frank's best efforts, the killer was never caught.

Doc Sheddon was crouched beside the body, making notes. He looked up. Doc was a small man, five-eight, over-weight, almost totally bald, with a round face that usually sported a jovial expression, but not today. For some reason, not his appearance, he always reminded me of Bilbo Baggins.

"Harry. I didn't expect to see you here." He glanced at Kate. "Unofficial, I take it."

Kate nodded. "Strictly unofficial."

"Time of death?" I asked.

"Between seven and nine this evening," Doc replied. "Multiple stab wounds to the chest and abdomen. One penetrated the heart. That was the kill shot, so to speak. The others..." He shook his head. "The others were overkill, or a message. Take your pick."

I studied the room. Aside from the body and the arranged

photos, it was neat, like the rest of the house. A desk with a computer. Filing cabinets. Bookshelves. A bulletin board covered with notes, photos, and maps connected by red string.

"Was anything taken?" I asked.

"Hard to tell," Kate said. "Nothing obvious. No signs of forced entry. Mrs. Packard said the door was unlocked but not open. Frank's wallet was still in his pocket with cash and credit cards. Watch, ring, everything of value seems to be here. His gun was still in the desk drawer."

"No, this wasn't a robbery," I said, shaking my head. "Whoever it was had an agenda. The photos, the positioning... It's a statement."

Doc stood up with a grunt. "I'll know more after the autopsy. From what I can see, though, he put up a fight. Defensive wounds on his hands and forearms. Bruising consistent with being held down. Whoever did this had to be strong—Frank was a big man—or there was more than one attacker."

"Any chance this could be a copycat?" I asked. "Someone mimicking the Strangler cases?"

Kate shook her head. "The Strangler strangled. This is a completely different MO. No, this feels personal. Someone with a connection to Frank or the original case."

I moved closer to the bulletin board. It was covered with information about the Strangler cases. Photos of victims, timeline charts, witness statements, maps showing locations where bodies were found, all connected with a complex web of red string. Frank had been working this case hard.

"He never let it go," Kate said, coming to stand beside me. "After he retired, it became a full-time obsession. He kept saying there was something we all missed, some connection we failed to make."

"Once a cop, always a cop," I muttered, then turned to look at Kate and said, "Did he ever say that?"

"No. Just that he was getting close. Last time I spoke with him was three days ago. He called me. He sounded excited. He said he'd found something, a missing piece, and he wanted to check one more thing before he shared it."

I turned to look again at the body, at the man who'd been like a second father to me. Surrounded by the ghosts of his greatest failure, murdered before he could solve the case that had haunted him for almost a decade.

"Why am I here, Kate?" I asked quietly. "Beyond the obvious of identifying the body, which you didn't need me for."

Kate glanced around to make sure no one else was within earshot. "Because Frank didn't trust anyone else. Not with this case. He told me once that if anything ever happened to him, I should bring you in. He said you were the only one who might be able to see what he saw. So, you want in?"

It had been a while since the last time she brought me in as a consultant, but still. I grimaced. "You don't need me, Kate. You're as good a detective as I ever was and—"

"Oh, for Pete's sake, stop it," she snapped, cutting me off. "You're still the best detective I know. And Frank trusted you. Whatever he found, whoever killed him because of it, they're still out there." She held my gaze. "Will you help me, or not?"

I looked down at Frank's body one more time. The man who'd mentored me, who'd believed in me when others didn't, who'd taught me what it meant to be a good detective. I owed him this much.

I nodded slowly, tilted my head to the right, looked at her

and said, "Yeah. I'll help, but you'll need to clear it with the chief."

Kate nodded. "That shouldn't be a problem. Thank you."

"I'll need access to everything Frank was working on," I said. "All his notes, files, everything."

"That might be tricky," she replied." Officially, this is just a homicide. I can't divert resources to reopen the Strangler case without authorization."

"Then we'll do it our way," I said. "I'll get my team on it first thing tomorrow."

"I don't know about that…" she trailed off, staring at me.

"They're the best at what they do," I said. "If there's anything to find, we'll find it."

Kate nodded slowly. "Okay. But keep me in the loop. This is still my case."

"Always," I promised.

As we turned to leave, something caught my eye. A small notepad on Frank's desk, partially obscured by an overturned coffee mug. I pointed it out to Kate.

"Was that processed yet?"

She shook her head. "I don't think so."

Carefully, using a pen from my pocket, I moved the mug. The notepad was blank except for a single line scrawled across the top page: "Catherine Wells is alive."

Kate's sharp intake of breath told me she recognized the name immediately.

"Catherine Wells," she said. "Victim number four."

I stared at the words. If Frank was right; if a supposedly dead victim of the Riverside Strangler was actually alive after all these years...

"Things just got a lot more complicated," I said.

"If Frank was right," Kate replied, "then everything we

thought we knew about the Riverside Strangler cases was wrong."

I took one last look around the room, at the meticulous murder board, at the photos arranged around Frank's body, at the cryptic note. Frank had found something, something worth killing for.

"I'll find who did this, buddy," I muttered. "And I'll finish what you started."

As we left, I could already feel the weight of Frank's last case settling onto my shoulders. Ten years of unanswered questions. Ten victims—or maybe nine, if Catherine Wells really was alive. One obsessed detective now murdered.

And somewhere out there, a killer who'd just made a very big mistake.

2

GHOSTS AND REVELATIONS

SATURDAY, AUGUST 13

I RETURNED HOME TO FIND AMANDA WAITING IN THE LIVING room looking more than a little concerned. She'd changed into her silk pajamas and robe, but I could tell she hadn't been sleeping. The empty wine glass on the coffee table and the way she was curled up in her chair told me she'd been worrying.

"How bad is it?" she asked as I closed the front door behind me.

I walked over and kissed her forehead before settling into my usual spot on the sofa. "Bad. Really bad. Someone stabbed Frank multiple times in his home office, then made it look like it was connected to the Riverside Strangler case."

"The serial killer from ten years ago?"

I nodded. "Ten victims over eighteen months, then nothing. The case went cold, but Frank never stopped working it. Even after he retired three years ago, it consumed his life. He was convinced there was something they missed, some connection that would crack the whole thing wide open."

Amanda leaned forward, her pale green eyes reflecting the lamplight. "And tonight someone killed him for it?"

"That's what it looks like. The killer arranged crime scene photos from all ten Strangler murders around Frank's body. Ten photos in a perfect circle, like some kind of sick tribute."

Her hand went to her throat. "My God, Harry. Who would do such a thing?"

"Someone who either knows that case intimately, or someone who wants us to think they do." I rubbed my eyes; I was tired. "Frank left a note. It said Catherine Wells is alive."

"Catherine Wells?"

"The fourth victim of the Riverside Strangler. Except maybe she wasn't a victim at all. Maybe she survived and Frank found out about it."

Amanda was quiet for a moment, processing this information. She'd covered enough crime stories as a journalist to understand the implications.

"If she survived," she said slowly, "then everything about that case changes."

"Everything," I agreed. "And if Frank was close to proving it, that might be motive enough for murder."

"You're going to work it, aren't you?" she asked quietly

I looked at her, this woman who knew me better than I knew myself. "Kate asked me to consult. Unofficially."

"Then you should. Frank was important to you. He deserves justice." She paused, then added, "But what about tomorrow? You promised Jade you'd take her fishing."

I heaved a deep breath, grimaced, then said, "Amanda, I hate it, but I'll have to cancel. I need to get my team on this right away, and I want to go through Frank's house again when it's not crawling with crime scene techs."

Amanda nodded, understanding but clearly not happy about it. "She's going to be heartbroken. You know that, right?"

"I know. But this can't wait. Frank's killer is out there, and every hour we delay gives them more time to cover their tracks or disappear entirely. I'll make it up to her. I promise—" I could have bitten my tongue off.

"Another promise, Harry?" she asked as she rose to her feet. "Come on. We both need to get some sleep."

The next morning, I had one of the worst conversations of my parenting career. Jade was already dressed in her fishing clothes when I came downstairs: little pink coveralls and a Tennessee Volunteers cap that was too big for her head. She was in the kitchen, bouncing with excitement.

"Daddy, I got the tackle box ready!" she announced, pointing to the small pink plastic box Amanda had bought her for her birthday. "And I made us sandwiches!"

My heart sank as I looked at the lopsided peanut butter and jelly sandwiches she'd attempted to make, more filling on the counter than between the bread slices. This was going to be even harder than I'd thought.

"Jade, sweetheart, we need to talk."

Her face fell immediately. At six years old, she was already learning to read the tone in adult voices that meant disappointment was coming.

"We're not going fishing, are we?" she asked, her voice small.

"I'm sorry, princess. Something very important came up with work. A friend of mine was hurt, and I need to help find out who did it."

Her face crumpled, and the tears came fast and hard. "But you promised, Daddy," she sobbed, her small body shaking with disappointment. "You told mommy promises to little girls are sacred. I heard you."

The words hit me like a punch to the gut because they were my own words, thrown back at me by my six-year-old daughter. I knelt down to her level, my hands on her shoulders.

"I know, princess. And I'm sorry. Sometimes grown-ups have to deal with very serious problems, even when we don't want to. Even when it means breaking promises we want to keep."

"Is it because of the bad man who hurt your friend?"

Trust Jade to cut right to the heart of it. "Yes, sweetheart. I have to help catch the bad man."

She wiped her nose with the back of her hand and looked up at me with those huge jade-green eyes. "Will you catch him soon so we can go fishing?"

"I'm going to try my very best," I replied, sincerely.

Amanda appeared in the doorway, still in her robe, and took in the scene with a single glance. She knelt down beside Jade and pulled her into a hug.

"How about this, baby girl?" Amanda said. "When Daddy catches the bad man, we'll have a special celebration fishing trip. Just the three of us, and we'll pack a picnic lunch with all your favorite foods."

Jade's tears slowed. "With peanut butter and jelly sandwiches?"

"With peanut butter and jelly sandwiches," Amanda confirmed. "And those little cheese crackers you love, and maybe some of those cookies from the bakery downtown."

"The ones with the sprinkles?"

"The ones with the sprinkles," Amanda replied, smiling at her.

Jade considered this for a moment, then looked back at me. "Promise you'll catch the bad man quick, Daddy."

"I promise I'll do everything I can."

She thought about this, then nodded solemnly. "Okay. But next time, can the bad man wait until after fishing?"

Despite everything, I found myself smiling. "I'll see what I can do."

Amanda walked me to the garage twenty minutes later, after we'd gotten Jade settled with cartoons and her favorite stuffed animal.

"She'll be okay," Amanda said, reading the guilt on my face. "Kids are resilient."

"I hate disappointing her."

"I know. But she also needs to understand that sometimes duty comes before pleasure. You're teaching her something important about responsibility."

I kissed her goodbye, breathing in the familiar scent of her shampoo. "I'll make it up to her."

"I know you will. Just be careful, Harry. If someone was willing to kill Frank..."

"I'll be careful," I promised, though we both knew that careful wasn't always possible in my line of work.

An hour later, I was at my downtown office, assembling my team in the conference room. The morning sun streamed through the tall windows, casting long shadows across the polished oak table where my investigators waited for their briefing.

Tim Clarke sat hunched over his laptop, fingers already flying across the keyboard. At twenty-seven, he looked more like a college student than one of the most skilled digital investigators in the Southeast. His dark hair was perpetually disheveled, his glasses slightly crooked, and his t-shirt proclaimed "There Are Only 10 Types of People: Those Who Understand Binary and Those Who Don't." He'd already consumed what looked like his third cup of coffee, judging by the empty cups scattered around his workspace.

TJ Bron occupied his usual chair at the far end of the table, his seventy—two year-old frame still ramrod straight despite the early hour. The Marine veteran's steel-gray hair was cut military short, and his weathered hands were folded precisely in front of him. Despite his age, he was still one of the most dangerous men I knew. His service record included two tours in Vietnam and more classified operations than I cared to think about.

Heather Stillwell sat between them, looking professional in dark slacks and a navy blazer that concealed her service weapon. At forty-five, she maintained the kind of fitness that made both criminals and clients take her seriously. Her short brown hair was perfectly styled, and her sharp brown eyes missed nothing. She'd been taking notes in her neat handwriting even before I'd started talking.

Jacque Hale sat at the opposite end of the table from TJ, her posture as perfect as always despite the early hour. My business partner and personal assistant was thirty-five but looked a decade younger, her coffee-and-cream skin flawless and her bushy black hair pulled back in a professional style. She wore a charcoal business suit that managed to look both authoritative and elegant, and her dark eyes were already focused on the legal pad where she'd been taking notes in her precise handwriting. Born in Jamaica, Jacque had earned her MBA from Vanderbilt and a bachelor's in criminology from The University of Tennessee, Knoxville, making her far more than just an assistant. She ran the business side of our operation with the same attention to detail that made her invaluable during investigations, and her protective instincts about our clients and our reputation made her the perfect gatekeeper for sensitive cases like this one.

"What do we have?" Heather asked as I took my seat at the head of the table.

While Jacque took notes, I spent twenty minutes walking them through everything I'd observed at Frank's crime scene. The positioning of the body, the arranged photographs, the note about Catherine Wells, and Frank's decade-long obsession with the Riverside Strangler case.

"Ten victims over eighteen months," I concluded. "Then the killing stopped. Frank was convinced the investigation missed something crucial, and he'd been working the case privately for years, even after retirement."

TJ leaned back in his chair, his expression thoughtful. "Eighteen-month killing spree ending abruptly suggests either the killer died, was imprisoned for something else, or moved away."

"Or got scared when one of the victims survived," Heather added, making another note.

Tim looked up from his screen, pushing his glasses up his nose. "I'm already pulling everything I can find on Frank's digital life. Computer files, internet searches, email accounts, phone records. If he was researching Catherine Wells, there'll be a trail. Frank was old school, but he understood the value of digital documentation."

"Good," I said. "But be careful about how you access police databases. We want everything legal and defensible."

"Define legal," Tim said with a grin.

"Tim!" I said, staring at him, my eyes narrowed.

"Okay, okay. Mostly legal. I'll be careful."

I turned to my field investigators. "I also want comprehensive background checks on all ten original victims and their families. That's a lot of people who might have strong feelings about the case never being solved."

TJ nodded, already making notes in his leather-bound notebook. "We'll start with the families," he said, "then expand to friends, coworkers, and anyone who had a connection to the victims. Ten murders means dozens of people who felt let down by the investigation."

"What about Frank's personal enemies?" Heather asked. "Thirty-three years as a cop means he put a lot of people in prison. Any of them might hold a grudge."

"Kate's handling the official investigation into Frank's background, but see what you can find independently. Cross-reference any recent releases from prison with the timing of Frank's murder."

"I can run those databases," Tim offered. "Prison releases are public record, and I can cross-reference with known associates, family members, anyone who might have held Frank responsible for their conviction."

"Do it," I said. "Also look for any cases Frank worked where the conviction was overturned or where there were allegations of misconduct. Sometimes the guilty hold grudges, but innocent people wrongly convicted can be just as angry."

Heather leaned forward. "What's our timeline on this? If Frank's killer thinks they've successfully misdirected the investigation toward the old serial case, they might be planning to disappear."

"We work fast but thorough," I said. "Tim, I want you to crack Frank's computer encryption as soon as possible. If he was building a case around Catherine Wells, his files will tell us what he found."

"Already on it," Tim said, his fingers resuming their dance across the keyboard. "Frank used pretty good security, but I've seen better. Give me a few hours."

My phone rang, interrupting our planning session. Kate's name appeared on the screen.

"Kate, what's up?"

"Harry, I've got preliminary autopsy results from Doc Sheddon. Can you come down to the station?"

"On my way." I ended the call and turned back to my team. "Get started on those assignments. I'll be back in a couple of hours with more information. Jacque. I need a minute, please."

As the team filed out, I gestured for Jacque to stay behind. She closed the conference room door and turned back to me.

"What do you need?" she asked, taking out her phone and opening her scheduling app.

"I need you to clear my calendar for the next week," I said. "Cancel everything non-essential, reschedule what you can."

"Done," she said as her fingers flew over the screen. "What about the McIntyre insurance fraud case? You're supposed to testify on Wednesday."

"See if they can postpone it. If not, we'll work around it." I leaned against the conference table. "I also need you to work with Kate. She's going to be sharing information with us, and we need to make sure everything stays above board."

Jacque nodded, making notes. "And your status at the PD?"

"Kate called while I was on the road. Chief Johnston approved it this morning. But Jacque, this case has some unusual legal implications. I need you to research something for me."

"What kind of implications?"

I chose my words carefully. "What are the legal ramifications if we discover someone who was officially declared dead is actually alive? Someone who's been living under a false identity for years."

Jacque's eyebrows rose slightly. "That's... complicated. Are we talking witness protection?"

"Maybe. Or maybe someone who faked their own death. I need to know what we're walking into if we find this person. What laws might have been broken, what our obligations are, how it affects any insurance payouts or legal proceedings from when they were presumed dead."

"Identity fraud, insurance fraud, possibly tax evasion depending on how long they've been using false documents," Jacque said. "And if they were running from something criminal..." She trailed off. "Harry, this sounds dangerous."

"It might be. Frank was killed because of what he discovered. Just research the legal angles for now. I need to know what we're dealing with before we go any further."

Jacque studied my face for a moment. "Be careful, Harry. And keep me posted on everything. If this gets complicated legally, I want to know immediately."

"Always do," I said, heading for the door. "Hold down the fort while I'm gone."

THE CHATTANOOGA POLICE DEPARTMENT OCCUPIED A MODERN, two-story building on Amnicola Highway. Kate met me in the lobby and escorted me to her office on the second floor.

"So," she said, settling in behind her desk. "Here we are again. Thanks, Harry. I appreciate it more than you know."

"You really don't need me, Kate," I said. "You're a great

detective and…" I reached down to scratch Samson behind the ears, "…you have a great team."

"Yeah, well," she replied, a little self-consciously, I thought. "Let's get to it shall we?"

"Doc worked through the night on Frank's autopsy. It's complete."

She handed me a folder containing Doc Sheddon's preliminary report. I scanned the technical language, translating the medical terminology into plain English.

"Seven stab wounds total," I said, reading aloud. "One to the heart was fatal, the others were…" I looked up at Kate. "Torture?"

"That's Doc's assessment," she replied. "The non-fatal wounds were inflicted first, probably to get information. The killer took their time."

"Military-style knife," I said as I made notes on the report margins. "Six-inch blade, thin, probably a stiletto or something similar. Interesting." I looked up at her. "I take it the weapon hasn't been found." She shook her head. "Defensive wounds?" I asked.

"Extensive. Frank fought hard. Doc recovered textile fibers from under his fingernails, so we'll have something to work with, but no DNA, unfortunately. He sent the fibers to the lab for processing."

"How long will that take, I wonder?"

"He put a rush on it, so maybe forty-eight hours." Kate said, leaning forward. "There's more, Harry. Frank's neighbors reported seeing a dark sedan parked on his street around seven PM yesterday. It was gone by the time uniforms canvassed the area."

"Any description of the driver?"

"No. But there's something else." Kate pulled out another

file. "I went through Frank's phone records. He'd been getting calls from unknown numbers for the past six weeks. Short conversations, usually less than a minute."

"Threatening calls?" I asked.

"That's what I thought initially. But I talked to Mrs. Packard, Frank's neighbor. She said Frank had mentioned getting calls from 'crackpots who won't let sleeping dogs lie.'"

I looked up from the autopsy report. "People tired of his questions about the Strangler case, I suppose."

"That was Frank's take on it," she said. "But what if they weren't random calls? What if someone was monitoring his investigation and warning him to back off?"

"And when he didn't back off, they killed him," I muttered as I watched Samson wander back to his bed under the window.

Kate nodded grimly. "It fits the timeline. The calls started about six weeks ago, which matches when Frank's research into Catherine Wells intensified."

My phone buzzed with a text from Tim: "Need you back at office ASAP. Found something big."

"I have to get back to the office," I told Kate. "Tim's found something."

"Keep me posted," she said.

———

TWENTY MINUTES LATER, I WAS BACK IN MY CONFERENCE ROOM, where Tim was practically vibrating with excitement. His laptop was connected to the large wall monitor displaying a complex file directory.

"I cracked Frank's computer encryption," he announced. "And Harry, this is incredible. Frank was building a complete database of everything that was wrong with the original investigation."

The monitor showed folders labeled with dates, victim names, and investigative categories. Hundreds of files, representing years of meticulous work.

"He documented every inconsistency, every piece of evidence that didn't fit the official narrative," Tim continued. "Look at this folder labeled 'Financial Irregularities,'" Tim said, clicking on it to reveal dozens of files.

"Financial irregularities?" I asked, moving closer to his screen.

"Frank was tracking money flows that didn't make sense," Tim explained, opening several spreadsheets. "Look at these bank records. Someone's been moving substantial amounts of cash through shell companies over the past several years."

Heather leaned closer to the screen. "How much money are we talking about?"

"Hundreds of thousands," Tim replied. "And the timing correlates with several dismissed criminal cases in Chattanooga. Every time a major case got thrown out on technicalities, money moved between these accounts within days."

"Someone's been paying for case fixing," TJ observed grimly.

I studied the financial data Tim was displaying. "Frank was following the money trail. He suspected corruption, not just an unsolved serial case."

"There's more," Tim said, opening another file. "Frank had been documenting evidence tampering in multiple cases over the past decade. Missing files, altered witness statements, compromised chain of custody procedures."

"All connected to the Riverside Strangler investigation?" I asked.

"Not all of them," Tim replied. "But there's definitely an overlap. Someone's been systematically corrupting investigations, and it looks like Frank was getting close to identifying who."

I leaned back in my chair, processing the implications. "This isn't just about solving old murders," I said. "Frank had stumbled onto active corruption, and someone killed him to shut him up."

"The question is," Heather said, "was it about the Strangler case specifically, or did Frank threaten to expose something bigger?"

"Maybe both," I replied. "We need to dig deeper into these financial records. Keep at it, people. In the meantime, I'm going to take another look at the crime scene."

Twenty minutes later, I was at Frank's house. The crime scene tape was still up, but the uniformed officer at the door recognized me and let me in. I stood for a moment in Frank's living room. The silence hung heavy around me. The house felt empty in a way that went beyond the absence of furniture or people. It felt... hollow, the air thick. It felt like it was, a place where something terrible had happened, and the walls themselves remembered.

I made my way to Frank's office, stepping carefully around the bloodstain that marked where he'd died. In the light of day, with no crime scene techs bustling around, I could see details I'd missed the night before.

The murder board dominated one entire wall, but now I understood what I was looking at. It was a methodical dismantling of an official investigation that Frank believed had been either botched or deliberately sabotaged.

I studied the photographs of all ten victims, arranged in chronological order. Jennifer Morrison, the first victim, smiled out from her college graduation photo. Lisa Haldon, the waitress, looked tired but happy in what appeared to be a candid shot. Sarah Mitchell wore scrubs in her photo—the nurse who'd dedicated her life to helping others.

Each victim had their own section on the board, with notes about inconsistencies in their cases.

I found myself focusing on the fourth victim's photograph. Catherine Wells had been twenty-three when she was attacked, a graduate student in art history with dark hair and intelligent eyes. According to the case file, she'd been jogging along the river path when the Riverside Strangler grabbed her. Her body was supposedly found the next morning, but Frank had circled several inconsistencies in red ink.

"No body recovery photos," read one note. "Cremation ordered immediately." Another said, "Family refused viewing —claimed too traumatic."

But the most telling note was recent, written in Frank's careful handwriting: "Insurance payout $500,000 despite no body. No follow-up investigation."

I took out my phone and took pictures of Frank's murder board, focusing on the Catherine Wells section. Tim would want to see this when we compared it to the digital files he'd recovered.

As I worked, I heard a car door slam outside. I moved to the window and saw a dark sedan parked across the street— the same type of vehicle Kate had mentioned from the neighbor reports.

My hand moved instinctively to my weapon as I watched the car. The windows were tinted too dark to see inside, but someone was definitely sitting in the driver's seat.

I decided to take the direct approach. I walked out of Frank's front door and straight out into the street toward the sedan, my hands visible but ready to draw my weapon if necessary.

The car started immediately and pulled away from the curb, accelerating quickly down the residential street. I got a partial license plate—Tennessee tag beginning with "HDL"—but the driver remained invisible behind the dark glass.

Someone was watching Frank's house. The question was whether they were watching for me, or for Catherine Wells.

I called Kate as I walked back to the house.

"Kate, someone just ran surveillance on me at Frank's house. Dark sedan, Tennessee plates starting with HDL. Can you run that partial?"

"On it. Are you okay?"

"Fine. They took off when I approached the car." I paused at Frank's front door, looking back down the empty street. "Kate, I think we're being watched. Someone knows we're investigating this case."

"Then we'd better solve it fast," she replied.

I ended the call and went back inside Frank's house, but the peaceful atmosphere was gone. Someone out there was keeping track of our investigation, which meant Frank's killer was still in the game.

3

DIGITAL FOOTPRINTS

SATURDAY AFTERNOON, AUGUST 13

I WAS BACK AT MY OFFICE BY FOUR-THIRTY THAT AFTERNOON, my mind churning over the surveillance car and what it meant for our investigation. Someone was definitely keeping tabs on our movements, which suggested Frank's killer was still actively involved rather than hoping the misdirection would be enough.

Tim was exactly where I'd left him, hunched over his laptop with the wall monitor displaying what looked like a digital archaeological dig through Frank's computer systems. Coffee cups littered his workspace, and his hair stood up at odd angles from running his hands through it.

"Frank was paranoid," Tim said, finally looking at me through his slightly crooked glasses. "He created multiple backup systems and dead-man switches. I think the guy was preparing for exactly what happened to him."

I stared up at the wall monitor. It showed a complex directory structure with hundreds of folders organized by date, case number, and subject matter. It represented years of obsessive documentation.

"He'd been using dark web resources to track people living under new identities," Tim continued, clicking through folders. "Expensive stuff, Harry. Frank was paying serious money for information that's not easy to come by."

"How much are we talking about?" I asked.

"Based on his financial records, he spent over forty thousand dollars in the past year alone. Bitcoin transactions, encrypted communications, the works. He was buying access to databases that most law enforcement agencies can't even touch."

I whistled low. "On a cop's pension?"

"That's what's interesting. Frank had money coming in from somewhere else. Look at this." Tim opened a financial spreadsheet showing Frank's bank accounts. "His pension was sixty-two thousand a year, but he was paying out, like, an additional forty to fifty thousand annually, but I haven't yet been able to figure out where his money was coming from."

"Consulting work, you think?" I said.

"Maybe. But there's no paper trail, no invoices, no business records. Just regular cash deposits over the past three years since retirement."

I studied the financial data, feeling a chill settle in my chest. "Tim, show me the timeline again. When did these extra payments start?"

Tim pulled up another screen. "First one was about six months after Frank retired. Then they became regular—usually three to four thousand dollars every month."

"Frank was paying someone for something," I muttered. "The question is, what?"

Tim switched to another file. "I also found encrypted communications between Frank and someone using the handle 'DeepThroat72.' Geez, how original is that? Anyway, they were discussing irregularities in evidence processing from the original Strangler investigation."

"Can you trace the other user?" I asked.

"Working on it, but whoever it is, they know their way around digital security. The communications were routed through multiple proxy servers and encrypted with military-grade software, but I was able to crack them," he said proudly and grinned at me.

Tim opened one of the communication logs. The messages were brief but intriguing:

DeepThroat72: *Package delivered as promised. Lab records show tampering in multiple cases.*

FCCallahan: *Payment sent. Need specifics on chain of custody violations. Who had access to alter the evidence logs?*

DeepThroat72: *That's going to cost extra. Very dangerous territory. Department brass involved.*

FCCallahan: *Name your price. Those families deserve the truth.*

I leaned back in my chair, processing the implications. "So Frank was buying information about evidence tampering in the Strangler cases."

"That's what it looks like," Tim agreed. "Someone with access to the police lab was feeding Frank proof that evidence had been deliberately compromised or destroyed."

My phone rang. It was Heather.

"How's the canvas going?" I asked.

"TJ and I have been working the neighborhoods around Frank's house, talking to people who might have seen something the night he was killed. Most folks were already asleep by nine PM—what's with that?—but we found a couple of interesting witnesses."

"Oh yeah? Talk to me, Heather," I said.

"Mrs. Patterson, three houses down from Frank, says she saw a dark sedan parked on the street around eight-thirty that night. She noticed it because it sat there for about twenty minutes with the engine running, then drove off slowly."

"Did she get a license plate?"

"Nope. It was too dark, but she could tell it was a Tennessee tags, but here's the interesting part - she saw the same car driving through the neighborhood twice the week before Frank was murdered."

"Someone was doing reconnaissance," I observed.

"That's what we're thinking. We also talked to old Mr. Henderson who lives across the street. He's got insomnia, spends most nights looking out his window. He says he saw someone walking around Frank's backyard with a flashlight around ten-fifteen."

"After Frank was already dead," I said. "D'you think the killer was looking for something?"

"Either that or they were making sure they hadn't left any evidence behind. Henderson said the person seemed to know the layout of Frank's property, and walked around the place without any hesitation. Okay, call me back if you find anything else."

I hung up and turned again to Tim, but it wasn't ten minutes later when TJ called.

"Harry, we've also been looking into Frank's recent activities. The man was definitely working on something big."

"All right," I said. "Tell me."

"Heather and I have been digging into Frank's activities during his final weeks. His neighbors say he'd been getting a lot more mail than usual: packages, overnight deliveries, stuff that required signatures."

"What kind of packages?" I said.

"According to Mrs. Patterson next door, mostly manila envelopes and small boxes. She noticed because her dog would bark every time the delivery trucks showed up, which was happening almost daily."

"Maybe Frank was ordering research materials," I observed.

"That's what we're thinking. We also talked to his barber, Larry Kozlov at the shop on Market Street. Frank had been going there for fifteen years, and Larry says Frank seemed excited about something in recent weeks. More talkative than usual, asking questions about old-timers who used to work in law enforcement."

"He was building a network of sources," I said. "Trying to get information from people who might remember details that weren't in the official files."

"Larry mentioned Frank asked specifically about retired cops. He was looking for people who'd be willing to share their memories off the record."

"Which means Frank suspected the official investigation missed something important," I said. "Keep working those angles. If Frank was gathering information from multiple sources, someone might have noticed him getting too close to sensitive territory."

I thanked Heather and ended the call, then turned back to Tim. "Keep digging into those encrypted communications. Frank's research was making someone nervous enough to kill him for it."

"Already on it," Tim said, his fingers resuming their dance across the keyboard. "But Harry, there's something else you need to see before you go. It wasn't just the Strangler he was investigating. He was also investigating several people *connected* to the original Strangler investigation. "Frank suspected the Riverside Strangler investigation was being deliberately sabotaged," Tim explained. "He documented evidence tampering, witness intimidation, missing files, and what he believed to be a systematic cover-up involving multiple people."

I studied the file names. I shook my head. "Geez, what the hell had he gotten himself into? More to the point, what the hell have I gotten myself into?"

"And then there's this," Tim said, opening another file. "Frank had evidence that several high-ranking officials were involved in systematic evidence tampering across multiple cases over the past decade."

The file contained photographs of documents, financial records, and what appeared to be surveillance photos of meetings between unknown individuals in various locations around the city.

"Frank wasn't just investigating the Riverside Strangler case," Tim continued. "He was documenting a pattern of corruption that affected dozens of criminal investigations. Look at these financial transfers."

Tim highlighted several suspicious transactions between shell companies and what appeared to be personal accounts. "He'd found out that someone's been paying substantial amounts to someone to ensure certain cases never resulted in convictions."

"And it wasn't just street-level corruption," Tim said, opening another file filled with financial records and surveillance photographs. "Frank had documentation of suspicious activities involving several high-ranking city officials: unusual financial transactions and meetings with people who had no apparent connection to legitimate city business."

The photographs showed various officials meeting in restaurants, parking lots, and other locations around Chattanooga, but the image quality was poor, which made it difficult to identify specific individuals clearly.

"Frank was building cases against multiple targets simultaneously," Tim continued. "He suspected the corruption network extended well beyond just the police department into other areas of city government."

"Who is that?" I asked, squinting as I pointed to one of the photographs. "He looks familiar."

"I've no idea, but I'll see what—"

He was interrupted by my phone buzzing with a text from Kate: "Need to see you ASAP. Something big's happened."

"Tim," I said, stuffing my phone back in my pocket, "back up everything you've found and send copies to my secure server. Also encrypt the backup drives and store them off-site."

"You think someone's going to try to destroy the evidence?"

"I think Frank was killed to prevent this information from becoming public, and that we may be next on the list."

Thirty minutes later, I was back in Kate's office, where I found her pacing in front of her desk while Samson watched from his bed under the window. Kate looked a little... disheveled. Wisps of hair hung from her ponytail and her shirt was wrinkled.

"We have a problem," she said. "A big one."

"Talk to me?" I said.

She handed me a manila envelope. "This was delivered to

the front desk an hour ago. No return address, paid for with cash, dropped off by someone wearing a hoodie."

Inside the envelope were photographs: surveillance pictures of me leaving Frank's house, Tim working at his computer, TJ and Heather in downtown Chattanooga, and Kate herself entering the police station.

"What the hell?" I muttered as I flipped through them. "How the hell did they get the picture of Tim?"

"Someone must have hacked Tim's system and turned on his webcam; at least that's what Jack thinks."

Jack North was Kate's IT specialist, and if he said that's what happened, he was probably right.

I called Tim and told him what happened. His first reaction was one of disbelief—people didn't hack into Tim's equipment—but he knew Jack and was smart enough to take the warning. "Don't worry, Harry," he said. "I'll fix it." And he hung up before I could answer.

"Someone's been watching all of us," Kate said. "They know exactly what we're doing and where we're going."

The street photographs were professional quality, taken with high-end equipment from concealed positions. Whoever was tracking us had resources and expertise.

"There's more," Kate continued, handing me a single sheet of paper. "This was included with the photos."

The message was brief and typed in a generic font: "Drop the Frank Callahan investigation or face the consequences. Callahan learned the hard way what happens to people who ask too many questions."

I studied the paper, looking for any distinguishing marks or clues about its origin. The printer was probably a common office model, the paper standard stock available anywhere.

"They're escalating," I said. "Frank's murder was supposed

to end it, but we're getting too close to something they can't afford to have exposed."

Kate nodded grimly. "The question is what."

"Maybe it's not just about Frank," I said, thinking about Tim's discoveries. "Frank found evidence of corruption in high places. Frank might just be one small piece of a much larger puzzle."

"Corruption?" she said, wrinkling her brow. "What kind of corruption?"

I told Kate about the financial records and the unexplained payments, Frank's communications with the mysterious informant, and the files documenting suspected evidence tampering and case manipulation by several law enforcement officials.

"It's a mess, Kate. Frank had evidence that could have exposed widespread corruption within the department."

Kate sat down heavily in her chair. "If Frank had evidence of corruption..."

"It would destroy careers, end pensions, and send people to prison," I finished for her. "No wonder someone killed him. The question is, who?"

My phone rang. It was Tim. I put him on speaker.

"Harry, you need to get back here. I found something huge."

I sighed. "Come on, Tim. I can't come back right now. I have... Tell me what you found."

"I cracked the encryption on Frank's DeepThroat72 communications. I know who was selling him information."

Kate and I exchanged glances. "Don't say anymore," I snapped. "We're on our way. And tell Jacque to lock the front door."

As we hurried out of the police station, Samson padding

alongside Kate, I couldn't help but think we were walking into a trap. The surveillance photos proved that someone with significant resources was tracking our every move, and Frank's fate served as a clear warning about what happened to people who got too close to the truth.

But we were past the point of backing down. Frank had spent his final years building a case that someone was desperate to bury, and now it was my responsibility to finish what he'd started.

Back at my office, Tim pulled up the decrypted communications on his wall monitor.

"Frank's informant was Detective Marcus Sullivan," he announced. "The same Marcus Sullivan who supposedly died in a car accident six months ago."

Kate stepped closer to the screen. "Sullivan was one of ours," she muttered. "He was a good detective. He worked organized crime."

"According to these messages, Sullivan was working undercover for the FBI," Tim continued. "He'd been investigating corruption in the Chattanooga Police Department for three years before his death."

"No way! You've got to be kidding," Kate said.

"I'm not kidding," Tim said looking up at her. "Look at this."

The communications log showed extensive exchanges between Frank and Sullivan, with Sullivan providing classified information about evidence tampering, case fixing, and what appeared to be a systematic network of corruption involving multiple law enforcement agencies.

"So Sullivan was Frank's source," I said.

"He was," Tim said, scrolling to more recent messages. "Sullivan also discovered that the Riverside Strangler case wasn't so much botched, as deliberately sabotaged to protect someone."

Kate leaned over my shoulder to read the screen. "Does it say who?"

"That's what Sullivan was trying to find out when he died," Tim replied. "His last message to Frank was sent two days before his car accident. He said he'd identified the person the cover-up was designed to protect, and he was planning to make arrests."

I studied the final message, dated just six months ago:

MSullivan: *Package ready for delivery. Target identified and evidence secured. Moving to arrest phase next week.*

FCCallahan: *Be careful. These people have killed before.*

MSullivan: *I know. But we can't let them get away with it. Justice for the victims.*

FCCallahan: *Keep me posted. Will provide backup if needed.*

There were no more messages after that. Three days later, Marcus Sullivan died in a single-car accident on a mountain road outside Chattanooga.

"Hmm!" Kate pursed her lips, then, shaking her head, said, "There's no way Sullivan's death was an accident. That would be too much of a coincidence. He was murdered to shut him up."

I nodded. "And six months later, they killed Frank to shut him up, too."

Tim opened another file. "And then there's this," he said. "Sullivan's FBI handler was an Agent Julie French. She's still active and working out of the Atlanta field office."

"We need to contact her," I said. "If Sullivan was working an official FBI investigation, French might have copies of his files."

Kate was already reaching for her phone. "I'll make the

call. Police to FBI carries more weight than private investigator to FBI."

As Kate stepped away to make her call, I studied the communications between Frank and Sullivan. Two dedicated law enforcement officers who'd stumbled onto something big and were killed for it.

"Back it all up, Tim," I said. "Store copies off-site, with different people, in different locations."

"Already done," Tim replied. "I've got backups in the cloud, with Jacque, my home computer, and three different secure servers."

Kate returned from her phone call, her expression grim. "Agent French is driving up from Atlanta tomorrow morning. She wants to meet. She sounded scared, Harry."

"Scared?" I asked. "Of what?"

"She wouldn't say over the phone. But she confirmed that Sullivan was working an official FBI corruption investigation involving the Chattanooga Police Department. When he died, the case was classified and sealed."

"Did she say why?"

Kate shook her head. "She wouldn't tell me. She said it was too dangerous to discuss anything except in person."

I nodded. Tomorrow was Sunday. Amanda would be... But it couldn't be helped. We had a killer to catch.

By then, it was growing dark outside, and I stepped over to the window and stared out at the river. The city lights were coming on casting golden reflections on the rippling surface, turning into a cauldron of liquid fire. It was beautiful, but somewhere out there, a killer was planning their next move. Someone with access to classified and sealed information, and the resources to conduct an in-depth, professional surveillance.

So far two people, that we knew of, had died trying to expose the truth about the Riverside Strangler case and the corruption that surrounded it.

The game, as Sherlock Holmes would have said, was afoot, and the stakes were life and death. But we had something Frank and Sullivan hadn't: we knew we were being hunted, and we were ready to fight back.

Tomorrow's meeting with Agent French might finally give us the answers we needed to identify Frank's killer. But for now, I was tired. And so I called it a day and went home to my family.

4

THE FEDERAL CONNECTION

Sunday, August 14, 2024

Kate and I met Agent Julie French at a coffee shop on Broad Street at nine-thirty Sunday morning, a neutral location Kate had suggested to keep the meeting away from official channels. The place was nearly empty, just a few early risers reading newspapers over their morning caffeine fix.

Agent French was not what I'd expected. She was in her early forties, average height with shoulder-length auburn hair and intelligent hazel eyes that seemed to catalog every detail of our surroundings. She wore jeans, a navy blazer, and carried herself well. She was confident with an air of authority that only comes with senior rank. But I could see the tension in her shoulders and there were dark circles under her eyes. *She's not been sleeping well,* I thought.

Kate made the introductions, and French gestured for us to take a corner booth away from the other customers. She'd already ordered black coffee and was nursing it like it was medicinal.

"Thank you for meeting with me," she said, her voice was quiet, but had an edge to it. "I apologize for being cryptic on the phone yesterday, Captain, but we have to be extremely careful."

"Marcus Sullivan was working for you when he died," I said, after Kate and I had settled into the seat across from her.

French nodded, her expression growing somber. "Marcus was one of our best undercover operatives. He'd been working a corruption investigation in Chattanooga for over three years when he was killed."

"Killed?" Kate asked. "His death was ruled accidental."

"That's the official line, yes. But we know better." French reached into her briefcase and pulled out a manila folder, keeping it closed on the table. "Marcus was investigating a network of criminal activity that we believe spans multiple law enforcement agencies throughout the Southeast."

I leaned forward. "What kind of criminal activity?"

"The kind that gets federal agents and retired detectives murdered," French replied caustically. "And PIs, too, if they're not careful," she added, giving me a cold look. "I can't go into specifics about an ongoing investigation, but I can tell you that Marcus had documented evidence of systematic corruption involving money laundering, evidence tampering, witness intimidation, and... murder."

"And Frank Callahan?" I asked.

French's jaw tightened. "Frank wasn't officially part of our investigation, but he'd stumbled onto some of the same evidence Marcus was collecting. When Marcus died, Frank became our only remaining source of information."

Kate pulled out her notebook. "What was Marcus investigating specifically?"

"I can't name names or discuss active suspects," French said carefully. "But I can tell you that the network involves people in positions of significant authority. People with access to police files, evidence lockers, and the ability to influence investigations."

"The Riverside Strangler case?" I asked.

French hesitated, then nodded slowly. "Among others. We believe several major criminal cases over the past decade were deliberately mishandled or covered up to protect members of this network."

I stared at her. What she was saying was astonishing. "How high up does this go?" I asked.

"High enough to have federal agents killed," French replied grimly. She opened the folder slightly, revealing the edge of what looked like surveillance photographs. "Marcus was preparing to make arrests when he died. The evidence he'd gathered would have exposed a conspiracy involving dozens of people across multiple agencies."

"Do you have his files?" Kate asked.

"Some of them. Marcus was careful. He kept backup copies. But when he died, several of his key files disappeared before we could secure them."

"Disappeared how?" I asked.

"Someone with high-level access cleaned out his safe deposit box, his home computer, and his office files within hours of his death being reported. It was professional, coordinated and efficient."

French took a sip of her coffee, her eyes scanning the nearly empty coffee shop. "What we did recover was enough to confirm the scope of the conspiracy, but not enough to identify all the participants."

"That's where Frank came in," I said.

"Exactly. Frank had been conducting his own investigation for years, and his findings corroborated much of what Marcus had discovered. More importantly, Frank had sources and methods that complemented Marcus's work."

Kate leaned back in the booth. "So when Frank was killed..."

"We lost our last direct link to the evidence needed to expose this network," French finished. "Which is why I'm here talking to you." She smiled grimly.

I studied the FBI agent's face, trying to read what she wasn't saying. "You want us to continue Frank's investigation."

"Unofficially, yes." She nodded. "The federal investigation is stalled without the evidence Frank had collected. We need someone outside official channels to pick up where he left off."

"That's dangerous," Kate said. "If this network is willing to kill federal agents and retired cops..."

"They'll kill private investigators and police captains too," French agreed. "I won't lie to you about the risks. But if we don't stop them now, they'll disappear. We have intelligence suggesting several key figures are preparing to leave the country."

"What kind of timeline are we looking at?" I asked.

"Weeks, maybe less. Once they realize Frank's investigation didn't die with him, they'll accelerate their escape plans."

French reached across the table and slid the folder toward me. "This contains copies of some of Marcus's files; the ones we can share without compromising other ongoing investigations. It also includes a secure communication protocol if you need to contact me."

I opened the folder enough to see surveillance photographs, financial records, and what looked like intercepted communications. "What exactly do you need from us?" I asked.

"Find Frank's evidence. All of it. His files, his sources, his proof of the corruption. Marcus's investigation provided the federal framework, but Frank had the local details and personal connections needed to make cases stick."

"And in return?" Kate asked.

"Full federal protection during and after the investigation. New identities if necessary. And the resources of the FBI to ensure successful prosecutions."

I closed the folder and looked at Kate. She gave me a slight nod.

"We'll do it," I said. "But we do this our way, with our people, using our methods."

"Agreed," French said, sounding relieved. And she leaned back in her seat for a moment, closed her eyes, then opened them again. "But take care. This network has been operating for years, and they have resources you can't imagine. They've killed before, and they won't hesitate to kill again."

She stood up from the booth, leaving a ten-dollar bill on the table. "My direct number is in the folder. Use the encryption protocols I provided. They're monitoring standard communications."

After French left, Kate and I sat in the coffee shop reviewing the materials she'd provided. The photographs showed surveillance of various individuals meeting in secluded locations, but the faces weren't clear enough for positive identification. The financial records documented suspicious transactions but used account numbers rather than names.

"She's being careful," Kate observed. "Giving us just enough information to be helpful but not enough to compromise their investigation."

"Smart," I agreed. "But also frustrating. We're walking into this blind, not knowing who we can trust or how far the corruption extends."

"What about our own departments?" Kate asked quietly. "If this network has people in multiple agencies..."

"We have to assume everyone's potentially compromised until proven otherwise," I said. "That means we keep this investigation completely separate from official channels."

Kate nodded, but I could see the concern in her eyes. The possibility that her own colleagues might be involved in Frank's murder was a betrayal that went to the heart of everything she believed about law enforcement.

"Are you going to bring the chief into it?" I asked.

"I have to," she replied, "and he won't be happy."

"You want to go do it now?" I asked.

She thought for a moment, then said, "Well, I know he's working today, and the department will be quiet, so... Yes, let's do it and get it out of the way."

An hour later, Kate and I and Samson were seated in Chief Johnston's office, watching him read through the FBI materials with growing concern. His polished head reflected the afternoon sunlight streaming in through the windows, and his famous mustache twitched as he processed the implications of what Agent French had shared.

"So what you're telling me," Johnston said, setting down the folder, "is that we have federal agents and retired detectives being murdered in my city, and there's a network of corruption that involves people in my department."

"That's what the evidence suggests, Chief," Kate replied carefully. "Agent French couldn't give us specifics about suspects, but she made it clear that this goes deep."

Johnston leaned back in his chair, his expression unreadable. "And what about you, Harry? You've been working with her."

"With your approval, Chief," I replied. "Frank Callahan's murder is officially your case, but he was my friend and mentor."

"But now it's become something much bigger." Johnston stood and walked to his window, looking out across the fire department next door. "Kate, if there are corrupt officers in this department, people involved in Frank's murder, how do we know who we can trust?"

"We don't," Kate said honestly. "That's why I'm bringing this to you. Agent French warned us to keep the circle small."

Johnston turned back to face her. "What does the FBI want from us?"

"They need Harry to continue Frank's investigation. Unofficially. They believe Frank had evidence that could expose the entire network, but it died with him unless Harry can find it."

"And you support this approach?" he asked.

Kate hesitated. "Chief, Frank Callahan was a good cop who died trying to expose corruption. If there are people in this department who were involved in his murder, then yes, I support using whatever means necessary to catch them."

Johnston nodded slowly. "All right. But I want to know everything. Any developments, any discoveries, any threats. I need to be kept in the loop. And Kate?"

"Yes, sir?"

"Be very careful who else you trust with this information. If Agent French is right about the scope of this conspiracy, we may be the only two people in this building who aren't compromised." Then he turned to me and said, "Harry, try to stay out of trouble, don't cross any lines and, above all, keep that geek of yours in line. We don't want any trouble from the FBI."

We left the chief's office, and, as we walked the familiar hallways of the police department, I couldn't help but wonder which of her colleagues might be involved in Frank's murder.

We'd just walked out through the main entrance doors when my phone buzzed with a text from Amanda: "How's the meeting going? Jade wants to know if you'll be home for lunch."

I showed Kate the message. "Family time. I promised Jade I'd make up for yesterday's canceled fishing trip."

"Go," Kate said. "I'll review Tim's files more thoroughly and see what I can cross-reference with our investigation. We'll pick this up tomorrow."

As I walked to my car, I had a feeling that Agent French had told us only part of the truth. The federal investigation was obviously much larger and more complex than she'd revealed, and the timeline for the network's potential escape told me we were running out of time. But I shook it off, deciding to go home and have a nice Sunday afternoon with my family.

Back home, I found Amanda and Jade in the kitchen, making what could only be described as the world's messiest pancake lunch. There was flour everywhere, and Jade had batter in her hair, but they were both laughing.

"Daddy!" Jade squealed, running to hug me with flour-covered hands. "We're making special pancakes!"

"I can see that," I said, lifting her up and getting flour all over my shirt. "What makes them special?"

"They're shaped like fish!" she announced proudly. "Because we couldn't go fishing yesterday."

Amanda smiled at me over Jade's head, and I felt some of the tension from the morning's meeting begin to ease. This was really what mattered: my family and me, safe and happy in our kitchen, making memories that would last long after Frank's case was closed.

But even as I helped flip the misshapen fish pancakes and listened to Jade's chatter about her imaginary underwater adventures, part of my mind was still processing Agent French's revelations. Somewhere out there, there were God only knew how many corrupt officials planning their escape, and we had only weeks to stop them.

The federal investigation added resources and legitimacy to our case, but it also raised the stakes. We were trying to expose a conspiracy that reached into the highest levels of law enforcement. Scary, huh? But you know what? Suddenly, I found it… exhilarating.

After lunch, while Jade napped and Amanda worked on her laptop, I retreated to my home office to study Agent French's files. The financial records showed a pattern of payments, regular coordination between multiple parties, but without names or account holder information, it was impossible to identify specific individuals, and it was obvious to me that the lack of detail was intentional. *But why?*

The surveillance photographs were more intriguing. They showed meetings in locations around Chattanooga—parking lots, restaurants, parks—where people exchanged envelopes or briefcases. All probably shot by Marcus Sullivan during his undercover work.

One photograph caught my attention: a meeting in what appeared to be the Elder Mountain Golf Club parking lot. Two figures stood beside expensive cars, one handing a manila envelope to the other. The image quality wasn't good enough for facial recognition, but both individuals appeared to be well-dressed, professional types.

I made a note to have Tim try to enhance the photographs. If we could identify even one of the participants in these meetings, it might provide a crack in the network's security.

My secure phone buzzed with an encrypted message from Agent French: "Review complete? Need to discuss timeline."

I typed back: "Files reviewed. Timeline understood. Will proceed with investigation."

Her response came quickly: "Be careful. They know you're investigating. Take all precautions."

The warning sent... I won't say a chill ran through me, but maybe a small quiver of a thrill. The game was now truly afoot. The surveillance photographs Kate had received yesterday proved that the network was already watching us, and Agent French's warning meant the danger was escalating.

I walked to my window overlooking the city and Tennessee River almost two-thousand feet below, watching the afternoon sunlight dance on the water, knowing Frank had stood at similar windows during his investigation, probably feeling the same mixture of determination and dread that I was experiencing now.

Tomorrow, Kate and I would visit the Wells family to understand why Frank had become so fixated on their daughter's case after all these years. We'd also need to follow up on

Tim's discoveries about the corruption files and the mysterious payments Frank had been receiving.

But tonight, I was going to spend time with my family,
because Agent French's warning made it clear that my investigation of Frank's murder might cost me more than I wanted
to pay.

I knew the people who killed Frank and Marcus Sullivan
wouldn't hesitate to target Amanda and Jade if they felt
threatened. That meant I had to be smarter, more careful, and
more ruthless than them.

Frank's murder had started as a case about justice for a
mentor and friend. Now it had become personal, and the
stakes couldn't be higher.

5

THE WELLS FAMILY

Monday, August 15, 2024

The Wells family home sat on a quiet tree-lined street in North Chattanooga, a modest two-story brick house that had probably been built in the 1960s. The neighborhood had that settled, comfortable feel of a place where families had put down roots and stayed for decades. As Kate and I pulled up to the curb, I noted the well-maintained yard, the fresh paint on the shutters, and the late-model Buick in the driveway. *Hmm. Looks like they're not too badly off, then*, I thought as I opened my door.

"Nice place," Kate observed as we walked up the front path. "Doesn't look like they're struggling."

"My thoughts, exactly," I replied. "Life insurance money can go a long way if you're careful with it," I said as I pressed the doorbell.

The woman who answered the door was clearly Margaret Wells, though ten years had aged her considerably since the newspaper photos I'd seen from Catherine's funeral. She was in her mid-sixties now, with silver hair pulled back in a neat bun and intelligent brown eyes that studied us with obvious wariness. She wore a simple blue dress and practical shoes, and her posture was that of someone accustomed to being in control.

"Mrs. Wells? I'm Harry Starke, and this is Captain Kate Gazzara with the Chattanooga Police Department. We'd like to speak with you about your daughter Catherine, if you have a few minutes."

Her expression hardened immediately. "If this is about that awful man Frank Callahan and his theories, I have nothing more to say. I told him repeatedly that Catherine died more than eight years ago, and I found his suggestions to the contrary deeply offensive."

"Mrs. Wells," Kate said gently, "Frank Callahan was murdered three days ago. We're investigating his death, and we believe it may be connected to his research into your daughter's case."

Margaret Wells' hand went to her throat, and for a moment her composed facade cracked. "Murdered? But... how?"

"May we come in?" I asked. "This is a conversation we should have privately."

She hesitated, then stepped aside to let us enter. The interior of the house was as neat and well-maintained as the exterior, with traditional furniture and family photographs covering every available surface. Many of the photos showed a young woman with dark hair and Catherine's distinctive bone structure at various ages. It was clearly the daughter they'd lost.

"Howard!" Margaret called toward the back of the house. "We have visitors."

Howard Wells, a tall, thin man in his seventies with thinning gray hair and nervous eyes, wore khakis and a button-down shirt that hung loosely on his frame, and his handshake was weak when Kate introduced us.

"Please, sit down," Margaret said, gesturing to the living room sofa. "Can I get you some coffee?"

"That would be nice, thank you," Kate replied.

While Margaret busied herself in the kitchen, Howard settled into a recliner that was obviously his regular spot, judging by the reading glasses and newspaper on the side table.

"So Frank Callahan is dead," Howard said quietly. "I can't say I'm surprised. The man was obsessed."

"You were listening," I said.

"Always," he replied with a smile.

"What do you mean by obsessed?" I asked.

Howard glanced toward the kitchen, then lowered his voice. "He'd been calling here for months, asking the same questions over and over. About Catherine's friends, her habits, where she liked to go. Margaret kept telling him Catherine was gone, but he wouldn't listen."

"What kind of questions specifically?"

"About her art supplies, her sketchbooks, whether she had any particular jewelry she always wore. Strange questions for someone investigating her death." Howard shifted uncomfortably. "Then he started showing up here with photographs."

"Photographs?" Kate asked.

"Pictures of a woman in Knoxville. He claimed it was Catherine, living under a different name. It was... disturbing.

The woman looked similar, I'll grant you, but Catherine is dead. We buried her nine years ago."

Margaret returned with coffee for four and placed the tray on the coffee table. I watched as she poured. Her hands were steady despite the emotional conversation.

"Mr. Wells," Kate said, "I understand you worked for Greaves Enterprises before you retired."

Howard's cup rattled slightly against his saucer. "That's right. I was a project manager there for twenty-eight years."

"And you retired shortly after Catherine's death, didn't you?" she asked.

"Well, yes. Margaret and I... we needed time to grieve. The company was very understanding about early retirement."

"With full benefits?" I asked.

Howard's eyes darted to his wife, then back to me. "I don't see how that's relevant to Frank Callahan's murder."

"We're just trying to understand the timeline," Kate said smoothly. "Grief can certainly affect someone's ability to work."

Margaret set down the coffee pot with more force than necessary. "My husband took early retirement because we'd just lost our only child. The company was generous with the severance package, and combined with Catherine's life insurance, we were able to maintain our lifestyle. I don't see anything suspicious about that."

"Life insurance can be complicated when the body isn't recovered," I observed.

"The police investigation concluded that Catherine had been murdered," Margaret replied firmly. "The insurance company honored their obligation after the appropriate waiting period."

"How much was the policy for?" Kate asked.

Margaret's lips tightened. "I hardly think that's appropriate to discuss."

"Mrs. Wells, we're investigating a murder. Frank Callahan died trying to prove that Catherine survived her attack. If there's any possibility he was right..."

"He wasn't right," Margaret snapped. "My daughter is dead. I identified her belongings myself when they were recovered from the crime scene."

"Her belongings?" I asked, pulling out my notebook.

Margaret hesitated. "Her running shoes, her wallet, some jewelry she always wore."

"What kind of jewelry?" Kate asked.

"A silver necklace with a small cross. Her grandmother's ring. A tennis bracelet I'd given her for her twenty-first birthday."

I made notes, comparing her description to what I remembered from the case files. "Mrs. Wells, would it be possible to see Catherine's room? Sometimes seeing someone's personal space helps us understand them better."

Margaret and Howard exchanged glances, and I caught something passing between them: fear, maybe, or warning.

"I suppose that would be all right," Margaret said slowly. "Though I should warn you, I've kept it exactly as it was when she... when we lost her."

We followed Margaret upstairs to a bedroom at the front of the house. When she opened the door, I felt like I was stepping back in time. The room was frozen just as it was nine years ago, with posters of bands I barely remembered and an obsolete laptop computer. But it was the art supplies that caught my attention. Easels, canvases, paints, brushes, sketchbooks; enough equipment for a serious artist. The work displayed on the walls showed real talent, mostly landscapes and portraits with a distinctive style that could only have come from formal training.

"Catherine was very artistic," Margaret said, her voice softening. "She was studying art history at UTC, but she was also a painter. She'd been accepted to a graduate program in Atlanta."

I walked around the room, studying the paintings and examining the personal items scattered on Catherine's desk and dresser. Something seemed... I dunno. I couldn't put my finger on what it was.

"Mrs. Wells, you mentioned that Catherine always wore certain jewelry. I see a jewelry box here."

"Yes, though most of her good pieces were... were found at the crime scene."

I opened the jewelry box carefully. Inside were the usual items you'd expect a young woman to own: earrings, bracelets, and several necklaces. But I also noticed something interesting: there were empty spaces in the jewelry box's compartments, indentations where specific pieces had obviously been stored regularly.

"It looks like some pieces are missing from here," I said.

Margaret nodded. "The pieces she was wearing when she died. The police gave them back to us eventually, but I... I couldn't bear to put them back in her jewelry box."

Kate was examining the art supplies. "These are expensive brands," she observed. "Professional quality."

"Catherine was serious about her art," Howard said from the doorway. "We wanted to support her talent."

I moved to Catherine's desk, where several sketchbooks lay open. The drawings showed the same artistic skill as the paintings, but there was something darker in the sketches:

shadowy figures, distorted faces, scenes that suggested the artist was troubled or frightened.

"Mrs. Wells, did Catherine ever mention feeling threatened? Being followed or watched?"

"Well, there was..." Margaret stopped, glancing at her husband. "There were some phone calls she mentioned, a few weeks before she died. Hang-ups mostly, but they seemed to upset her."

"Did she report them to the police?" Kate asked.

"She said she was going to, but then... then it was too late."

I continued examining Catherine's belongings, comparing what I saw to my memory of the police reports. Something was definitely off, but I needed to check the actual case files to be sure.

"Mr. Wells," Kate said, "you seem nervous about discussing your former employer. Was there any particular reason you left Greaves Enterprises when you did?"

Howard's face flushed. "I told you, we were grieving. I couldn't concentrate on my work."

"But Greaves is a major company," I said. "They must have had grief counseling, family support services. Why not take a leave of absence instead of early retirement?"

"There were... there were some changes happening at the company," he replied, hesitantly. "Restructuring, like, you know? It seemed like a good time to go."

Margaret moved protectively closer to her husband. "Howard had worked there for nearly three decades. He was entitled to retire when he chose."

I closed the sketchbook I'd been examining and turned to face both of them. "Mrs. Wells, Mr. Wells, I'm going to be direct with you. Frank Callahan was murdered by someone who didn't want him to continue investigating the Riverside

Strangler case. He believed Catherine survived. Now, maybe he was wrong, but someone thought his investigation was dangerous enough to kill him for it."

Margaret's face went pale. "You're saying Catherine's supposed survival got Frank killed?"

"I'm saying someone is willing to commit murder to keep certain information secret. If Catherine is alive, she might be in danger. If she's not alive, then someone is using her name to cover up something else entirely."

Howard stood up abruptly. "I think this conversation is over. You've upset my wife enough."

"Mr. Wells—" Kate began.

"No, I want you to leave. Now."

As we prepared to go, Margaret walked us to the front door. At the threshold, she grabbed my arm gently but firmly.

"Mr. Starke," she said quietly, making sure her husband couldn't hear. "Frank Callahan spent months asking us about Catherine, about her death, about the investigation. But I think he was asking the wrong questions about the wrong people."

"What do you mean?"

"He kept focusing on whether Catherine survived, on whether she might be living somewhere else. But maybe the question isn't who Catherine became; maybe it's who benefited most from keeping the Strangler case unsolved."

"Who do you think benefited?"

Margaret glanced back toward the house, then met my eyes. "The same people who always benefit when investigations fail, Mr. Starke. The people who have something to hide."

With that cryptic statement, she closed the door, leaving

Kate and me standing on the front porch with more questions than we'd arrived with.

The people who have something to hide, I thought. It was something and nothing, and yet...

As we walked back to our cars, Kate slowed her pace, shook her head, and said, "Well, that was interesting, but I'm not sure how much it helped."

"Maybe more than you might think," I said, taking out my phone. "I need Tim to do some research for me."

"Research?" she asked. "Like what?"

"I want him to compare the inventory of Catherine's belongings from the crime scene with what we just saw in her bedroom. Something doesn't match, and I think Margaret Wells knows more than she's telling us."

I dialed Tim's number as we reached our vehicles. "Tim, I need you to pull the complete evidence inventory from the Catherine Wells crime scene and cross-reference it with a list of items I'm going to send you."

"You're looking for discrepancies?" Tim asked.

"Exactly. Also, I want you to dig deeper into Greaves Enterprises. I want to know what kind of 'restructuring' was happening around the time Howard Wells took early retirement, and whether there's any connection to the Riverside Strangler investigation."

"On it. Anything else?"

"See what you can find about life insurance payouts for murder victims when the body hasn't been recovered. There might be some legal requirements or waiting periods that could tell us more about the Wells' family's timeline."

As I ended the call, Kate leaned against her car. "You're not happy, are you?" she said. "What's your gut telling you, Harry?"

"They're hiding something," I replied. "The question is whether they're hiding Catherine's survival or covering up something else entirely."

"Like what?"

"Like maybe Howard Wells didn't retire from Greaves Enterprises voluntarily. Maybe he was forced out because he knew something about the company's involvement in the Strangler case cover-up and was paid to keep his mouth shut."

Kate considered this, then said, "Gotcha. And don't forget Margaret Wells was a police forensic photographer. She would have had access to crime scene evidence and the expertise to manipulate photographs or documentation."

"Oh, I hadn't forgotten," I said. "It might explain why some of Catherine's belongings don't match between the crime scene inventory and her bedroom," I said. "How about this: let's say Catherine is alive. Her parents could have helped stage her death, right? But, if she's really dead, someone could be using her identity as part of a larger deception."

"Either way," Kate said, thoughtfully, "Frank Callahan died because he got too close to the truth."

"You can say that again," I muttered. "Look, I gotta go. I'll call you later, or you can call me."

She nodded, "Stay safe, Harry."

"Always," I said, as I turned away and went to my car.

I slid into the driver's seat of my car, started the engine and then sat back in my seat for a moment to think. My mind was in a whirl. I couldn't shake Margaret Wells' parting words: 'asking the wrong questions about the wrong people.' Was she trying to tell us something without betraying her family's secrets? There was no telling, but I intended to find out.

Back at my offices, I found Tim already deep into his research, with Jacque helping him organize files and cross-reference information.

"What did you find?" I asked, settling into a chair beside Tim's workstation.

"Some interesting discrepancies," Tim said, pulling up two lists on his monitor. "According to the police evidence inventory, Catherine Wells was wearing a silver cross necklace, a diamond tennis bracelet, and her grandmother's sapphire ring when she was attacked."

"That matches what Margaret told us."

"But here's the thing," Jacque said, consulting her notes. "According to the insurance claim filed by the family, Catherine was wearing additional jewelry not mentioned in the police report. A gold watch, pearl earrings, and a second necklace with her initials."

"So either the police missed those items, or the family inflated the insurance claim," I said.

"Or someone removed the items from the crime scene before the police processed it," Tim added.

"What are you going to do about it?" Jacque asked, looking up at me.

"Right now, we document everything," I said, leaning back in my chair. "We need to be methodical about this. The jewelry discrepancy could be innocent. Maybe the family was confused about what Catherine was wearing that night, or maybe they listed items they thought she might have been carrying."

"But you don't think it's innocent," Tim observed.

"Eh," I said, scrunching up my face. "Right now, I really don't know what I think. Hmm, perhaps Howard's nervous behavior suggests the Wells family knows more than they're telling us." I stood up and walked to the window. "But we can't jump to conclusions. We need to build a solid case based on facts, not suspicions."

"So what's the next step?" Jacque asked.

"First, Tim, I want you to pull the actual police evidence photos from Catherine's crime scene and compare them with the insurance claim documentation. If there are items listed on the insurance claim that don't appear in the crime scene photos, that's evidence of fraud."

"And if the photos match the insurance claim?" Tim asked.

"Then either the police missed documenting some items, or someone added jewelry to the scene before the photos were taken. Either way, it points to problems with the original investigation."

I turned back to face them. "We also need to approach this carefully. If the Wells family is involved in insurance fraud, that's a separate issue from Frank's murder. We can't let one investigation compromise the other."

"What about Margaret's warning?" Jacque asked. "You know; about asking the wrong questions about the wrong people?"

"That's what bothers me most," I admitted. "She seemed genuinely concerned about pointing us in the right direction, but was she also protecting her family's secret? We need to figure out what she was really trying to tell us."

"I have more," Tim said. "I found records of Howard Wells' employment at Greaves Enterprises. He was involved in land acquisition and zoning applications."

"And?" I asked. "What kind of properties?"

"Mostly properties along the Tennessee River. Including

several locations where Riverside Strangler victims were found."

At that, I sat back in my chair and narrowed my eyes. "Are you telling me Greaves Enterprises owned the land where the murders took place? That's one hell of a coincidence."

"Not owned, but they had development interests in several of those areas. Howard Wells would have been familiar with all of them: access points, security, traffic patterns, and so on."

It was food for thought. If Howard Wells had inside knowledge of Greaves' development sites, he could have passed that information on to someone planning the murders. Or worse, he could have been directly involved in selecting the locations. Yeah, I know, it's a stretch, but after interviewing the man...

"Tim, I want you to map every Greaves Enterprise property development project for the past fifteen years. Cross-reference them with all violent crime locations in those areas, not just the Strangler murders."

"On it," Tim said, his fingers flying over the keyboard. "And Harry, there's something else you need to see. I was able to access Howard Wells' financial records from his early retirement."

Tim pulled up bank statements showing the Wells family's finances before and after Catherine's death. The numbers told a clear story.

"They received four hundred fifty thousand from Catherine's life insurance," Tim said. "But they also received an additional two hundred thousand from something called 'Greaves Development Consulting' over the following two years."

"Consulting fees for what?"

"The payments are listed as 'land use consultation' and

'zoning advisory services.' But here's the interesting part: Howard Wells was officially retired. Why would a retired employee be receiving consulting fees?"

Jacque looked up from her legal research. "Those payments could be hush money. You know, to keep him quiet about something he learned while he was working for them."

"Or payment for ongoing services," I said grimly. "What if Howard Wells was actively helping someone use those sites for... I dunno. Criminal purposes?"

It was a disturbing picture. Howard Wells had inside knowledge of secluded locations along the Tennessee River. His wife Margaret had access to police forensic photography equipment, and their daughter supposedly died at the hands of the Riverside Strangler. But the evidential inventory didn't match the family's insurance claims. *What the hell was going on?*

"Harry, if this family was involved in staging Catherine's death or covering up the Strangler murders, why would Margaret Wells give us that hint about asking the wrong questions?"

"Because maybe she wants the truth to come out now that Frank is dead," I said. "Or maybe she's trying to redirect our investigation away from her family and toward someone else."

"Someone like who?"

"Someone who benefited from keeping the Strangler case unsolved. Someone who used the mystery and fear to cover their own criminal activities."

I got up from my seat and went to my office where I stood at the window looking out over the river, thinking. *Have we uncovered a conspiracy that goes much deeper than Frank's murder or even the Riverside Strangler case? Are we looking at a network of criminal activity that's been operating for over a decade, protected by corruption, cover-ups, and murder?* I took a long deep breath, slowly shaking my head.

Frank Callahan had died trying to expose the truth about Catherine Wells. But maybe the truth wasn't about whether she survived. Maybe it was about who used her death to hide their own crimes. *If she's really dead! If not... Who the hell knows?*

6

FOLLOWING THE MONEY

I ARRIVED AT MY OFFICE THE NEXT MORNING TO FIND TIM HAD been at his workstation since five that morning, surrounded by coffee cups, energy drink cans, and the paper wrappers from three egg, sausage and bacon bagels. His hair disheveled, and his eyes had the slightly glazed look of someone who'd been staring at computer screens for too many hours.

"Please tell me you went home at some point last night," I said, settling into a chair beside his workspace.

"Yeah, home. I went. I was back here at five," Tim replied without looking up from his monitors. "I've been working on Frank's financial investigation."

I shook my head. There was no point in admonishing him. Tim was what he was. "Find anything interesting?" I asked.

Tim turned his chair so he faced me. He really did look like hell, but I could see from his expression he was also excited. "Oh yeah, Harry," he said as he shoved his glasses further up the bridge of his nose with a forefinger, "what I found is more than interesting. It's terrifying."

He gestured to one of the four monitors, which displayed a complex flowchart connecting dozens of names, bank accounts, and transactions spanning several years.

"Frank wasn't just investigating the Riverside Strangler case," Tim continued. "He was onto something else; something big. That's a breakdown of a network of corruption that's been operating in Chattanooga for at least a decade."

I studied the chart, recognizing several prominent names connected by lines representing financial transactions. "Walk me through it, Tim."

Tim clicked through several screens, showing bank records, property transfers, and what appeared to be coded communications. "Frank had been tracking money flows between various individuals and organizations. Look at this pattern."

He opened another file showing a timeline of cases and corresponding financial activity. "Here's what's really disturbing. Frank had identified at least twelve major criminal investigations that were compromised, and in every case, someone received payment shortly afterward."

I leaned closer to examine the timeline. The cases ranged from drug trafficking to white-collar crime to violent felonies, all involving suspects with connections to Chattanooga's business and political elite.

"Who was making the payments?"

"Now that's where it gets complicated," Tim said, pulling up another screen. "The money was laundered through multiple shell companies and offshore accounts, but Frank managed to trace several of them back to their sources."

The screen showed a web of corporate entities, many with

names that meant nothing to me. But a few stood out: Greaves Development Holdings, Elder Mountain Investment Group, and Tennessee River Properties.

"Greaves again," I muttered.

"Not only Greaves, but … Harry, you're not going to believe this, but it looks like Frank was also investigating Commissioner Reynolds as part of his overall investigation, as well as Judge Henley and a Dr. Marsh."

"Reynolds," I said. "You're kidding me! And Henley? What the hell? And who's this Dr. Marsh?"

"No I'm not. I don't know who Marsh is. But I do have this," Tim said and clicked to a new document. "Frank discovered that several of the shell companies were purchasing properties along the Tennessee River, the same areas where Riverside Strangler victims were found. According to the property records, development projects that never got built. But look at this." Tim highlighted several transactions. "The properties were purchased for well above market value, held for a few years, then sold at losses. It's a classic money laundering operation."

"That's all well and good," I began, "but what about—" I was about to drag him back to Commissioner Reynolds when my phone buzzed with a call from TJ. I put him on speaker.

"Heather and I have been doing follow-up interviews in Frank's neighborhood," TJ said. "We found a couple of people who weren't home during the initial canvas."

"What did they tell you?" I asked.

"Mrs. Whitmire, who lives two blocks over, walks her dog every night around nine PM. She remembers seeing an unfamiliar car parked at the end of Frank's street the night he was killed; a dark sedan with the engine running. When she walked by again twenty minutes later, it was gone."

"Did she get a description of the driver?"

"No. It was too dark to see much, but she said there was definitely someone behind the wheel. The interesting part is she'd noticed the same car in the area twice the week before Frank's murder, always in the evening hours."

TJ paused and I heard him flipping through his notes. "We also talked to Mr. Kowalski," he continued, "who works night shifts and gets home around ten-thirty. The night Frank was killed, he saw someone walking quickly away from Frank's street toward the main road. He said the person seemed to be in a hurry and kept looking back over their shoulder."

"Any description?" I asked.

"Average height, wearing dark clothing and some kind of hat or hood. Kowalski thought it was odd because most people in that neighborhood drive everywhere."

"Anything else?"

"The mail carrier mentioned Frank had been getting a lot more packages lately - overnight deliveries, registered mail, things that required signatures. She said it was unusual for a retiree to have that much mail traffic."

"Okay, TJ. Good work. Let's close it down. Come on in," I said and hung up.

Police Commissioner Reynolds, I thought. *It's impossible. There must be some mistake.*

I turned back to Tim's financial analysis. "Now, Tim, show me what Frank found about Reynolds, Henley, and Marsh. And you'd better be right, Tim. Reynolds is the police commissioner."

"You think I don't know that," he muttered as he pulled up individual files for each suspect. The financial records painted a picture of systematic corruption spanning years.

"Commissioner Reynolds has been receiving regular

payments through a consulting company called 'Public Safety Solutions,'" Tim explained. "But the company doesn't seem to provide any actual services. There are no employees, no office, no contracts with legitimate clients."

"How much has he received?"

"Over two hundred thousand dollars in the past three years alone. Always in amounts just under the federal reporting requirements."

I sat back in my chair, trying to process the scope of what Frank had uncovered. "The Riverside Strangler case was just a part of a much larger investigation of crime and corruption. No wonder someone decided to shut him up, permanently."

"Exactly," Tim agreed. "And Harry, there's something else, and it's really important."

"Saving the worst for last, huh?" I muttered.

"You could say that, yeah." He did that thing with his glasses and then continued. "I found email communications between Frank and Marcus Sullivan that Agent French didn't include in the files she gave us."

I frowned. "Go on."

Tim opened a new window showing message logs between Frank and Sullivan dating back several months before Sullivan's death.

"Sullivan was feeding Frank information about federal investigations into Chattanooga corruption. Look at this message from two weeks before Sullivan died."

The message read: "Frank, my superiors are getting nervous about your investigation. They think you're compromising our operation. Be very careful who you trust."

"So Sullivan was trying to protect Frank?" I said.

"And Frank was trying to protect Sullivan," Tim replied, showing me Frank's response: "I have backup plans in place. If anything happens to either of us, the evidence will go public automatically."

"Backup plans?" I muttered. "What backup plans?"

"That's what I've been trying to figure out since five this morning," Tim said. "Frank mentions dead-man switches and insurance policies in several messages, but I can't find the actual files or mechanisms he set up."

My secure phone buzzed with a message from Agent French: "We need to meet immediately. There have been some developments."

I showed the message to Tim. "Can you keep working on Frank's backup systems while I meet with Agent French?"

"Of course," Tim said, turning back to his computers. "But Harry, be careful. If Frank and Sullivan were both killed to prevent them from exposing this network, I'd say you're definitely on their target list now."

Before I left, I called TJ and told him to start surveillance on Commissioner Reynolds.

An hour later, I met Agent French at a different coffee shop, this one on the outskirts of Chattanooga near the Georgia border. She looked even more stressed than during our first meeting, with dark circles under her eyes and a nervous energy that told me she hadn't been sleeping.

"Thank you for coming," she said, gesturing to a corner booth. "We have a problem."

"What kind of problem?" I asked as we sat down opposite one another.

"The kind that gets federal agents transferred to desk jobs in North Dakota," French replied grimly. "My superiors want me to back off the Chattanooga investigation."

"Oh yeah?" I said. "Why?"

"The reason I was given was that the case is going nowhere

and is consuming money and resourses that could be used elsewhere, but I think it's because it involves too many prominent people, and that someone at the Bureau is worried about political fallout."

I leaned forward. What I was hearing made no sense. "What about Marcus Sullivan's murder? What about Frank Callahan?"

"Officially, Sullivan died in an accident and Callahan was killed by an unknown assailant during a robbery gone wrong. That's the story my bosses want to stick with."

"And unofficially?"

French pulled out a manila envelope similar to the one she'd given us before. "Unofficially, I'm sharing information with a private investigator who's working a related case."

I opened the envelope. Inside were surveillance photographs, financial records, and transcripts of recorded conversations.

"Those are from Sullivan's personal files," French explained. "The ones he kept hidden from the Bureau. He was… stepping outside the box, shall we say?"

The transcripts showed conversations between various Chattanooga officials discussing case fixing, evidence tampering, and elimination of threats to their operation. Several mentioned Frank Callahan by name as a problem that needed to be resolved.

"This proves they were planning to kill Frank," I said.

"It proves someone was planning to silence him," French corrected. "But proving who actually carried out the murder is a different matter entirely."

"What do you need from me?"

"Find Frank's backup evidence. Sullivan's notes indicate Frank had documentation that could bring down this entire network, but it's hidden somewhere safe. If we can locate it, I might be able to convince my superiors to reopen the official investigation."

French stood to leave, then paused. "Stay safe, Harry. These people are dangerous and stop at nothing."

Back at the office, I found Tim still working frantically at his computer.

"Any luck finding Frank's backup systems?" I asked.

"Maybe," Tim said, pointing to a complex file structure on his monitor. "I think Frank created multiple dead-man switches designed to automatically release information if he failed to check in regularly."

"Where would the information be released to, d'you know?"

"No, nor will I until we find the actual files. What I can't understand is why haven't they been triggered already? He's been dead now for several days, they should have fired automatically. Which means either the systems failed, someone disabled them, or Frank never had a chance to set them up properly before he was killed."

Jacque looked up from her legal research. "There's another possibility. Maybe Frank's backup plan required manual activation by someone he trusted."

"Like who?"

"Like Sullivan or... you," she said simply. "You were Frank's friend, and he specifically requested your involvement in this investigation. Maybe he left instructions for you to follow if something happened to him."

I considered this possibility. Frank had been paranoid enough to create elaborate security systems and backup plans. It made sense that he'd want a trusted friend to handle the final step.

"Where would he hide something like that?" She asked.

I didn't answer, but it made sense, sort of. I went back to my office and flopped down in my chair to think. Nothing. My mind was in a whirl. I tried to think back over the years, over the thousands of conversations Frank and I had had. Nothing! In the end, I gave it up for the night and went home, thinking... Hell, I don't know what I was thinking.

7

THE MEDICAL CONNECTION

WEDNESDAY, AUGUST 17, 2024

I LAY AWAKE STARING AT THE CEILING FOR MOST OF THE NIGHT, my mind churning through everything we'd discovered about Frank's investigation. *Commissioner Reynolds?* I thought. *Geez. That's not going to go down well with chief, or Kate. I hope to hell Frank was right... What the hell am I thinking? Of course he was right. Frank was always right.* The network of corruption, the financial connections, the mysterious backup files; it all swirled together in an endless loop that prevented any hope of sleep.

At three-fifteen, Amanda rolled over and placed her hand on my chest.

"You're thinking so loud you're keeping me awake," she said softly.

"Sorry. I didn't mean to disturb you."

"Harry, you've been tossing and turning for hours. What's eating at you?"

I turned to face her in the darkness, grateful for her presence. "It's Frank's backup files. Tim thinks Frank created some kind of dead-man switch to automatically release his evidence if something happened to him, but we can't find it."

"Maybe he didn't set up an automatic system," Amanda suggested. "As a journalist, I know that automation can fail or be discovered by the wrong people. What if Frank's backup plan required personal action by someone he trusted?"

"That's what Jacque suggested. But where would he hide instructions for me? We searched his house thoroughly."

Amanda was quiet for a moment, thinking. "When I'm working on a sensitive story, I don't hide important information in obvious places like my office or home. I put it somewhere that has personal meaning but wouldn't be obvious to outsiders."

"Like where?"

"A place connected to shared memories, inside jokes, significant moments. Somewhere only the intended recipient would think to look."

I considered this. Frank and I had worked together for years, shared countless conversations about cases, life, philosophy. But nothing immediately came to mind about where he might have hidden something specifically for me.

"There might be something," I said slowly. "Frank was always full of surprises. If he left something for me... You're right, it would be somewhere meaningful to both of us."

"Well, when you think of it, you'll know," Amanda said, settling back onto her pillow. "Frank trusted you for a reason."

At seven AM, I was already dressed and heading downstairs when I heard Jade's voice from the kitchen.

"Daddy, mommy said you look tired. Are you sick?"

I found my daughter at the breakfast table, still in her princess pajamas, eating cereal and swinging her legs.

"Not sick, sweetheart. I just didn't sleep very well."

"Because of the bad man who hurt your friend?"

I smiled at her perceptiveness. "That's part of it, yes."

She studied my face, frowning. "When you catch the bad man, will you sleep better?"

"I think so."

"Good, 'cause mommy says you need your sleep to think good thoughts."

Amanda appeared in the doorway, already dressed for work. "Out of the mouths of babes," she said, smiling. "Coffee's ready, and there are bagels if you want breakfast."

"Just coffee. I want to get to the office early this morning."

I poured coffee into a travel mug and kissed my girls goodbye. "I'll call you later."

At the office, I found Tim exactly where I'd left him the night before, though he'd apparently showered and changed clothes at some point. The coffee cup in his hand was steaming, and his eyes looked slightly more focused.

"Please tell me you got some actual sleep," I said.

"Four hours on the couch in the conference room," Tim replied. "I found nothing about Frank's backup files, but I did make progress on his computer systems and started digging deeper into Dr. Benjamin Marsh's background."

"That's good," I said. "What did you find?"

Tim pulled up several files on his monitor. "Frank was definitely investigating Marsh, but not just for the Riverside Strangler connection. He was building a case for medical malpractice and possibly murder."

"Show me," I said.

Tim clicked through various screens showing medical

records, prescription databases, and patient files. "Ten years ago," he began, "Marsh was briefly considered a suspect in the Riverside Strangler case because of his medical knowledge and access to locations where bodies were found. But he was cleared when he provided alibis for the crucial dates. There are hospital records showing he was on duty during several of the murders. But I found some interesting inconsistencies when I hacked into the hospital's personnel database."

Tim highlighted several of them on his screen. "Shift schedules that were changed after the fact, patient logs that don't match the official timeline, even electronic keycard access to records that show Marsh leaving and returning to the hospital during times when he was supposedly working."

"So he did have enough time to commit the murders," I said.

"More than enough," Tim replied. "And Harry, I also accessed the state medical board's prescription monitoring database. Marsh has been prescribing unusual amounts of certain controlled substances over the years."

Tim opened another file showing prescription records. "Sedatives, paralytic agents, substances that could be used to incapacitate victims. The quantities he's been ordering go way beyond what would be normal for emergency room procedures."

"Has anyone ever questioned him about it?" I asked, frowning.

Tim shook his head. "Every time there's been an inquiry, the investigation was either dropped or transferred to someone else. It's like he's being protected."

"Okay... Good, so, what about the jewelry? Did you find anything?" Tim pulled up two documents on his monitor. "I accessed the original police evidence inventory from

Catherine Wells' crime scene and compared it with the insurance claim filed by the family six months later."

"And?"

"According to the police report, Catherine was wearing a silver cross necklace, a tennis bracelet, and her grandmother's ring when she was attacked. All three items were recovered and logged into evidence." Tim highlighted the relevant entries. "But look at the insurance claim."

The insurance document listed the same three pieces, but also included a gold watch, pearl earrings, and a second necklace with Catherine's initials - items worth an additional $3,200.

"So either the police missed some jewelry at the scene, or the family inflated their claim," I said.

"Yep," Tim continued, opening another screen. "I also traced the insurance payout. The company paid out $8,900 total for Catherine's personal effects, but there's no record of the extra jewelry ever being recovered or returned to the family."

I leaned closer to study the documents. "What about the jewelry box in Catherine's room? I noticed empty spaces that looked like pieces were missing."

"That's what made me dig deeper," Tim said. "If Catherine was wearing her most valuable pieces when she was attacked, and they were recovered by police, why would her jewelry box still show empty spaces? Unless..."

"Unless someone removed items from the crime scene before the police processed it," I finished.

Tim nodded. "Or the family staged the bedroom to support their insurance claim. Either way, it appears there's deliberate deception involved."

"Can you trace what happened to the police evidence?"

"I dunno. The evidence room records for that period are incomplete. Several entries are missing or have been altered." Tim's expression darkened. "Harry, this fits the pattern of evidence tampering we've been seeing in other cases."

I thought about Margaret Wells' parting words about asking the wrong questions. "Tim, I want you to dig deeper into the Wells family finances. Look at their insurance payouts, and any other irregularities you can find."

"You think the family is involved in Frank's murder?" he asked, his eyes narrowed as he looked at me.

"I think someone's been lying about Catherine Wells for nine years, and Frank died because he got too close to the truth."

My phone rang. It was Kate.

"Harry, you're not going to believe this. Dr. Marsh was the emergency room doctor who treated Catherine Wells nine years ago."

Now that was a game changer. "You mean if she survived her attack?" I asked.

"No… Maybe… I don't know," she replied. "Marsh signed the death certificate, but the medical records from that night have either been lost or destroyed. There's no way to verify what actually happened to Catherine Wells."

"We need to put surveillance on Marsh," I said. "What's his current status?"

"I've already got a unit watching his house," she replied. "But here's something else: Marsh has been making regular visits to a private medical facility outside Chattanooga; Mountain View Recovery Center."

"I've heard of that place," I said. "Private's the operative word. It's more difficult to get into than the county jail is to get out of. What do we know about it?"

"Nothing, but I'll look into it."

After ending the call with Kate, I called Heather and put her onto watching Marsh, then I turned again to Tim. "Keep digging into Marsh's background. I want to know everything about his medical practice, his financial situation, and any connections to the other suspects. And do a little digging and see what you can find out about this Mountain View Recovery Center." And with that, I turned to leave. It was almost eleven-fifteen.

"Will do," Tim said, his fingers flying over the keyboard. "But hold on a minute, Harry. You should know that Marsh has been involved in a suspicious number of patient deaths over the years. Look at this."

Tim pulled up a spreadsheet showing patient mortality data. "Twelve patients in the past ten years. All of the deaths involving drugs prescribed by Marsh, and all were ruled accidental or natural causes. But when you look at the pattern..." He paused for a second, then turned, looked up at me and continued, "I did a little digging into their backgrounds. They were mostly elderly, isolated individuals without close family members. People whose deaths wouldn't generate much interest. But there are also several younger patients who were involved in legal cases, potential witnesses, people with information that could be damaging to certain high-status individuals."

That got my attention. "You think Marsh has been murdering patients?" I asked.

Tim shrugged. "Maybe. Either for personal gain or to protect someone. Look at this timeline." Tim highlighted several dates. "Every time one of these patients died, Marsh received a substantial payment through one of those shell companies we identified yesterday."

I studied the financial connections. "So he's not only covering up the Strangler case, he's a paid assassin."

"Wow, I hadn't thought of it like that," Tim replied, "but yes, that's what it looks like. And here's another thought, Harry: What if Frank's investigation threatened to expose him...?"

"Then Marsh would have a powerful motive for murder," I muttered. "I gotta go to work, Tim. I'll be in my office if you need me. Keep up the good work, and keep me informed."

It was almost one in the afternoon when TJ called in with an update from his surveillance of Commissioner Reynolds. "Harry, Reynolds is definitely spooked," he began. "I did a little nosing around, talked to some people. Apparently, he's hired private security, and yesterday he met with Judge Henley and Dr. Marsh at the Elder Mountain Golf Club."

"But you don't know what they discussed?" I asked.

"Not the details, no, but my source told me they were passing documents back and forth and everyone looked stressed. The meeting lasted about an hour, then they left separately. "

"I think you'd better go home and get some rest. Kate has a cruiser watching Marsh's home, so I'll have Heather take over Reynolds for a while."

It wasn't ten minutes later that Heather called with her surveillance report on Dr. Marsh. "This guy knows what he's doing, Harry," she said. He varies his routes, checks for followers."

"Geez, where did all that come from, I wonder?" I replied.

I heard her snort. "Either someone's taught him how to avoid detection, or he's got military or law enforcement background we don't know about. Hey, did you know there's an unmarked cruiser watching him?"

"Yes, I did. I was going to call you. That's Kate's guy, so you can take a break from watching Marsh and take over from TJ for a while. He was watching Commissioner Reynolds. I want to know if he visits the Mountain View facility. And I want to know why the place is shrouded in secrecy. Stay safe, Heather." And I hung up.

At a little after two that afternoon, Tim tapped on my door, opened it and stepped inside, his laptop balanced in the crook of his arm. "You got a minute, Harry?"

I nodded. He sat down in front of my desk. I leaned back in my chair and waited.

"I've been accessing hospital databases and medical records from multiple facilities where Marsh had worked over the years," he said, after rubbing his eyes and adjusting his glasses. "Harry, this guy's been moving around a lot. He's worked at five different hospitals in the past ten years, usually leaving right before or after a suspicious patient death"

I nodded. "That sounds like a pattern of running when things get too hot?"

"Exactly. But here's the thing: each time he moves, he gets a positive recommendation from his previous employer, even when there were questions about his performance."

"And from that, you think...?"

"Well, someone must be protecting him, right? Or someone's paying the right people to provide him with clean references. Look at this." Tim rotated his laptop and showed me financial records for the hospital administrators who had provided Marsh's recommendations. "They all received substantial payments around the time they wrote his letters of recommendation."

I could only shake my head at the enormity of what I was hearing, and at the scope of the intrigue. And I couldn't help but wonder, *What the hell was Frank thinking, trying to handle it on his own? Surely he must have known they would eventually come after him.*

At a little after three, Kate called back with more information about the Mountain View Recovery Center. "I had Jack do some research on this facility, Harry," she said. "It's officially licensed as a drug rehabilitation clinic, but they only treat a very exclusive clientele. Patients who pay cash, use assumed names, and demand complete privacy."

"It sounds like the perfect place to hide someone like Catherine Wells," I replied. "What are you thinking?"

"I'm thinking that if she survived her attack and needed ongoing medical care, reconstructive surgery, or psychological treatment, this facility would be the place. No questions asked, no official records."

"But why would anyone do that for her?" I asked. "Why not just treat her in a regular hospital and be done with it. What would they gain?"

I could almost see her shaking her head. "I don't know," she replied. "I can only think that someone, for some reason, wanted her to stay dead, but also wanted her to live... if that makes any sense?"

I grinned. "Yeah, Kate, it makes sense. But the only way we're going to find the answers is to find her. Can we put surveillance on the facility?"

"Yes, I already have two people on the way over there. But Harry, the property is heavily secured with cameras, motion sensors, and private security. Getting close enough for meaningful surveillance is going to be challenging."

As the afternoon progressed, the evidence against Dr. Marsh continued to mount. Tim discovered that Marsh had been prescribing medications to patients who didn't exist, billing insurance companies for phantom procedures, and maintaining multiple medical licenses under different names.

"This guy is running a complete, frickin' medical fraud operation," Tim said, with no little amount of awe. He showed me the falsified medical records and billing statements. "He's been stealing identities, creating fake patients, and collecting insurance payments for years."

"And all the while murdering real patients and covering up crimes for the corruption network," I muttered

"D'you think he treated Catherine Wells at that private facility... if she's still alive?"

At that, I could only shake my head.

The financial records showed that Marsh had received over half a million dollars through various shell companies over the past five years, far more than he could have earned through his legitimate medical practice.

"Someone has been paying him very well for his services," I observed.

"And if Frank's investigation threatened to expose all of this..."

"Marsh would certainly have every reason to kill him."

By late afternoon, we had built a compelling case that Dr. Benjamin Marsh was not only involved in the original Riverside Strangler cover-up but had been operating as a professional killer and medical fraud specialist for years. His connection to Catherine Wells' treatment—if that's what happened—his suspicious patient deaths, and his financial ties to the corruption network made him one of our primary suspects for Frank's murder. But we still needed concrete proof of that, and we still needed to determine whether Catherine Wells was alive and being treated at his private facility.

"Tomorrow we need to get a closer look at the Mountain View Recovery Center," I said. "If Catherine is there, she might be the key to solving this entire case."

"And if she's not there?" Tim asked.

"Then we keep building our case against Marsh and the others until we have enough evidence for Kate to make arrests."

By six that evening I was ready to give it up and go home, so I did. I said goodnight to Jacque and went to my car thinking about the day's events. And I continued to think as I drove up Scenic Highway. I now knew that whatever else he was, Dr. Benjamin Marsh was my prime suspect in Frank's murder. And even if he had nothing to do with it, he was a key player in a criminal conspiracy that had been operating in Chattanooga for more than a decade.

But whether he was protecting Catherine Wells or had eliminated her as a threat remained to be seen. Tomorrow's investigation of the Mountain View facility might provide the answers we needed.

But, deep in my gut, I had the feeling there was more, much more.

8

JUDICIAL CORRUPTION

THURSDAY, AUGUST 18, 2024

I WAS LATE GETTING INTO THE OFFICE THURSDAY MORNING, arriving a little after ten to find Tim deep into his investigation of Judge Patricia Henley's financial records. He'd set up a complex display on his wall monitors showing bank statements, property records, and what appeared to be a web of shell companies and consulting arrangements.

"You didn't go home again last night, did you?" I said, settling into a chair beside his workstation.

"I did, actually," he replied, grinning at me. "I got a whole six hours of sleep."

I had to admit, he did look surprisingly refreshed.

"But I've been here since seven working on Henley's finances, and Harry, what I found is going to blow your mind."

He gestured to the main monitor, which displayed a timeline of Judge Henley's income and expenditures over the past decade. "Judge Henley's official salary is one hundred sixty-five thousand a year. But look at her actual spending patterns."

Tim clicked through several screens showing luxury purchases, expensive vacations, and real estate transactions. "In the past five years alone, she's spent over two million dollars on items that would be impossible to afford on a federal judge's salary."

"Geez, how the hell is she hiding that kind of income?" I asked.

"Very carefully," Tim said, pulling up another set of records. "She's been receiving payments through a complex series of financial arrangements designed to look like legitimate consulting fees and speaking engagements. But the amounts far exceed what any judge could reasonably earn from work on the side."

Tim opened a spreadsheet showing payment records. "Look at these speaking fees. She's supposedly been paid fifty thousand dollars for a one-hour presentation to the 'National Legal Education Foundation.' But when I researched that organization..."

"Let me guess," I said. "It doesn't exist?"

"Oh, it exists, but it's a shell company with no employees, no office, and no record of conducting any actual educational seminars. It's just a front for funneling payments to Henley."

I studied the financial data. "Any idea what kind of cases she's been fixing?" I asked.

Tim pulled up court records and case files. "Everything from organized crime to white-collar fraud to violent felonies. Frank had documented at least thirty major criminal cases over the past decade where Henley's decisions seemed to favor defendants who had connections to our corruption network."

I nodded slowly, thinking, then said, "Any with a connection to the Riverside Strangler investigation?" I asked.

"Uh huh," Tim said, opening a new set of files. "Frank had documented several instances where Henley influenced legal proceedings that could have exposed the Strangler cover-up. Whenever someone tried to file civil suits related to the investigation, or when family members of victims sought to have evidence reexamined, Henley found procedural reasons to dismiss or delay the cases."

My phone buzzed with a call from Kate. "Harry, I've been reviewing some of the court cases Tim sent me earlier this morning. Judge Henley's about as corrupt as I've ever seen."

"So tell me, what did you find?"

"I cross-referenced her decisions with our list of suspects. In every single case involving Reynolds, Marsh, or anyone connected to Greaves Enterprises, Henley ruled in favor of the defendants."

"That's a pattern that would be hard to explain as coincidence," I said.

"Hah, it's impossible to explain," she replied. "And there's something else. I found records showing that several key witnesses in these cases either disappeared or recanted their testimony shortly before trial."

"Witness intimidation, d'you think?" I asked.

"Or worse," she said. "Three potential witnesses have died in the past five years, all in accidents or from natural causes. But the timing is suspicious: each death occurred within weeks of being scheduled to testify in cases before Henley's court."

"Three witnesses? Kate, that can't be a coincidence either," I replied. "They're eliminating threats."

"That's what I'm thinking. And Harry, if they're willing to kill witnesses to protect Henley's corrupt decisions..."

"Then Frank's murder fits the pattern," I finished. "He was getting too close, wasn't he?"

"Exactly. We're not just looking at bribery and case fixing, we're looking at murder to protect a criminal conspiracy."

After ending the call with Kate, I turned back to Tim's investigation. "Sorry, Tim," I said. "Show me the financial connections. I want to know who's been paying Henley?"

Tim pulled up a complex flowchart showing money movements between various accounts and shell companies. "The payments are laundered through at least six different organizations, but I traced them back to their sources. Greaves Enterprises, the Elder Mountain Investment Group, and several other companies we've been investigating."

"The same network that's been paying Reynolds and Marsh," I muttered

"Exactly," Tim replied as he adjusted his glasses. "They've been using Henley to control the judicial system while using Reynolds to control police investigations and Marsh to eliminate problems."

I sat back in my chair and thought about it for a moment. "What we have here," I said, "is complete corruption of the justice system. These people can commit crimes, cover them up through police corruption, and ensure that anyone who threatens them either disappears or faces a corrupt judge."

"And Frank's investigation threatened to expose all of it," Tim said. "Which gives every one of them motive for murder."

"Keep digging, Tim," I said as I pushed my chair back. "If you find anything significant, give me a buzz."

He nodded and I left him to it.

Around eleven that morning, Amanda called with more disturbing news. "Harry, I've been investigating Judge Henley's lifestyle and financial situation for a potential story, and I'm getting pushback from management."

"I bet you are," I replied. "Who and what?"

"Jack Sharp, my news director called me into his office this morning and suggested I focus on 'more current stories' instead of what he called 'speculative investigations into respected public officials.'"

"That doesn't sound like normal editorial guidance," I said.

"That's what I thought," she replied. "So I did some digging into Channel 7's ownership structure. Harry, you're not going to believe this, but one of our parent company's major investors is the Elder Mountain Investment Group."

"You're kidding me," I said, stunned by the revelation. "That's the same shell company that's been funneling money to our suspects."

"And it seems they have enough influence to control which stories we cover and which ones get killed. When I started asking questions about Henley's expensive lifestyle, someone made a phone call."

"Amanda, you need to be careful. If they're willing to kill Frank and potentially other witnesses..."

"I know. But Harry, this proves the corruption extends beyond law enforcement and into the media."

"As I said, be very careful who you talk to and what you dig into," I said. "I don't like it, Amanda. Not one bit."

"I'll be fine," she said, "and I'll be careful. You be careful, too."

"Always," I replied, and hung up.

It was later that morning, around noon, when Kate called

with a proposal. "Harry, I want to investigate the Mountain View Recovery Center officially. I think I can get a warrant from Judge Strange."

"That's a much better approach than external surveillance," I said. "What's your plan?"

"I'll take my team—Corbin Russell, Tony Cooper, and Tracy Ramirez. We'll approach it as a wellness check related to a missing person case. But Harry, I want you there, too."

"You sure that's wise? If this facility is what we think it is..."

"That's exactly why I need you there. Your investigation has already uncovered connections we might miss. Besides, you're officially consulting on Frank's murder case."

"Okay," I replied. "If you say so."

An hour later, I met Kate and her team at the courthouse where she was meeting with Judge Henry Strange to obtain a search warrant. Judge Strange was one of the good guys; a longtime friend of my father's and someone I'd known since childhood. His integrity was beyond question, which made him the perfect choice for this sensitive operation.

"You ready?" she asked.

I nodded.

"Then let's go. We have an appointment and we don't need to keep him waiting."

"Harry," Judge Strange said, shaking my hand warmly. "Kate tells me you're consulting on the Callahan murder. Frank was a good man. I'm sorry for your loss."

"Thank you, Judge. We're hoping to find some answers."

Strange looked at Kate, his eyebrows raised in question.

Kate presented her case, explaining that Catherine Wells had been presumed dead but might be receiving treatment at Mountain View under an assumed name. She carefully avoided mentioning the broader corruption investigation, focusing only on the missing person angle.

"The facility's privacy protocols make it impossible to conduct a normal welfare check," Kate explained. "We need legal authority to verify whether a potential crime victim is being treated there."

Judge Strange reviewed the warrant application carefully. "This is highly unusual, Kate. Private medical facilities have significant patient privacy protections."

"Which is why we're being careful to follow proper procedures," Kate replied. "We're not seeking to violate legitimate patient confidentiality, just to determine if someone who was reported dead is actually alive and receiving care."

After twenty minutes of careful questioning, Judge Strange signed the warrant. "Be respectful of patient privacy," he warned. "And Kate, be careful. If your suspicions are correct, you may be walking into a dangerous situation."

An hour later, our little convoy approached the Mountain View Recovery Center. Kate drove the lead vehicle with Samson in the back seat wearing his badge and K9 harness. I rode up front with her while Corbin Russell and Tony Cooper followed in a second police vehicle, and Tracy Ramirez brought up the rear.

The facility was even more impressive than in the photographs. Nestled in the mountains just outside Chattanooga, it looked like a luxury resort rather than a medical facility. The main building was a sprawling modern structure with floor-to-ceiling windows and carefully landscaped grounds. But the high fences, security cameras, and armed guards made it clear this was no ordinary treatment center. Hell, it looked like a fancy internment compound.

"That's a lot of security for a rehab clinic," Corbin observed over the radio.

"Stay alert," Kate replied. "Remember, we're conducting a welfare check on a missing person. Be professional but prepared for anything."

The guard at the main gate examined our warrant carefully before calling the facility's administration. After a tense five-minute wait, the gates opened, and we were directed to park in front of the main building.

Dr. Angela Taggart, the facility director, met us at the entrance. She was a woman in her fifties with graying hair and a severely professional demeanor, but I could see tension in her eyes as she reviewed our warrant.

"This is highly irregular," Dr. Taggart said. "Our patients come here specifically for privacy and confidentiality. A police investigation could compromise their treatment."

"We understand your concerns," Kate replied. "We're not here to disrupt treatment or violate patient privacy. We're simply trying to verify whether a specific individual who was reported deceased might actually be alive and receiving care here."

Dr. Taggart led us into a comfortable conference room while she departed to review our warrant with someone whose name was never mentioned, and I had to wonder why not. Through the windows, I could see patients moving around the grounds: people of various ages engaged in what appeared to be therapeutic activities.

"The individual we're looking for would be approximately thirty-three years old now," Kate explained when Dr. Taggart returned. "Dark hair, approximately five-foot-six, admitted approximately nine years ago for treatment of traumatic injuries, possibly under an assumed name."

Dr. Taggart's poker face was impressive, but I caught a slight reaction when Kate mentioned the timeline. "I'll need to review our patient records," she said. "This will take some time."

While we waited, Tony Cooper and Tracy Ramirez conducted a walkthrough of the public areas of the facility. The place was indeed luxurious: private rooms, gourmet dining, extensive recreational facilities, and what appeared to be a state-of-the-art medical wing.

"This place would cost a fortune," Tracy observed quietly. "Who pays for treatment here?"

"People who value privacy above all else," I replied.

Samson, meanwhile, was providing his own form of investigation. The big German Shepherd was alert and focused, his nose working as he catalogued scents throughout the facility. Kate watched him carefully, knowing he would pick up things humans might miss.

After an hour, Dr. Taggart returned with a file folder. "We did have a patient who matches some aspects of your description," she admitted. "A woman admitted approximately nine years ago for treatment of severe traumatic injuries and psychological trauma."

Kate leaned forward. "Can you provide details about her treatment or current status?"

"I can only tell you that she completed her initial treatment program and was discharged into an outpatient care arrangement. She is no longer a resident of this facility."

"When was she discharged?"

"Approximately eighteen months ago."

"Do you have records of her outpatient treatment or current location?"

Dr. Taggart shook her head. "Patient privacy laws prevent

me from providing that information without additional legal authorization. I can confirm that we provided the care requested and that the patient was successfully treated for her injuries."

Kate and I exchanged glances. We weren't going to get much more information without a more specific warrant, but we'd confirmed that someone matching Catherine Wells' description had been treated at the facility.

"Did Dr. Benjamin Marsh ever provide treatment for this patient?" I asked.

Dr. Taggart's professional composure slipped slightly. "Dr. Marsh has consulted with our facility on various cases over the years. I cannot discuss specific patient-doctor relationships."

"One more question," Kate said to Dr. Taggart. "Do you maintain security footage of your facility?"

"For safety purposes, yes. But again, patient privacy concerns would prevent us from sharing that without specific legal authorization."

As we drove away from the facility, Kate's team debriefed over the radio.

"They're definitely hiding something," Corbin said. "That place has more security than most government buildings."

"And did you see the medical equipment in that wing?" Tony added. "That's not standard rehab equipment; that's trauma surgery and reconstructive surgery gear."

"Expensive equipment," Tracy observed. "And Dr. Taggart knew more than she was telling us."

Kate looked at me as we drove down the mountain road. "What do you think?"

"I think Catherine Wells was there, and I think she may have been there much longer than they're claiming. The question is whether she left voluntarily or whether she's been moved somewhere else. Kate, we've confirmed that the facility has been treating... questionable patients, that they have connections to Dr. Marsh, and that they're hiding information about a patient who matches Catherine Wells' description. That's enough for a more specific warrant."

As we drove back toward Chattanooga, I sat back in my seat thinking about the facility. It was obviously more than just a private rehab clinic. It was a place where people could go to disappear from their old lives and emerge with new identities. The question was whether Catherine Wells had been hidden there as a protected victim or as a criminal being sheltered by... *Who the hell knows?* One thing I did know was that we needed to dig deeper into the facility's connections and try to track down where Catherine Wells had gone.

But tonight, I needed to process what we'd learned and continue my search for Frank's missing backup evidence. The answers were out there somewhere, waiting to be discovered by someone smart enough to think like Frank Callahan. And Frank must have thought that was me, because, as far I as I knew, there was no one else.

The judicial corruption investigation would have to wait another day. Right now, the Mountain View facility had given us our most promising lead yet in the search for the truth about Catherine Wells and Frank Callahan's murder.

As the afternoon progressed, Tim continued uncovering evidence of Judge Henley's corruption. He found records showing that she'd been influencing not just criminal cases but also civil proceedings, contract disputes, and even family court matters.

"She's been selling justice to the highest bidder for years," Tim said, showing me case after case where Henley's decisions favored parties with connections to influential people. "Divorce settlements that awarded assets to abusive spouses, custody decisions that ignored child welfare, business disputes resolved in favor of companies that were clearly in the wrong."

"How many lives has she destroyed for money, I wonder?" I muttered.

"Dozens, maybe hundreds. And Harry, there's something else that really bothers me. Several of the families affected by her corrupt decisions have children who later ended up in the juvenile justice system. That's not right."

Late in the afternoon, I heard from Agent French. "Harry, my superiors are getting nervous about the scope of your investigation. They're worried about political fallout if this goes public."

"Oh yeah? You want to tell me about it?" I asked, caustically.

"The kind of fallout that comes from exposing systematic corruption involving federal judges, police commissioners, and major business leaders. They want assurances that any arrests will be based on ironclad evidence."

"You can tell your bosses we're working on that," I said, "but we need more time."

"You may not have much time," she replied. "My sources tell me that important members of the network are already preparing their exit strategy."

"We're doing the best we can," I replied. "That it? Are you done?" I wasn't happy. Getting pressure from the locals was one thing. Getting it from the FBI was quite another.

She was quiet for a moment, then said, "Yes, that's it for now."

"Then you have a good evening, Agent French," I said and hung up.

That evening, before I left for home, I went to Tim's lair to see how he was doing. The upshot of that was: "I found something else that's really disturbing," he said. "It appears Henley's been coordinating with officials in other cities."

"Why am I not surprised?" I muttered wearily. "Look, Tim, I need you to focus on the timeline around Frank's death. Look for any communications between Henley and the other suspects in the days leading up to his murder. Also check for any cases or legal proceedings that Frank's investigation might have affected."

"Okay…" Tim said.

I told him to close up shop for the evening and go home and get some rest, and that I'd see him bright and early in the morning. And I made sure he went. I walked him out to his car, watched him settle and then drive away, but not before I warned him I didn't want to see him in the office before nine the following morning. "And get some frickin' proper sleep, you little monster."

Me? I drove home that evening, my mind churning. Frank's missing backup evidence remained elusive, despite my continued efforts to think of where he might have hidden it. But even without Frank's files, we were building a compelling case against Judge Henley and maybe even other members of the network.

Tomorrow, I knew we'd need to dig deeper into the Mountain View facility and try to determine what role it played in the conspiracy. If Catherine Wells was still being hidden there, she might be the key to understanding the entire operation. If not, where the hell was she? And what if she was involved in the murders rather than a victim? It seemed to me as I made the turn onto East Brow that judicial corruption was just one piece of a much larger puzzle, and we were running out of time to solve it.

Finally, as I turned in through the gates to my home, I remembered what Frank had told me more times than I could remember: 'Justice is worth fighting for. But sometimes the fight comes at a price higher than anyone was prepared to pay.'

9

FAMILY SECRETS

I WOKE UP FRIDAY MORNING TO THE SOUND OF JADE'S laughter drifting up from the kitchen, followed by Amanda's voice trying to maintain some semblance of order during what was obviously an elaborate breakfast production. The clock on my nightstand read six-thirty; early for a six-year-old to be up and causing mayhem.

I found them in the kitchen, where Jade was standing on a step stool at the counter, covered in flour and wielding a wooden spoon like a magic wand. Amanda stood beside her, equally flour-dusted, trying to salvage what appeared to be an attempt at making pancakes from scratch.

"Daddy!" Jade announced without turning around. "We're making surprise breakfast!"

"I can see that," I said, kissing Amanda's cheek and noting the fine coating of flour in her hair. "How surprised should I be?"

"Very," Amanda replied with a grin. "Your daughter decided we needed 'special detective pancakes' to help you catch the bad man."

"Detective pancakes?"

Jade turned to face me, her jade-green eyes bright with excitement. "They're shaped like magnifying glasses! See?" She held up a misshapen blob of batter that, with considerable imagination, might resemble a magnifying glass.

"That's perfect, princess," I said, lifting her down from the step stool. "Every detective needs proper fuel for solving cases."

"Will they really help you catch the bad man?" she asked, suddenly serious.

I knelt down to her level. "They'll definitely give me the energy I need to keep working on it."

"Good," she said, nodding solemnly. "Because mommy says the bad man made you sad, and I don't like it when you're sad."

"I'm not sad when I'm with my girls," I said, pulling both of them into a hug that left us all even more flour-covered than before.

Breakfast that morning was an adventure, but turned out surprisingly good.

I arrived at my office at eight-thirty that Friday morning to find Tim hunched over his workstation, surrounded by the usual debris field of coffee cups and energy drink cans.

"I thought I told you I didn't want to see you here before nine?" I scolded him. "I've a good mind to send you home for the rest of the day."

I wasn't angry with him, and he knew it, because he grinned up at me and said, "But you won't, will you, boss?"

"No, I won't. Did you get some sleep?" I said, settling into the chair beside his workspace.

"I did, and seven hours, which is a lot for me," Tim replied distractedly without looking up from his monitors.

"Okay, so what have you got?" I asked, resignedly.

He said nothing for a minute, then, "I've been analyzing the financial connections between our suspects, and there are some patterns that don't make sense."

He gestured to his main display, which showed what appeared to be a complex network diagram with financial transactions, shell companies, and bank transfers spanning several years.

"I've been tracing money flows between Commissioner Reynolds, Judge Henley, Dr. Marsh, and Thomas Greaves," Tim continued, adjusting his glasses. "There's been a lot of activity over the years."

I leaned closer to study the display. The screen showed interconnected transactions between various accounts and corporate entities, with amounts ranging from thousands to hundreds of thousands of dollars.

"So tell me about it," I said.

Tim clicked through several screens, showing bank records, property transfers, and what appeared to be coded communications. "Systematic money laundering," he said, "case fixing, evidence tampering, and witness elimination. Look at this pattern."

"Yeah, I see it," I said. "We've already established the pattern, but how does all this tie in with Frank? Show me what Frank found about Reynolds, Henley, and Marsh."

Tim pulled up individual files for each suspect. "Commissioner Reynolds has been receiving regular payments through Public Safety Solutions," Tim explained.

"Okay, so how much has he received?"

"Over two hundred thousand dollars in the past three years alone. Always in amounts just under the federal reporting requirements."

Tim switched to Judge Henley's records. "Henley's been even more careful. Her payments come through a law firm that specializes in 'judicial education seminars.' She's supposedly been paid speaking fees for conferences that either didn't happen or had no record of her participation."

"And Dr. Marsh?" I asked.

"Medical consulting fees from a research company that doesn't conduct any actual research. It's another shell operation designed to hide bribery payments."

Tim sat back in his chair, linked his hands together behind his neck, swiveled his chair a little, and stared at me.

"So?" I said.

"So, you asked what Frank had discovered. This is it. It's no wonder they killed him."

I shook my head, blew a deep breath out through my lips, and said, "Yeah, you're right, Tim. The Riverside Strangler case was just a part of a much larger investigation of crime and corruption. It's no wonder someone decided to shut him up… permanently."

"Exactly," Tim agreed. "And Harry, there's something else, and it's really important."

He lowered his arms, swiveled his chair back to face his display and typed quickly, highlighting a series of transactions between multiple shell companies. "Every time a major criminal case was dismissed, or evidence disappeared, money moved between these accounts within forty-eight hours. And Commissioner Reynolds appears to be the one coordinating the entire operation."

Again, I shook my head. I couldn't help it. I mean, a police commissioner. It's... It was beyond belief.

"How much money are we talking about?" I asked, leaning back in my chair.

"Millions of dollars over the past five years alone. Reynolds has been using his position to facilitate various criminal activities while..." He paused, then said, "What are we going to do about it, Harry?"

I studied the financial data. It was obvious, even to me, that the scope of the conspiracy went far beyond Frank's murder.

"I don't know, Tim," I said, staring at the monitors. "All this..." I nodded at the displays. "It's beyond me. How the hell did Frank get himself entangled in this mess?"

"I think he must have stumbled onto it while investigating the Riverside Strangler case," Tim said.

"That's what it looks like," I replied. "Frank was meticulous. If there's a link between the Strangler case and this"—I waved a hand at the main screen—"His methodical approach to the investigation would have inevitably led him to the financial irregularities that would have exposed the entire network."

My phone rang. I frowned at the interruption. "Geez, will this thing never stop ringing?" I said as I struggled to retrieve it from my pocket. I looked at the screen. It was Kate.

"Harry, I need you at the station," she said when I answered. "Chief Johnston wants a briefing on our findings, and Captain Morrison is here to coordinate departmental resources for the investigation."

"Morrison?" I asked. I knew the name. In fact, I'd worked with her once, back when I was a cop. She was a sergeant then, and a good cop, as I recalled.

"Yeah, Lisa Morrison is one of our senior captains. She worked with Frank years ago and has been helping coordinate the official response to his murder. The chief wants her involved in any federal cooperation."

"Okay. I'll be there in thirty minutes," I said.

"Good, and bring Tim with you."

"The chief asked for Tim?" I said, as he looked round at me.

"No," she replied. "That would be me."

Thirty minutes later, Kate led Tim and me to a secure conference room at the police department, where Chief Johnston waited with the woman I recognized as the onetime Sergeant Morrison.

Detective Captain Lisa Morrison was a woman in her mid-forties with short brown hair and intelligent dark eyes. "Harry Starke," she said, smiling as she stood up and offered me her hand. "We meet again. It's been a long time. How are you?" Her handshake was firm; her skin warm to the touch. "I'm sorry for the loss of Frank Callahan. He was a good detective and a good man. I worked with him briefly when I was a sergeant, and I have nothing but respect for his dedication."

"Thank you," I replied. "Kate tells me you're coordinating departmental resources for the investigation."

Morrison nodded. "Chief Johnston"—she looked round at him—"asked me to ensure our department provides full cooperation with the federal authorities and, of course, your involvement in the investigation. Frank's murder is priority one for all of us."

Chief Johnston gestured for everyone to take seats around the conference table, then looked at Tim and said, "Welcome, Tim. It's been a while."

Tim looked embarrassed as the Chief introduced him to Morrison. He stood, coughed, cleared his throat, poked at his glasses, and then offered her his hand. "Nice to meet you, miss... I mean, Captain."

She smiled at him and said, "It's nice to meet you, too, Tim. I've heard a lot about you."

Tim nodded, his face red, and sat down.

"Well, Harry, what have you found?" Johnston asked, leaning back in his chair, his arms folded across his chest.

I looked at Tim, who connected his laptop to the conference room's display screen. He cleared his throat, took a deep breath and began, "We've uncovered evidence of a criminal conspiracy involving several prominent individuals, including Commissioner Reynolds."

At that, Johnston unfolded his arms, leaned forward and snarled, "This had better be damn good, Harry."

Tim blanched. His face went white.

Morrison leaned forward, studying the financial diagrams Tim displayed. "It's okay, Tim. Take it easy. We're all friends here. But these are serious allegations. What kind of evidence are we talking about?"

Tim walked them through the money laundering patterns, case-fixing correlations, and communication intercepts that pointed to corruption involving Reynolds' network. And as he did so, Morrison asked detailed questions about the evidence, taking careful notes and offering observations about police procedures and legal requirements.

Morrison studied the financial diagrams. "Someone with serious administrative access set this up. Reynolds has that kind of authority, but we'll need a mountain of evidence to make charges stick against a commissioner."

"That's why we're taking this slow," Kate said. "One

screwed-up procedure and his lawyers will get everything thrown out."

Morrison nodded approvingly. "Frank would have approached it the same way," She said, paused, then added, "I remember him saying that justice delayed is justice denied, but justice rushed is justice destroyed."

Slowly shaking his head, Johnston studied the financial evidence. "What do you need from the department, Harry?"

"Access to case files, evidence lockers, and any records that might show how investigations were influenced or misdirected," I replied. "Tim also needs to analyze database access logs to understand how information was being shared within the network."

"Captain Morrison can coordinate that access," the chief said. "She'll be your departmental liaison for any official requests."

Morrison made notes on her pad. "I'll start gathering the files immediately," she said.

As we prepared to leave, Morrison approached me. "Mr. Starke, Frank told me you had the best instincts for reading crime scenes he'd ever seen. He told me about that warehouse case where you spotted the evidence everyone else missed. He said you never gave up on a case once you sank your teeth into it."

"Thank you. That means a lot," I said. "Frank was my mentor."

"He believed in doing things the right way, no matter how long it took or how difficult it became," Morrison replied. "I hope you'll approach this investigation with the same dedication."

"Oh, I intend to," I said with a wry smile. "Whatever I am, I owe most of it to Frank. Look, I have to go, but I'll leave Tim with you. If you could see he has what he needs, I'd be grateful."

"Of course," she said, offering me her hand. "Thank you for coming, Harry."

An hour later, I met Agent French at a small café near the courthouse. She looked more stressed than during our previous meetings, with the kind of tension that comes from handling explosive information.

"Your investigation is moving in the right direction," French said after the usual niceties and the delivery of two cups of black coffee. "It certainly looks as if Commissioner Reynolds is at the center of a criminal network we've been tracking for months."

"What can you tell me about the federal investigation?" I asked.

"It goes deep, Harry," she replied. "Reynolds appears to be heading a sophisticated operation with connections to organized crime throughout the Southeast."

She pulled out a manila folder but kept it closed on the table. "Marcus Sullivan was building a case against Reynolds when he was killed. His files contain evidence of financial crimes, evidence tampering, and what appears to be a systematic approach to corrupting law enforcement and judicial proceedings."

"How close was Sullivan to making arrests?" I asked.

"Very close," French said grimly. "But his death set back the federal investigation significantly. Reynolds and his associates became more careful, making it harder to gather the additional evidence we need."

French slid the folder across the table. "This contains what we can share about Reynolds' network. Use it carefully. If Reynolds realizes he's under federal investigation, he'll either disappear or take steps to eliminate all the remaining witnesses."

I nodded as I opened the folder just enough to see surveillance photographs and financial documents, then closed it again. I looked again at French. She was obviously stressed, and the fact that what she was sharing wasn't lost on me. This was federal evidence in an active investigation, and she was risking her career by providing it.

"What kind of timeline are we looking at?" I asked.

"Weeks, maybe less," French replied grimly. "Reynolds and his associates are already showing signs of preparing exit strategies. If they realize how close we are to making arrests, they'll accelerate those plans."

"And you think they'll eliminate the witnesses? Any idea who they might be?"

French's expression darkened. "That much I can't share, but Frank and Sullivan are proof they won't hesitate to kill anyone who threatens their operation. Your investigation has already made you a target, Harry. Be very careful who you trust."

I tucked the folder inside my jacket. "What about Kate and my team?"

"Federal protection is available if needed, but it comes with restrictions that might compromise your investigation. For now, stay alert, I suggest you vary your routines, and assume you're being watched."

"Understood," I muttered.

French stood to leave, then paused. "Harry, Reynolds has been a police commissioner for eight years, before that he was the county's chief deputy. He knows how investigations work, he has access to resources and personnel, and, though I doubt he did it personally, he's already demonstrated he's willing to kill law enforcement officers. Don't underestimate what he's capable of."

"One more thing," I said as she gathered her things. "If this network is as connected as you say, how do we know our communications are secure? Reynolds has access to police resources, and if he's monitoring our investigation..."

French paused. "We've been using encrypted channels, but you're right to be concerned. Assume any police department communications could be compromised. If you need to reach me urgently, use the secure number in that folder and the encryption protocols we provided."

"And if things go sideways before you're ready to make arrests?"

"Then you call the number in the file immediately and get your family somewhere safe. We'll worry about the legal niceties later."

As I drove back to my office, I let my mind wander, thinking how the investigation was expanding beyond Frank's murder to encompass a much larger criminal conspiracy. Reynolds appeared to be the central figure, but what about Judge Henley, Dr. Marsh, and Thomas Greaves? I shook my head as I drifted across the road and decided to concentrate on my driving, rather than the several ways I knew these guys could and would kill to protect themselves.

Back at the office, I found Jacque organizing files and preparing legal briefs for the various aspects of our investigation.

"How much trouble are we in if Reynolds realizes we're onto him?" I asked.

"Serious trouble," Jacque replied. "A police commissioner has access to all sorts of resources and information."

I nodded. "Tim back yet?" I asked.

"He is. He's back in his hidey hole," she replied.

"Okay," I said. "I'll go have a quick word with him, then I'll be in my office, if you need me."

Tim looked up from his computer. "Hey, Harry. I've been analyzing the communication patterns between the suspects, and they've been coordinating their activities more frequently since Frank's murder."

He pulled up phone records and email logs. "Regular communications, meetings at unusual times and locations, financial transactions that suggest they're implementing some kind of contingency plan."

"You think they're getting ready to run?" I asked.

"Maybe," he replied. "Either that or they're planning to eliminate remaining threats. I'm thinking our investigation must have gotten their attention."

"Stay on it, Tim, and keep me updated with any new developments."

I went to my office and settled down to catch up on some paperwork. I was still at it when Kate called. I looked at my watch. It was almost five.

"Kate. What's up?" I asked.

"I thought I'd let you know that Captain Morrison has provided access to department files. She's arranged for us to review evidence from several cases that might have been influenced by Reynolds' network."

"You know she and I worked together on a case, back in the day," I said

"No, I didn't. How did you get along with her?"

"We got along well together. She's professional and thorough."

"She knew Frank well and seems committed to seeing his killer brought to justice."

I nodded to myself. "It's good to know we have at least one ally in the department."

"Oh, come on, Harry. We have more than one. I trust my entire team with my life. I gotta go. I have stuff to do, and I don't want to be here all night. Talk to you tomorrow." And she hung up.

I put the phone down, leaned back in my chair, linked my hands together behind my neck and stared up at the chandelier, thinking. Nah, not really thinking; wondering what the hell I'd gotten myself into this time.

I was still there, still staring up at the chandelier when Jacque came in thirty minutes later to tell me it was time to lock up and go home. So I did, determined to have a quiet evening and a good night's sleep.

10

FOLLOWING THE MONEY

SATURDAY, AUGUST 20, 2024

I WOKE SATURDAY MORNING TO THE SMELL OF BACON AND coffee drifting up from the kitchen. Amanda was already up, standing at the stove in her silk robe, her hair pulled back in a loose ponytail. She looked over her shoulder when I appeared in the doorway.

"Good morning, sleepyhead," she said, flipping bacon in the skillet. "Jade's still asleep, so I thought I'd make us a proper breakfast for once."

"What's the occasion?" I asked, wrapping my arms around her waist from behind.

"No occasion. I just wanted to spend a few minutes with my husband before he disappears for another day of chasing criminals."

I kissed her neck, breathing in the familiar scent of her shampoo. "I promise I'll be careful."

"I know you will," she said, leaning back against me. "But Harry, if this gets too dangerous..."

"We'll cross that bridge when we come to it," I said, though we both knew the investigation was already more dangerous than either of us wanted to admit.

"Just promise me you won't take any unnecessary risks," she said, turning back to the stove. "Jade needs her daddy."

"I need her daddy too," I replied, wrapping my arms around her again.

We ate breakfast together in the quiet kitchen, the morning sunlight streaming through the windows making everything feel normal despite the gathering storm clouds over the Frank Callahan investigation..

Forty minutes later, at eight-twenty-five, fortified by Amanda's bacon and eggs, I arrived at my office to find Jacque at her desk, TJ and Heather in their offices, and, predictably, Tim in the conference room, the wall monitors displaying a series of complex flowcharts, bank records, and transaction histories. "Hey, Harry," he said, brightly when I poked my nose inside.

"Tell me you went home last night," I said, stepping inside.

"Of course I did," he replied, grinning at me. "What d'you think I am? I was home by seven, in bed at nine, and I came in at six," he said, adjusting his glasses.

I narrowed my eyes. "Tim, if I thought..." I didn't complete the thought, instead, I said, "I'm gonna take that key away from you, if you don't do as I say. No one can run on just four hours sleep. Okay, so what have you got for me? Anything good?"

"I'll let you be the judge of that," he said, sitting back in his chair and gesturing to the main display, a one-hundred-inch wall monitor, which showed an intricate web of financial transactions between multiple accounts and shell companies. "I've been diving deeper into the money flows around Commissioner Reynolds, and it's pretty extensive."

I studied the charts. The network showed large, regular transactions between Reynolds, Henley, Marsh, and Greaves, with connections to dozens of other accounts and businesses.

"Walk me through it," I said.

Tim clicked to a detailed breakdown showing millions in transactions over five years. "This is Reynolds' operation. Look at these patterns."

He highlighted a series of transactions. "Every time a high-profile criminal case gets dismissed or evidence disappears, money flows from Greaves Enterprises to accounts controlled by Judge Henley. Then smaller amounts move to Dr. Marsh and other accounts we haven't identified yet."

"How much are we talking about?" I asked.

"Three point seven million dollars in traceable transactions. Probably double that when you factor in cash payments and offshore accounts." Tim opened another screen. "Greaves has been running fake construction projects to launder money, Henley's been fixing cases at the federal level, and Marsh has been eliminating problems."

I leaned back in my chair, studying the data. "And Frank stumbled onto all of this while investigating the Riverside Strangler case?"

"That's what it looks like," he replied. "Frank was famous for 'following the money.' I'm thinking his investigation into old evidence and case files led him to discover these irregularities."

Tim pulled up another display. "And then there's this," he continued. "There are some older financial transactions that don't seem connected to Reynolds' network at all. A different pattern, smaller amounts, going back further."

"How far back?" I asked.

"It starts about ten years ago," he replied. "Someone else has been receiving payments for something, but it doesn't appear to be part of the big money laundering operation."

My phone buzzed with a text from Kate: "Morning, Harry. Morrison has received permission to access the evidence lockers. Can you meet us at the PD? And bring Tim with you."

"Grab your gear," I said to Tim. "Kate wants us at the PD."

"Good timing," Tim said, saving his work. "I'd like to cross-reference these financial patterns with actual case files."

I told Jacque where I was going, and TJ and Heather to keep an eye on Reynolds and Marsh respectively, and then we left. And, less than ninety minutes after I arrived at work, Kate led Tim and me to the department's evidence locker, where Captain Morrison was waiting with a stack of file boxes and a cart loaded with evidence containers.

"I pulled everything I could find related to cases involving Reynolds," she explained, gesturing to the cart. "Financial crimes, dismissed cases, anything where he had administrative oversight."

She handed Kate a detailed inventory. "I also included some cases that Frank had requested access to in recent months. I thought they might be relevant."

I thanked her, and she moved away, sat down and folded her arms. Me? I studied the file labels. Most were recent cases involving drug trafficking, money laundering, and organized crime, and I immediately noted the pattern, a pattern that wouldn't readily be noticed had they not been gathered together: cases that should have resulted in convictions but ended in dismissals or reduced charges.

"This is exactly what we need," Kate said. "Tim, can you cross-reference these case numbers with your financial data?"

"I reckon I can," Tim replied, opening his laptop. As he worked, I noticed Morrison watching him.

"He's impressive," Morrison said quietly after catching my look. "Frank always said a good investigator needs to adapt to new technology."

"Tim's the best at what he does," I agreed. "What was Frank's impression of how these cases were handled?"

Morrison's expression grew thoughtful. "He had concerns about procedural irregularities, and he believed someone was manipulating the outcomes."

Kate pulled out a case file from three years ago. "Look at this," she said. "This is a drug trafficking case with enough evidence to put away a major distributor but then key evidence becomes inadmissible due to search warrant technicalities."

"Judge Henley's court," Morrison noted, reading the file. "She ruled the warrant was improperly executed."

Tim looked up from his laptop. "That case shows up in my financial analysis. Two days after the dismissal, one hundred thousand dollars was moved from a Greaves shell company to one of Henley's consulting accounts."

"There's our connection," I said. "Reynolds identifies profitable cases, Greaves provides funding, Henley dismisses charges, and everyone gets paid."

Over the next two hours, we reviewed dozens of case files while Tim cross-referenced them with his financial data. The pattern was clear: Reynolds' network had been manipulating criminal cases for years, generating millions in profits while criminals walked free.

"Hundreds of criminals back on the streets," Morrison said grimly.

My phone buzzed with a message from Agent French: "New intel. Need to meet."

"Agent French wants to meet," I told Kate.

"Go," Kate said. "Lisa and I will continue reviewing these files."

An hour later, I met Agent French at a small park outside the city where our conversation couldn't be overheard or recorded.

"Your financial analysis is confirming what we suspected," French said. "Reynolds' network has been operating for years. Money laundering, case fixing, contract killings."

"How close are you to making arrests?"

"Closer than we were before your investigation," French replied. "But there's something else. We think there might be additional criminal activity that's not part of Reynolds' operation."

She pulled out a manila folder. "Marcus Sullivan found evidence tampering and case manipulation that predates Reynolds' network. Someone's been corrupting investigations for over a decade."

"A different organization?" I asked frowning.

"We're not sure. Sullivan believed it might be an individual operating independently." French handed me the folder. "This contains what we can share about the older activities. Be careful with it."

I scanned the documents inside. Financial records, case files, and witness statements spanning ten years. "Any theories about who might be involved?"

"Sullivan had some ideas, but he was killed before he could

develop solid evidence. Whoever's behind these older activities is more careful than the Reynolds group. More subtle."

As I drove back to the station, I thought about the new revelation and how complex Frank's investigation had become. The Reynolds network was a clear case of organized crime on a grand scale with identifiable players and traceable money. But now there was something else, older and more deeply hidden.

Back at the police department, I found Kate and Morrison still reviewing the evidence files.

"What did Agent French have to say?" Kate asked.

I pursed my lips before replying, then said, "She confirmed that Frank was also investigating something else. Something going back more than eight years that might not be connected to Reynolds at all."

Morrison looked up from her files. "That might explain some irregularities I found. Evidence tampering that doesn't fit Reynolds' methods."

"Such as?"

"More subtle. Witness statements with minor changes, evidence that disappears briefly then returns, crime scene photos that don't quite match the reports."

Tim connected his laptop to the conference room's display. "I also found some older financial transactions that don't connect to Reynolds' network. Different funding sources, smaller amounts, going back about ten years."

"So... That's it, then. It confirms that someone else *is* manipulating cases," I muttered.

"But for what purpose?" Kate asked.

Morrison studied the timeline Tim displayed. "Maybe Frank was investigating multiple cases without realizing they were separate. That would have made him dangerous to more than one criminal operation."

As the afternoon progressed, we continued building evidence against Reynolds' network while puzzling over the older, mysterious activities. Reynolds' operation was clear. It was a profitable conspiracy involving high-level corruption. But the older pattern remained a mystery.

"We need to identify what those older activities were about," Kate said as we prepared to wrap up for the day. "Frank's murder could be connected to either one."

Morrison gathered her files. "I'll continue reviewing the older cases tomorrow. If there's a pattern of evidence manipulation going back ten years, I should be able to find it."

"Thanks for"—I glanced around the files and evidence scattered across numerous tables—"all this access," I told her. "Frank would have appreciated your thoroughness."

"Frank deserves justice," Morrison replied simply. "So, whatever it takes."

I nodded. "Tim, we need to go. I need to get back to the office. Kate, we'll talk tomorrow. Thank you again, Captain Morrison."

It had been a good day, but as Tim and I headed out to my car, I had a deep-seated feeling that we were missing something important. Frank had been investigating the Riverside Strangler case when he was killed. Beginning ten years ago, the Strangler had killed ten young women over eighteen months and then stopped. But why did the killer stop? Frank's discoveries had led him from one thing to another, culminating in the Reynolds conspiracy. Were the two connected in some way? If so, I wasn't seeing it. I didn't know, but what I did know was that something didn't add up, and I had to figure out what that was.

"Tim, I want you to keep working on those older financial patterns," I said as I pulled out of the police department lot onto Amnicola Highway. "There's something there we're missing, and we need to figure out what, why, when and who."

"You got it boss," Tim replied. "But Harry, whoever's behind the older stuff is good at hiding their tracks. This might take some time."

"Frank had ten years to build his case," I said. "We need to do better than that."

As I drove home that evening, Agent French's words echoed through my mind. *Personal reasons rather than profit.* If she was right, someone had been corrupting investigations for a decade, but not for money. She *was* right about one thing: the older activity felt somehow different from Reynolds' network. It was… more desperate, more willing to kill to protect secrets.

Frank had been methodical in his investigation, following every lead wherever it took him. That thoroughness had ultimately cost him his life, but it had also provided us with evidence of criminal conspiracies spanning ten years.

As I turned onto Scenic Highway, I let out a deep breath and shook my head. *Tomorrow,* I thought, *we'll continue building cases against Reynolds and his associates and try to identify who'd been manipulating Frank's investigations. Both operations are connected in some way and are dangerous, but in different ways.*

Justice for Frank meant we had to solve both mysteries, no matter how long it took or how dangerous the investigation became. I was determined to finish what he'd started.

11

THE ATTACK

SUNDAY, AUGUST 21, 2024

I WOKE SUNDAY MORNING TO THE SOUND OF RAIN DRUMMING against the bedroom windows and Amanda already up, moving quietly around the room as she got dressed for a morning run.

"You're not seriously going out in this weather," I said, squinting at the clock that showed it was only six-thirty.

"It's just a light drizzle," she replied, putting on a baseball cap. "Besides, I need to clear my head before I tackle that investigative piece on city budget irregularities."

"Be careful," I said, sitting up in bed. "And take your phone."

She kissed my forehead. "Don't I always? Jade's still asleep, so you can have a quiet morning with your coffee and case files."

After Amanda left, I got up, showered, dressed, made coffee and settled at the kitchen table with Agent French's folder from yesterday. The older financial patterns Tim had discovered were troubling.

My phone rang at eight-fifteen. It was Kate.

"Harry, I need you to check out something for me. Can you swing by Detective Sullivan's old neighborhood this morning?"

"Kate, It's Sunday... Sure. What am I looking for?"

"Sullivan's landlord called yesterday. He said he found some boxes in the basement storage unit that belonged to Marcus. They might contain something related to his investigation."

"Why don't you handle it?" I asked.

"Because I'm going to be tied up with Chief Johnston all morning, going over security protocols after what you discovered about Reynolds yesterday. Besides, you knew Sullivan better than any of us."

"On a frickin' Sunday. What the hell's he thinking?"

"Oh, he's pissed," she replied. "This Reynolds thing is getting to him, I think."

"Well, all right, then," I said.

An hour later, after Amanda came home, I was driving through the Northshore district where Sullivan had lived in a converted warehouse apartment. The neighborhood was a mix of artists' lofts and young professionals, the kind of place where a federal agent could blend in without attracting attention.

The landlord, a nervous man in his sixties named Pete Kowalski, met me at the building's entrance.

"I feel terrible about this," he said, leading me toward the basement. "Marcus was a good tenant, never any problems. When he died, the FBI came and cleared out his apartment, but they missed the storage unit. There are three or four file boxes that look like official stuff. I didn't want to throw them away in case they were important, but I also didn't know who to call."

The basement was dimly lit, with rows of storage units separated by chicken wire. Sullivan's unit was in the back corner, secured with a combination lock that Kowalski cut with bolt cutters.

Inside were four banker's boxes labeled with dates spanning the past three years. I opened the first one and found it filled with case files, financial records, and surveillance photographs. All were related to corruption investigations in the Southeast.

"This is exactly what we need," I told Kowalski. "I'll make sure the FBI gets them."

A few minutes later, as I was loading the boxes into my Range Rover, I noticed a dark sedan parked across the street. The two men in the front seat were both wearing sunglasses despite the overcast morning. When I looked directly at them, the driver started the engine.

I finished loading the boxes, thanked Kowalski, got into my car, and pulled away. And, as I did so, the sedan pulled out behind me. *I see,* I thought. *I have company. Let's see if I can lose them.*

For the next ten minutes, I took a circuitous route through the residential streets, making random turns and doubling back. The sedan stayed with me, maintaining its distance, which confirmed it wasn't a coincidence.

I was approaching the intersection of Cherokee Boulevard and Riverside Drive when they made their move. The sedan accelerated and pulled alongside my Range Rover. The passenger window rolled down, and I caught a glimpse of tactical gear.

I floored the accelerator and yanked the steering wheel hard to the right, tires squealing as I took the corner onto Riverside Drive. The sedan followed, but my modified engine gave the Range Rover more power than they'd expected.

I reached for my phone to call Kate, but the sedan rammed my rear bumper, sending the Range Rover skidding toward the guardrail overlooking the Tennessee River. I fought to maintain control, adrenaline surging as I realized these guys were professionals and prepared to kill.

The sedan pulled alongside me again, and this time I saw the passenger clearly. Military haircut, tactical vest, assault rifle. He gestured for me to pull over, but I kept driving, weaving between traffic as we approached the Market Street Bridge.

They rammed me again, harder this time. The Range Rover's rear window exploded in a shower of safety glass, and I felt the vehicle start to spin. I managed to straighten it out, but the sedan was already positioning for another impact.

That's when I saw the Chattanooga Police Department cruiser approaching from the opposite direction. I flashed my headlights and honked the horn, hoping to attract the officer's attention. The sedan's driver saw the cruiser too and immediately backed off, taking the next exit at high speed.

The patrol officer, a young sergeant named Davis whom I recognized from Kate's unit, pulled over and approached my damaged vehicle with his hand on his weapon.

"Mr. Starke? Are you all right? What the hell happened here?"

"I don't really know," I replied, through the open window. "I'm thinking it was a professional hit team," I said, climbing out of the Range Rover to assess the damage. "They've been following me since I left the Northshore district."

Davis immediately called for backup and requested that Kate be notified. Within fifteen minutes, the scene was swarming with police vehicles, crime scene technicians, and federal agents.

Kate arrived with Captain Morrison, both looking grim as they surveyed my damaged vehicle and listened to my account of the attack.

"This was clearly intimidation rather than elimination," Morrison observed, studying the impact patterns on my Range Rover. "If they'd wanted you dead, they would have used different tactics."

"I think they wanted the files I recovered from Sullivan's storage unit," I said, gesturing to the boxes still intact in the back of my vehicle. "They were at Sullivan's house when I was loading the boxes. They followed me from there. Someone knew where I was going."

Kate's expression darkened. "Only three people knew about your trip this morning. Me, you, and the landlord."

"Which means either the landlord is connected to Reynolds' network, or they're monitoring our communications," Morrison said.

Tim arrived with his laptop a few moments later and immediately began to analyze the crime scene while Kate worked with federal agents who were processing my vehicle for evidence.

"Harry," Tim said, pulling me aside. "I found something yesterday that I didn't get a chance to tell you. There's monitoring software embedded in the police department's main database system."

"Are you frickin' serious?" I said, stunned. "Why the hell didn't you tell me, Tim? That kind of thing is important; real important."

He looked chagrined, shrugged, then muttered, "I know. I should have told you immediately, but with everything happening so fast, I didn't realize how critical it was."

I opened my mouth to speak, then closed it again. There was no point in chastising him further. He looked devastated.

"Never mind," I said. "It is what it is. Tell me about the monitoring."

"It's the kind that tracks every search, every file access, every communication that goes through the servers. Someone's been watching the investigation in real-time."

Morrison overheard him and joined our conversation. "That would explain how they knew about your meeting with the landlord. If Reynolds has administrative access to our systems, he could track all of our activities."

Kate called a secure meeting at a nearby restaurant, away from any police department communications that might be compromised. Over coffee and scrambled eggs, we discussed the implications of the morning's attack.

"I don't like this one bit," Kate began. "You said they were wearing tactical gear, Harry. That lifts this to a whole new level of danger."

Before I could answer, my phone buzzed with a call from Amanda. "Harry, where are you?" she asked. "There was a man here at Channel 7 asking questions about you and our family."

"A man? Who is he? What kind of questions?" I asked.

"I don't know who he is," she replied. "He was wanting to know personal stuff. Where we live, where Jade goes to school, what our routines are. Jack Sharp told him to leave, but Harry, he seemed to know things about us that aren't public information."

I felt a chill run through me. "Stay at the station. Don't leave until I get there."

After ending the call, I turned to Kate and Morrison. "They're targeting my family now. Someone was at Amanda's work asking questions."

Morrison immediately pulled out her phone. "I'm arranging protection for your family. This thing is escalating."

"What about the investigation?" I asked.

"We continue," Kate said firmly. "But with enhanced security protocols and the assumption that all police department communications are compromised." She turned to Tim. "Can you remove that monitoring software you found?"

Tim adjusted his glasses, considering. "Maybe. But if I do it too quickly or obviously, Reynolds will know we've discovered it. Better to leave it in place and feed it false information while we use secure channels for our real communications."

"You can do that?" Morrison asked.

"Sure. I can make it look like we're investigating dead ends while we pursue the actual leads through encrypted channels. Reynolds will think he's staying ahead of us when he's actually being misdirected."

Kate nodded approvingly. "Do it. Let Reynolds think he's controlling our investigation."

Morrison reviewed her notes. "I'll coordinate with Chief Johnston to implement counter-surveillance measures and revised security protocols. We also need to relocate this investigation to a secure facility outside the police department."

Over the next two hours, Morrison organized a comprehensive security response that included protective details for my family, secure communication systems, and a safe house operation managed through federal resources rather than local police.

"Captain Morrison's been invaluable," Kate told me as we watched her work with the various agencies. "She understands how Reynolds could use his position to monitor and intimidate us."

Chief Johnston arrived at the scene and immediately expressed concern about the escalating danger.

"Harry," he said after a moment of reflection. "This is not something we bargained for. Now your family is in danger. Are you sure you want to continue with this investigation?"

"Yeah, I do, and probably not for the reasons you think. They threaten me, it's one thing. They threaten my family, it's quite another. I'm not backing down."

As the afternoon progressed, we relocated our investigation to a secure federal facility outside Chattanooga, with Morrison coordinating the transfer of all relevant files and evidence.

Tim set up his computer systems in the new location and immediately began working on the PD's monitoring problem and analyzing Sullivan's recovered files.

"These files are incredible," Tim said, reviewing Sullivan's documentation. "He was building cases against corruption in four different cities. Reynolds' operation is just one piece of a much larger criminal enterprise."

Morrison nodded as she reviewed Sullivan's case files. "This explains why Frank's investigation was so dangerous," she said.

By evening, we had been able to establish secure operations and still maintain the investigation's momentum. The attack on me had proved that Reynolds' network viewed us as a serious threat; it also demonstrated their willingness to use violence.

At around six, Morrison gathered her files and said, "I'll continue coordinating departmental cooperation. Is there anything else you guys need before I leave? If not, I'll see you here in the morning. I usually get in around eight. Be sure to call me if anything urgent comes up."

There wasn't anything, so she said good night and left.

Me? I drove home in a rental vehicle wondering what the hell was coming next.

12

THE ANONYMOUS SOURCE

Monday, August 22, 2024

I woke the following morning to find Amanda already up. Ten minutes later I walked into the kitchen to find Amanda and Maria Boylen sitting at the kitchen table with cups of coffee and serious expressions, and I realized Amanda must have taken the previous evening's incident more seriously than I'd thought and made a phone call.

Maria, Jade's part-time nanny and family bodyguard who'd become more like family over the years, looked up as I entered.

Maria is quite a character. Age forty-five, she was a small, Hispanic woman with shining black hair and intelligent dark eyes that missed nothing. She graduated UA in 2003 with a degree in political science and applied to the ATF. The process took thirteen months, but she was finally inducted in 2004. She left in 2015 with the rank of G9 after eleven years on the job. Since then, she worked for two security companies specializing in personal protection. She was a bodyguard with a black belt in Krav Maga, a license to carry and an expert shot. She knew what I needed, and she loves kids, so I hired her.

"Harry," Maria said, standing to give me her usual hug. "Amanda told me what happened yesterday. Are you all right?"

"I'm fine, Maria," I replied. "A little banged up, but nothing serious. I need some coffee." I poured myself a cup, kissed Amanda, and settled into a chair beside them. "Where's Jade?"

"Upstairs doing homework," Amanda replied. "I thought it better to keep her occupied while we talked about what happened at the station."

Maria nodded.

"Tell me exactly what happened with the man who came to Channel 7," I said to Amanda.

Amanda's expression tightened. "He showed up around noon claiming to be a freelance journalist working on a story about local private investigators. But Harry, the questions he was asking weren't about your professional work."

"What did he want to know?"

"Personal details. Where we shop for groceries, what time Jade gets out of school, whether we have regular routines or schedules. He seemed particularly interested in when you're home versus when you're working."

Maria leaned forward. "Amanda called me right after it happened. This man, he was not a reporter."

"What makes you say that?" I asked.

"I have seen reporters before when they come to the houses where I work," Maria said. "They ask about the work, the cases, the success stories. This man, he was learning how to find your family when you are not there to protect them."

The chill I'd felt during Amanda's phone call returned. "Did he threaten anyone directly?"

"No, but he didn't have to," Amanda replied. "Jack Sharp finally told him to leave, but the damage was done. Harry, he knew things about us that he could only have learned by watching our house or following us around for weeks."

I narrowed my eyes. "Such as?"

Amanda consulted notes she'd written on a legal pad. "He knew I sometimes go running early in the morning. He knew Jade takes the bus to school at seven-forty-five. He even mentioned that we sometimes have dinner at Giuseppe's on Friday nights, and that you usually order the veal piccata."

Maria nodded. "I told Amanda we should change the locks, and check the cameras. But Harry, I think this is much bigger than locks and cameras can handle."

"You're right," I said. "Kate and Captain Morrison have arranged police protection. There are officers watching the house and following Amanda and Jade during their daily routines."

"Oh dear," Amanda said. "How long do I have to put up with that?"

"Until we finish this investigation and arrest everyone involved," I said. "Days, weeks, I don't know."

Amanda was quiet for a moment, then said, "Harry, I need to ask you something, and I want an honest answer. Is this case worth putting our daughter at risk?"

I looked at both women. They were genuinely concerned.

"That's... a bit unfair," I said. "After all we've been through together; the three of us. The years we had to put up with Shady Tree. It's what I do, Amanda. You knew that when you married me. You have to trust me," I said slowly.

Maria reached across the table and squeezed my hand. "Then we protect this family while you do what you must do."

Amanda nodded. "I'm sorry, Harry, but we didn't have Jade through the Shady Tree years. Now you do. I just needed to hear you say it, is all."

"I know that," I replied, "and I also want you to know that if you asked me to walk away right this minute, I would. You and Jade are more important than... anything."

"I know," she said, reaching for my other hand, "which is why I'm not asking."

We were interrupted by Amanda's phone ringing. She glanced at the caller ID and frowned.

"It's someone from work," she said, answering the call. "Hello? What? Slow down, I can barely understand you."

Amanda's face went pale as she listened. "Are you sure? When did this happen? Where are you now?"

After a tense three-minute conversation, Amanda ended the call and turned to us with a shaken expression.

"That was someone from Margaret Wells' photography studio. He says he has information about surveillance photographs related to your investigation, and he wants to meet."

"Information?" I asked. "What kind of information?"

"He wouldn't say over the phone, but he sounded terrified. He said people have been paying the studio to process surveillance photos of you and your team, and he's afraid he's in danger."

And then, within minutes of Amanda hanging up, Kate rang.

"Harry, we just got a call from someone claiming to have evidence about surveillance operations targeting our investigation. Amanda's name came up as a contact."

"She just got a call," I said. "He wants her to meet him. What do you think?"

"It could be a trap," she replied, "but if it's legitimate, this person could have the crucial evidence we need."

I looked at Amanda and Maria. They were both waiting to hear what I would decide.

"Set up the meeting," I told Kate. "But we do it safely, with backup and security protocols."

AN HOUR LATER, WE MET AMANDA'S CONTACT AT A BUSY downtown restaurant called The Foundry. The man who approached our corner booth was young, maybe twenty-five, with nervous eyes and the pale complexion of someone who spent most of his time in a darkroom.

"You're Harry Starke?" he asked, glancing around the restaurant. "I'm Jason Mills. I work part-time at the Wells Photography Studio."

Kate and Captain Morrison had entered the restaurant, both trying to appear casual. Morrison had positioned herself at the table opposite where she could watch both entrances but was still close enough to hear the conversation. Kate seated herself in the booth next to Amanda.

"You say you have information," Kate said. "Let's see it."

Jason pulled out a manila envelope and kept it on his lap. "For the past two weeks, we've been getting unusual processing jobs almost daily..." He paused for a moment then continued. "Surveillance photos, of you guys. You. Your team. Your families. All paid for in cash, premium rates for fast turnaround."

Amanda leaned forward. "Can we see the photographs?"

Jason nodded nervously, glancing around the restaurant one more time. "I made duplicates before I realized how dangerous this might be." He hesitated, his hands shaking slightly as he kept the envelope on his lap.

"It's all right," Kate said reassuringly. "We're here to help."

Jason took a deep breath then said, "There are photos of Mr. Starke at his office, Captain Gazzara at the police department, and... I don't know who the other people are."

He spread the photos on the table between us. Amanda gasped as she saw images of herself arriving at and leaving Channel 7, of Jade waiting for the school bus, of me walking to my car in the office parking lot.

"My God," Amanda whispered, her face going pale. "How long have they been watching us?"

Kate's jaw tightened as she studied a photograph of herself entering the police department. "These are professional surveillance shots. High-end equipment, concealed positions."

Amanda looked at me with fierce eyes. "Harry, this is why that man knew so much about our family."

I felt anger building in my chest as I stared at photos of my six-year-old daughter. "Jason, how many of these photos are there?"

"Dozens," he replied, his voice barely above a whisper. "Different locations, different times of the day."

Morrison spoke quietly. "Jason, who's been bringing in these jobs?"

"It was a different person each time, but they all have the same instructions. High quality prints, specific formats, and complete confidentiality. The payments are always cash, always overpaid."

"How much are we talking about?" Kate asked.

"Five hundred dollars for jobs that usually cost fifty.

Someone really wants these photos and wants us to keep quiet about them."

Jason glanced around the restaurant again, then pulled several more photographs from the envelope. "These show meetings between people I think you're investigating. Look."

The photographs showed Commissioner Reynolds, Judge Henley, Dr. Marsh, and Thomas Greaves meeting at various locations around Chattanooga.

"This proves they've been coordinating their activities," Kate observed, studying the fronts and backs of the photos. "These meetings happened over the past several weeks."

"There are more," Jason said, producing additional photographs.

Kate examined the timestamps on the photos. "Some of these were taken after Frank's murder. They've been meeting regularly to coordinate their response to our investigation."

"Jason," I said, "do you have any idea who's paying for this surveillance?"

He shook his head. "No names, but I can tell you it appears to be two different operations. One set of photos focuses on the people in suits meeting at restaurants and offices. The other set is more personal - families, homes, daily routines."

Amanda asked the question I was thinking. "Two different clients?"

"I don't know for sure," he replied, "but that's what it looks like. Different photography styles, different subjects, but all paid for in cash."

Morrison's radio crackled quietly with a message from the backup officers outside. She listened through her earpiece, then turned to us.

"We may have a problem," she said. "There's a vehicle with

tinted windows that's been circling the block since we arrived."

I was about to suggest we leave when the restaurant's front window exploded in a shower of glass. The sharp crack of a high-powered rifle echoed through the dining room as Jason Mills slumped forward, blood spreading across the table.

"Sniper!" Morrison shouted, leaping across the gap between the tables to cover Kate. She drew her weapon and shouted again, "Everyone down!"

Chaos erupted throughout the restaurant as patrons screamed and dove for cover under tables and behind chairs. I grabbed Amanda and pulled her to the floor while Morrison snapped at her backup officers through her radio, "Shots fired at The Foundry. Civilian down. Request immediate backup and medical response. Active shooter attack in progress."

Kate reached over to Jason and checked for vital signs. "He's gone," she muttered.

Through the shattered window, I could see people running on the street as police sirens approached from multiple directions. The sniper had fired only once, then disappeared.

"This was a professional hit, Kate," Morrison said. "They eliminated a witness and at the same time sent us a message."

Within minutes, the restaurant was swarming with police and sheriff's officers.

Kate secured Jason's surveillance photographs before we were moved to a booth at the far end of the restaurant. "I need copies of those," I said.

She nodded. "You know this changes everything?" she said as we waited for Detective Lieutenant Henry Clark to turn us loose.

All I could do was nod as I calculated the implications of what we'd just learned and what had happened.

Amanda sat beside me, visibly shaken but composed. "That young man died because he was trying to help us," she whispered.

Morrison sat down beside Kate and reviewed the surveillance photos. She shook her head. "They've been watching you for almost two weeks," she said. "This raises a lot of questions, Kate. The most pressing one is how did they know?"

"That's an easy one," I said. "They somehow bugged your communications. I need to call Tim." And I did. I told him to join us and that I needed a report.

He arrived with his laptop some twenty minutes later. "Harry, the counter-surveillance system is working, but it's not perfect. Reynolds' database monitoring has been neutralized. He's only hearing banter in the situation room and two of the detective's offices that are not involved."

"Do they know what you're doing?" Kate asked. "The detectives?"

"Oh yeah, I had to tell them to be careful, but they were okay with it..." He trailed off.

"But?" I asked. I could hear the hesitation in his voice.

"But that's just one intelligence source. If someone with legitimate access to our activities is sharing information directly with Reynolds, my digital countermeasures won't stop that."

"You're saying we have a leak?"

"Either that, or they're using old-fashioned human intelligence: physical surveillance, informants, people on the inside. My system only blocks their electronic monitoring."

"So that's how they knew about this meeting?" I asked.

"If someone told them about it directly, yeah," he replied. "The database shows we're investigating financial irregularities in the mayor's office, which is completely false. But if Reynolds has another source..."

I sat back in my seat, folded my arms and stared at Kate. She shrugged, but said nothing. But I could see she was thinking. If we had a leak at the police department... well, all bets were off.

"It looks like the sniper used a high-powered rifle, probably a 5.56 NATO or .223," Morrison reported after consulting with Mike Willis. "Pretty standard stuff these days. An AR-15 with a scope, I should imagine. And they had detailed knowledge of our meeting and the location."

"How did they know about Jason's meeting?" Amanda asked.

Kate looked at Tim. He just slowly shook his head.

"Either they were monitoring his communications," Kate said, "or someone on the inside leaked the information."

As the afternoon progressed, we relocated to the secure facility. Jason Mills' murder remained under local jurisdiction, but federal agents increased their involvement due to connections with Sullivan's corruption case.

"Those surveillance photographs Jason died providing are crucial evidence," Morrison said as we reviewed the materials in our secure location. "They prove Reynolds' network has been coordinating their criminal activities and planning responses to our investigation."

Kate studied the timeline evidence from the photos. "Look at these dates. They've been meeting regularly since Frank's murder, with increased frequency after we started investigating their financial operations."

"The question is," I said, "whether Jason's murder was ordered by Reynolds or by someone else, someone who's been running the older criminal activities."

Morrison said, "My money's on Reynolds. He has the resources and capabilities for this kind of operation."

By eight o'clock that evening, I felt like we'd hashed it to death, and I was bone tired. And I said so, and that it was time we called it a day.

Amanda rode home with me in the rental car followed by a blue and white cruiser. Even so, I didn't feel safe. Still, we arrived home without incident to find Maria waiting for us.

"Miss Jade is in bed," she said, "but you need to go tell her good night."

And we did, only to find her fast asleep. Amanda gently tucked her in, and we quietly left, leaving the door open a little way so we could hear her if she woke up.

"You know that could just as easily have been you?" she said as we joined Maria in the living room. She was seated in one of the wingback chairs, her Glock 17 on the table beside her.

"But it wasn't, and police protection will ensure it won't be," I replied.

"Sometimes you're so naïve," she replied. "Police protection didn't save Jason from a sniper and it won't save you. You can't be protected from what you can't see."

She was right, of course. Even so, I couldn't quit. It wasn't in my nature.

13

PROTECTIVE CUSTODY

Tuesday, August 23, 2024

I woke to the sound of Maria talking quietly to someone in the kitchen. The clock showed five-thirty, earlier than usual even for her. I found her sitting at the table with a man in a navy-blue suit. *A fed,* I thought, and I was right.

"Mr. Starke," the agent said, standing. "Agent Williams. We need to discuss relocation."

"Coffee first," I said, pouring a cup. "Then talk."

Maria handed me a plate of scrambled eggs. "The safe house is ready," she said as she sat down again. "They want us to move this morning."

"What about Jade's school?"

"Arrangements have been made," Agent Williams said. "Temporary homeschooling until the situation resolves."

Amanda appeared in the doorway, already dressed. "How long are we talking about?"

"Hard to tell," Williams replied. "Your family's safety is the priority now."

An hour later, we were loading essential items into two black SUVs while a moving crew handled the rest. Jade thought it was an adventure until she realized she wouldn't see her friends for a while.

"But I have a spelling test Friday," she said, tears starting.

"We'll practice together," Amanda told her. "Just you and me."

The safe house was a four-bedroom cabin in the mountains east of Chattanooga—in Blue Ridge, Georgia—isolated but comfortable. Federal agents established a security perimeter while Tim set up his communication equipment in the basement.

"This place is clean," he reported. "No surveillance, secure internet, encrypted phones."

Kate arrived with Samson and Captain Morrison to review the security. Morrison walked the perimeter with the federal team, checking sight lines and access points.

"The location is defensible," Morrison said, as she returned to the cabin with Williams. "There are multiple escape routes, good visibility. You should be safe here."

"Oh my God," Amanda said. "Are you serious?"

"As a heart attack," Williams said with a smile.

"What about the investigation?" I asked.

"We continue from the secure facility in Chattanooga," Kate replied. "Morrison's coordinating with Chief Johnston to maintain operational security."

"It's a hell of a drive from here to there," I said.

Kate simply shrugged. I mean, what could she say?

Tim connected his laptop to the cabin's communication

system. "I can monitor everything from here. Database access, financial tracking, communication intercepts."

"Any new developments on the surveillance software?" Kate asked.

"Reynolds is still seeing false information about investigating the mayor's office," Tim replied. "But someone leaked yesterday's meeting location to the sniper."

Morrison reviewed her notes. "We need to identify the source. Other than Jason himself, and whoever he told, only four people knew about the meeting."

"Who?" I asked.

"You, Amanda, Kate and myself," she replied.

Kate studied Morrison's list. "We need to check Jason's phone records, see who he called before contacting Amanda."

Over the next two hours, we established secure operations from the cabin.

"These photos prove Reynolds' network has been meeting regularly," Tim said, displaying images on his monitor. "Look at the timestamps. They seem to have moved things up since Frank's murder."

"All public places with good security," Morrison said, thoughtfully. "They know what they're doing."

"What about the personal surveillance photos?" Amanda asked.

Tim pulled up the images of our families and daily routines. "They're well done. Not taken with a phone; high-end equipment, careful positioning. Someone spent serious money on this."

Maria studied the photos of Jade waiting for the school bus. "They know her schedule," she said, "her route, her friends. Very dangerous."

Kate's phone rang. It was Chief Johnston.

"Chief, you're on speaker," Kate said.

"Harry, I've been reviewing the security arrangements with Morrison. This safe-house operation is costing serious money. How long do you need?"

"Until we arrest everyone involved in Frank's murder and the corruption network, I guess."

"That could be months."

Morrison spoke up. "Chief, these people are using professional killers. The family protection is necessary."

"I understand, but the budget..."

"Chief," I interrupted him, "they threatened my daughter. I don't care about the budget. You want me to pay for it myself; I'll do it."

Johnston was quiet for a moment. "No, that won't be necessary," he said. "But I need regular updates on your progress. Kate, you know the drill." He ended the call.

"Geez," I said. "That's not the kind of pressure we need, not now."

"We need to speed things up," Kate said. "The longer this drags out, the more likely someone else gets killed."

"What about Agent French?" I asked. "Any word from her?"

"She's supposed to check in this afternoon," Kate replied. "The FBI wants to coordinate arrests with our local investigation."

Tim looked up from his computer. "Hey, you two, I've been analyzing the financial data from Jason's photos. The meeting locations correspond to money transfers. It looks like they're planning something big."

"What are you talking about, Tim?" Kate asked.

"Large asset transfers to offshore accounts. I think maybe they're planning their escape. I'd say Reynolds' network is getting ready to disappear."

Morrison said, "If they're planning to flee, we need to move fast. Once they leave the country, extradition becomes complicated, if at all."

Kate took out her phone. "I need to check something with Agent French."

An hour later, Agent French arrived at the cabin with two of her agents.

"Take a look at these," I said, pointing to Tim's laptop, "and tell me what you think." French nodded and sat down beside Tim, took the mouse from him and began to scroll through the photographs. After a few moments, she looked up at me, her expression grim, and said, "These were taken by a pro. They match what we've seen from the Reynolds network. But these family shots were taken by someone else."

"And you know that how?" I asked.

"They're more intimate. More detailed. The Reynolds images are surveillance shots pure and simple."

She took her own laptop from her bag and set it up next to Tim's and he connected it to his system. "Can you cross-reference with other federal investigations?" he asked.

"I can," she replied as she pulled up one database search after another. "What we're looking for is similar surveillance patterns in other cities."

I was sitting outside on the front porch, ruminating and admiring the view of the mountains when I heard Tim calling for me. "Hey, Harry, c'mere. I found something in Jason's phone records."

I went inside and joined him and French at the worktable.

"He made two calls before contacting Amanda. One to Wells Photography Studio, one to an unknown number."

Kate leaned over Tim's shoulder. "Can you trace the unknown number?"

"I'm working on that now," he replied. "The call lasted seven minutes, so it wasn't a wrong number. "

"If Jason called someone else first," French said, "that might be the leak we're looking for."

"Or perhaps someone warned him about the danger," Amanda suggested.

Morrison turned to look at her, frowning. "Could be," she said. "Seven minutes is quite a long conversation. And we know Jason was scared out of his brains."

Tim's computer chimed with search results. "The unknown number belongs to a burner phone purchased with cash in Knoxville three weeks ago."

"Knoxville," Kate said. "That's interesting. Why would Jason be calling someone there?"

Morrison gathered her files. "We need to investigate the Knoxville connection. The call was seven minutes long, so we know it had to be something important. I think something must have spooked him, which is why he called you, Amanda. We also need to follow up on the call he made to Wells."

"So where are we, then?" Tim asked. "I'm hungry. I could eat Samson between two loaves of bread."

Samson looked up at him with his head cocked to one side.

"Geez, I didn't mean it, Sammy," he muttered, and the big dog lay down again.

"I'll make you a sandwich," Amanda said, smiling. "Ham and cheese alright?

"Perfect," he replied, first with a smile for Amanda, then a grin for Samson who ignored him.

"Tomorrow we follow up on the Knoxville connection,"

Kate said, preparing to leave. "And Lisa will work with the federal agents to track down the burner phone."

"What about Reynolds?" I asked.

"Federal surveillance continues. If they're planning to run, we'll know about it." She looked around. "Where's Agent Williams?" she asked.

"He left when I arrived," French said.

Morrison reviewed security protocols with the cabin's protection detail. "The federal agents will maintain perimeter security. You'll be safe here."

After Kate and Morrison left, Amanda and I sat on the front porch while Jade played inside under Maria's watchful eye.

"This isn't how I imagined our life when I married a private investigator," Amanda said, setting down her glass of red wine. Me? I was drinking Laphroaig that Amanda had thoughtfully brought with her.

"You married an ex-cop who became a private investigator," I said after taking a sip. "There's a difference."

"Is there? You're still chasing killers and putting our family at risk."

I didn't have a good answer for that, so I didn't reply.

Tim joined us on the porch with his laptop. "I wonder who that call from Knoxville was from," he said as he sat down next to Amanda.

"Tomorrow we find out," I said, watching the sun set over the mountains that now protected my family from the people who'd murdered my friend and mentor. Did I feel comfortable being sequestered up there in the middle of a mountaintop forest? Hell no, but what choice did I have? My family's lives were at risk, so I had to tough it out.

It was after nine when Maria put Jade to bed and Amanda

and I sat with her for a moment. She was asleep in minutes. I think the mountain air and the late—for her—night must have tired her out. By ten-thirty, we were, all four of us, still out on the porch. Amanda was talking quietly with Maria and I was gazing off into the moonlit distance. It was surreal. I was on my third glass of Laphroaig and feeling... a little heady. The truth is, I was ready for bed. I looked at Tim. He was, as usual, away with the birds, deep into something on his laptop. I leaned over, gently took it from him and closed it.

He frowned at me. "What..."

I smiled at him. "Not tonight, sonny. Tonight you get some sleep. Go to bed. You can have this back in the morning."

14

THE FEDERAL CONNECTION

WEDNESDAY, AUGUST 24, 2024

I WOKE WEDNESDAY MORNING FEELING MORE RESTED THAN I'D expected. The mountain air and Laphroaig had done their job, and for the first time in days, I'd slept through the night without thinking about snipers or surveillance photos.

I found Tim in the kitchen, already dressed and nursing his first cup of coffee. He looked at me expectantly.

"Yes, you can have your laptop back," I said, pouring my own coffee. "But remember what I said about sleep."

"I got eight hours," Tim replied, grinning. "First time in weeks."

I was drinking my coffee on the cabin's front porch when Kate's car appeared on the mountain road. She arrived at seven-thirty with Samson and Agent French, plus a briefcase full of files.

"Early start," I said as they walked up to the cabin, Samson padding alongside Kate.

"We've got a lot to cover," Kate replied. "The Wells Photography Studio, the Knoxville connection, and some new federal intelligence."

Inside, Amanda was making breakfast while Maria kept watch on Jade. Samson settled down beside Kate's chair as the cabin became our temporary command center.

"First things first," Kate said, settling at the kitchen table. "I called Wells Photography yesterday evening."

"Who did you talk to? What did they say?" I asked.

"I spoke to Margaret Wells. Jason Mills called the studio at eleven-fifteen Monday morning, twenty minutes before he called Amanda. He spoke with Margaret Wells herself."

Agent French took out a digital recorder. "We interviewed Mrs. Wells last night, and, with her permission, we recorded the conversation."

Kate pressed play on the device. And Margaret Wells' voice filled the cabin kitchen.

Jason was terrified. He told me someone had been asking questions about the surveillance photos we'd been processing. Then, on Sunday night, a man came to the studio, after we were closed. Jason saw him through the window, trying to get in.

French paused the recording. "Mrs. Wells also said Jason had been worried about the surveillance work for weeks."

French restarted the recording. *Jason said the man at the window looked like military or police, or something,* Wells continued, *and that he was taking photographs of our building, and writing down the license plate numbers of the cars parked outside.*

"So Jason was already being watched before he contacted us," I said.

"Exactly," French replied. "Someone in Reynolds' network must have identified Jason as a potential problem."

Tim looked up from his computer. "That could explain the

seven-minute call to Knoxville. Maybe he was reaching out for help."

"Maybe, but reaching out to whom?" Amanda asked.

No one answered, but Amanda was right; it was a bit of a stretch.

"Agent French has been working with the FBI to identify similar operations in other cities," Kate said pulling a stack of files from her briefcase. "Agent French. Would you do the honors, please?"

French nodded, grabbed one of the files, opened it, and took out a wad of photographs, which she proceeded to spread across the table. "Agent Sullivan had been investigating corruption throughout the Southeast; Tennessee, Georgia and Northwest Alabama in particular. This is what he found."

The photographs showed meetings between Reynolds and men I didn't recognize, all taking place in different cities. Atlanta, Nashville, Birmingham, Memphis and Chattanooga.

"From what we've been able to learn, it appears that Reynolds was running a criminal organization across the three states."

I shook my head, wondering what the hell we'd stumbled into.

"Including Chattanooga, which is central to the other four cities, we're talking dozens of corrupt officials and millions in laundered money," French replied. "Sullivan wasn't done with his investigation, but he was close. He'd managed to document evidence that it was Reynolds who was running the organization out of Chattanooga."

"What about Sullivan's evidence?" Amanda asked. "Were you able to recover it all? Do you have enough to arrest him?"

"No," French said. "Harry was able to recover some of

Sullivan's evidence from the locker in the building where he lived, and I have some, but the key elements are missing."

"Key elements?" Amanda asked.

"We don't have the organization's complete financial records, Nor do we have detailed proof of case fixing and evidence tampering, or documentation of the murders committed to protect the network. All we know for sure is that Sullivan and Jason Mills were murdered and, possibly Frank Callahan. But most important of all, we don't have the names of all the corrupt officials."

Tim whistled low. "That's why Frank's investigation was so dangerous to them."

"Yeah," I muttered, "and I still haven't been able to figure out what he did with his backup files. They're out there somewhere, if only I could figure out where."

I looked at Amanda. She gave me a wide-eyed shrug: nice, but not helpful.

"We, that is the FBI, have been working in all five cities," French continued. "But Sullivan's murder set us back at least six months and now, at the speed Reynolds is moving, it's doubtful if we can catch up. "

"What about the older criminal activities we discovered?" Amanda asked. "The ten-year timeline that doesn't connect to Reynolds?"

French hesitated. "Yes," she said after a moment, "Sullivan found evidence of evidence tampering and case manipulation that predates Reynolds' network. Someone's been corrupting police investigations for over a decade, but we think for personal reasons rather than profit."

"Any theories who it might be?" I asked.

She made a wry face and shook her head. "Sullivan

believed it was family-related," French replied. "Someone protecting a relative or close associate."

Morrison's radio buzzed. She took it outside, but quickly returned and said, "Kate, we have a problem. Reynolds has been making calls to Atlanta and Nashville since yesterday afternoon. It looks like he's on the move and preparing to run."

French pulled out her secure phone. "I need to contact the Atlanta field office," she said. "If Reynolds is planning to escape, we need to move up our arrest timelines."

"It's time you shared everything you have," I told her. And, reluctantly, she agreed. Over the next hour, while French worked with federal agents in the five cities, the rest of us continued to build cases against the Reynolds organization as best we could.

"Sullivan had been working the case for three years," French said. "He had no doubt that Reynolds was the central coordinator."

"How did Reynolds get so much power?" Amanda asked.

It was Kate who replied. "Well, for one, he's the police commissioner, and two, he has connections throughout the tri-state area. Who better than him to put such a network together? It looks like Reynolds was able to build relationships with every corrupt official in every major city. Geez, the man had his own mutual assistance network."

"The amount of money he generated is incredible," Tim muttered from the couch where he had his laptop on his knee. "He was taking percentages from criminal operations across the board. Whoever said crime doesn't pay, was wrong. I mean, it involves drug trafficking, money laundering, contract killings, case fixing. Any criminal enterprise that needed law enforcement protection paid into Reynolds' network. He was even taking money from Tren de Aragua."

At that, I turned from the table and stared at him. He simply shrugged, grinned and said, "It is what it is, Harry."

I turned back to the table, shaking my head. Not so much at Tim as at the scope of what he was describing.

"The Knoxville connection is still puzzling me," Morrison said, "and I'm wondering if it's related to the older criminal activities rather than Reynolds' network..."

"I agree," Amanda said. "Someone with a ten-year secret might be more desperate than Reynolds' profit-driven operation."

"Desperate enough to kill a photography studio employee," I agreed.

Kate's phone rang. It was Chief Johnston. She put him on speaker.

"Kate, the mayor's office has been getting calls from the FBI; something about expanded investigations. What the hell's happening?"

"It's quite simple, Chief," she replied, and proceeded to fill him in on what we'd learned.

"Geez, as if I didn't have enough on my plate," he muttered after she'd finished. "How does this affect our local investigation, Captain?"

It was Morrison who spoke up. "It doesn't, Chief, we're continuing to build cases against Reynolds and his network, and we're working to find out who killed Frank Callahan."

"Very well. Keep me updated," Johnston said and hung up.

"When can we expect arrests?" I asked.

"We're coordinating our operation across the five cities," French said. "But we need Frank Callahan's evidence to ensure successful prosecutions."

"Well, that's not about to happen," I replied. "I still can't figure out where he hid it, if at all."

Tim, who had been quietly analyzing data from the federal databases, looked up and said, "I think I found something that connects the network to the older stuff."

We all turned to look at him. "What? What have you found?" Kate asked.

"I found some odd financial transfers from one of Reynolds' accounts to someone in the Chattanooga area. Small amounts, irregular timing, going back more than eight years."

French leaned over Tim's shoulder to study the data. "Show me those transactions."

Tim pulled up a timeline showing payments between Reynolds' network and local accounts. "The amounts are always under federal reporting requirements, but they're consistent. Someone local has been receiving payments from Reynolds for years."

French studied Tim's analysis. "If Reynolds was paying someone locally for services, it might explain the leaks."

"I've been reading through Sullivan's files," Amanda said. "There's something here I don't quite understand. Something about witness protection arrangements that bypass normal federal procedures."

Kate turned to her and said, "What kind of arrangements?"

"Unofficial relocations," Amanda replied, "new identities created outside of normal channels, medical treatment provided through private facilities."

French looked perplexed.

Morrison leaned over Amanda's shoulder. "It looks to me like Sullivan found out that if someone needed to disappear, Reynolds could make it happen."

"I need to make a call," French said and turned her back.

French ended her call a few minutes later and turned to the group. "Reynolds has been contacting private aircraft companies in all five cities. We're out of time. FBI offices are coordinating simultaneous arrests for eleven PM Eastern tonight."

"Tonight?" Kate asked. "That's less than five hours."

"Asset transfers are accelerating. If we wait, they'll be gone by morning."

Tim looked up from his computer with concern. "If we arrest Reynolds' network tonight, what happens to the older criminal investigation?"

"We continue pursuing Frank's killer," Kate replied. "But eliminating Reynolds removes a major threat and source of evidence tampering."

Morrison reviewed the tactical plans with the federal agents while Kate kept Chief Johnston apprised of what was happening. The remote mountain cabin had become the command center for a multi-state law enforcement operation.

"Harry," Amanda said quietly, "if they arrest everyone tonight, do we get to go home?"

"Depends on if we find who killed Frank," I replied. "If it was Reynolds, then yes. If it was someone else..."

"We stay hidden until the killer is caught," she finished.

French was now in constant contact with the FBI surveillance in all five cities. "All primary targets are still in their respective cities," French reported. "Arrest teams are positioning now."

Kate received updates from Chattanooga where the police and sheriff's departments were preparing to arrest Reynolds, Henley, Marsh, and Greaves. The coordination required split-second timing to prevent the suspects from warning each other.

"What about the Knoxville connection?" I asked. "Jason's seven-minute call?"

"We'll follow up after tonight's arrests," Kate replied. "First we eliminate the obvious threats."

The arrests were scheduled for eleven PM Eastern, ten Central, to account for the difference in the time zones.

"Asset transfers are continuing," Tim said. "So are the travel arrangements."

"How much money are we talking about?" Amanda asked.

"Closing on one billion," Tim replied. "Reynolds has been moving assets to offshore accounts for the past week."

French reviewed the arrest warrants with Kate while federal agents and SWAT teams prepared to move in. The scope of the operation was beyond anything Chattanooga had ever participated in.

"Sullivan would have been proud," French said quietly. "His investigation is finally coming to fruition."

By the time evening fell that Wednesday, we had finally established that Frank's investigation had uncovered two separate criminal operations: Reynolds' regional network and something older and more personal. Both had reasons to kill Frank, but which one actually killed him; that remained elusive.

"Maybe after tonight we'll finally get some answers," Kate said, checking her watch. "But who knows? We might get a whole bunch of new questions instead."

"That's a little pessimistic, don't you think?" Amanda said, tiredly, as she scratched behind Samson's ears; something he was exceedingly partial to.

Tim closed his laptop and stretched. "I should probably get

some rest before the arrests start. I'd say it's going to be a long night."

"I thought you never slept," Kate said with a smile.

He gave her one of his looks. "And I'm hungry," he said. "What about dinner?"

"Patience, Tim," she replied. "It's only six-fifteen. The operation begins at eleven, but we'll be monitoring from here."

While we waited for dinner, Amanda and I went out onto the front porch to watch Jade playing with Samson under Maria's watchful supervision. The big German Shepherd seemed to be having a huge time as she threw sticks for him to fetch. Any other time it would have been an idyllic scene. As it was, it was simply a reminder that life goes on, even under the most extreme circumstances.

"Let's hope that after tonight we'll know who killed Frank and things can get back to normal," Kate said, watching her partner play with my daughter.

Amanda smiled as she watched Jade and Samson. "Well, at least *she's* having fun," she said. "This might be the only normal part of her day."

I nodded, my mind wandering over the mountains and valleys, wondering what the outcome of tonight's arrests would be. By this time tomorrow, dozens of corrupt officials would be in custody. But somewhere out there, Frank's killer was still free, and until that person was caught our investigation would remain incomplete. I heaved a sigh, shook my head, and watched the sun set over the Northwest Georgia mountains.

15

THE NETWORK FALLS

WEDNESDAY NIGHT/THURSDAY MORNING, AUGUST 24-25, 2024

I WAS DOZING IN THE CABIN'S LIVING ROOM CHAIR WHEN AGENT French's phone erupted at nine-forty PM. Kate jerked awake on the couch beside me while Tim looked up from his laptop.

"French here," she answered, then listened for thirty seconds before her face went white. "When? How long ago?"

Morrison appeared from the kitchen. Amanda came down the stairs, having put Jade to bed an hour earlier.

"Understood," French said, ending the call. She turned to us with a grim expression. "Reynolds is on the move. All of them."

"What happened?" Kate asked.

"Someone must have tipped them off," French replied. "Federal surveillance spotted Reynolds leaving his house twenty minutes ago with suitcases. Henley, Marsh, and Greaves are also on the move."

Morrison grabbed her radio. "All units, all units. Suspects are on the move. Execute arrest warrants immediately. I repeat, execute arrests now."

Kate was already on her phone with Chief Johnston. "Chief, we need every available unit. Reynolds and the others are running."

Tim's laptop was connected to federal communications. "I'm monitoring the operations in all five cities," he reported. "It's chaos. Nashville and Birmingham teams are scrambling."

"The Atlanta team has Marsh," French announced twenty minutes later. "But he was armed and shots were fired."

"Anyone hurt?" Kate asked.

"Two agents wounded, not life-threatening," French replied. "Marsh is in custody."

"Chattanooga units are en route to Reynolds' last known location," Morrison reported. "He's heading toward the airport."

"Private jet?" I asked.

"That's what surveillance indicates," she replied.

"Memphis team got their targets," Tim reported. "Nashville is still in pursuit. Birmingham has three of four suspects in custody."

"What about Reynolds?" Amanda asked.

Kate listened to her radio, then shook her head. "Nothing yet."

French slammed her hand on the table. "Dammit. Reynolds was the key to the whole network."

"Birmingham team is reporting," Tim said, listening to his earpiece. "Judge Henley attempted to run but she crashed her car. She's in custody but injured."

For the next two hours, we received updates as federal and

local teams swept the Southeast arresting network members. Some succeeded, others failed.

"Final count," French announced at one AM. "Eighteen arrests across five cities, seven escaped including Greaves."

"What about Reynolds?" Kate asked.

"Got him," Morrison replied with satisfaction. "Tennessee state troopers intercepted his vehicle less than a mile from the Cleveland, TN, jetport. He's in custody."

"Greaves?" I asked.

"Gone," Morrison said, shaking her head. "He made it to a small regional airport south of Valdosta, Georgia. The state police arrived just in time to see his plane take off. No flight plan was registered. He could be going anywhere."

So, the arrests had been largely successful, but seven key figures, including Greaves, had escaped.

"Someone warned them," French said, pacing the cabin's living room.

French grabbed Kate's arm and pulled her aside. While they talked quietly at the far end of the room, the rest of us continued processing the night's events.

"They've been preparing for this possibility for a long time," Morrison said.

"And someone told them exactly when to run," Amanda observed.

"Well, the good news," Tim reported, "is that we got their computers and financial records. The network's been disrupted even if some of the key players escaped."

I watched French and Kate's conversation. I couldn't hear what they were discussing, but French was obviously agitated about something. After several minutes, they returned to our group. French looked troubled. "As soon as Dr. Marsh was arrested," she said, "he started talking. The guy is terrified."

"Oh, and what did he want?" Morrison asked.

"He was trying to make a deal," French said

"Oh yeah," I snapped. "What kind of a deal?"

"Immunity. In return, he'll spill all he knows. He mentioned the unauthorized witness protection arrangements and relocations, the new identities created outside normal federal channels. Medical treatment for people who were supposed to be dead, the names of those involved, all in exchange for immunity from prosecution. He was in full panic mode."

"Uh huh," I said.

"But here's the thing," she continued, "Marsh mentioned the Riverside Strangler investigation."

Amanda looked at me with raised eyebrows.

Morrison leaned forward, her expression sharpening. "Did he give specifics?"

French shook her head. "Marsh said someone in law enforcement has been making payments. Someone who had access to the case files, evidence, and has, or had, the ability to manipulate the investigation, and others." French paused, studying our faces. "He specifically mentioned a case involving a supposed murder victim who was actually being treated for severe injuries at private medical facilities."

Kate's radio crackled with another update. She listened, then turned to us with a grim expression. "Chief Johnston wants a complete briefing at oh-eight-hundred. The mayor's office has been getting calls from the media about the arrests."

"How did the media find out so quickly?" Amanda asked.

Tim looked up from his laptop, where he'd been monitoring news feeds. "It's already on Channel 7's website. Your buddy Charlie Grove is having a field day describing a 'Multi-state law enforcement operation and dozens of arrests in a corruption investigation.' Someone leaked it fast."

"Charlie is not my buddy!" Amanda stated hotly.

"Or," Morrison said thoughtfully, "someone wanted the arrests to become public immediately to pressure the suspects into cooperating."

French checked her phone. "Marsh is being transported to the federal facility in Atlanta. He's requesting protective custody and full immunity."

"When can we interview him?" Kate asked.

"Federal prosecutors are meeting with him this morning," French replied. "If he provides useful information, they'll arrange for us to question him directly."

By two AM, the cabin had settled into an uneasy quiet. The immediate crisis was over, but the investigation was far from complete. We still didn't know who killed Frank, so Tim continued monitoring communications while the rest of us tried to process the night's events.

"Seventeen years on the force," Morrison said, staring out the cabin window at the dark mountains. "I've seen corruption before, but nothing like this. A police commissioner running a criminal network across three states. It's... unbelievable."

Amanda sat beside me on the couch, her hand finding mine. "At least it's over."

"Not quite," I muttered. "We still don't know who killed Frank or what happened to Catherine Wells."

French overheard and approached our conversation. "Actually, Reynolds might be able to provide those answers. He's also asking about plea arrangements."

Kate looked up from the tactical reports she'd been reviewing. "So when can we interview Reynolds?"

"Federal custody protocols require a cooling-off period," French replied, "but Chief Johnston has requested that Chattanooga detectives be involved in any questioning related to local crimes, and that includes Frank's murder."

Morrison gathered her files and radio equipment. "I should head back to coordinate with the chief and make sure the local investigation maintains momentum. The federal arrests are important, but our primary focus remains on finding Frank's killer."

Tim saved his work and closed his laptop. "I'm going back to the office," he said, "if that's all right with you. I'll keep monitoring the financial databases. With Reynolds' network disrupted, we might finally be able to trace those older payments now."

BY DAWN ON THURSDAY MORNING, REYNOLDS' CRIMINAL network had been severely damaged, but not destroyed. The escaped members would likely disappear permanently, but those in custody were already providing information about the organization's activities.

"Dr. Marsh is talking," French reported over the phone. "He's desperate to cut a deal."

"What's he saying?" Kate asked. "Anything worth listening to?"

"He confirms that Reynolds was running protection services for people with sensitive histories. New identities, medical treatment, relocation assistance, and so on and so on. He's also talking about a Catherine Wells."

I leaned forward. "Catherine Wells?" I said. "What about her?"

"He won't give details until he's made a deal,"

Kate stood and began pacing. "So, it looks like Catherine Wells survived, and that someone's been paying Reynolds to keep her hidden."

"But who?" Amanda asked. "And why?"

Morrison reviewed her notes. "I see nothing here about treatment. If Catherine did survive and had been severely injured, she would have needed ongoing care."

"The Mountain View Recovery Center," I said, nodding thoughtfully.

French confirmed that federal agents were preparing to execute a search warrant at the Mountain View facility based on Marsh's cooperation.

"They're moving this morning," she announced. "If Catherine Wells is there, we'll find her."

Kate grabbed her jacket. "I'm going with them."

"We're all going," I said, then looked at Amanda. "Except you. You stay here with Jade and Maria."

Amanda nodded reluctantly.

Two hours later, our convoy approached the Mountain View Recovery Center. Kate drove the lead vehicle with Samson in the back seat wearing his badge and K9 harness. I rode beside her while federal agents followed on behind. It looked like a presidential motorcade.

The facility looked different this time. The security gates were open, and there were no guards in sight. I was told later that federal agents had secured the perimeter an hour earlier.

"Looks like they cleared out," Kate observed as we drove along the driveway.

Agent Clark, the federal team leader, met us at the entrance. "The facility's been abandoned since yesterday evening. Most of the staff and patients were evacuated within hours of Dr. Marsh's arrest."

"Any sign of Catherine Wells?" I asked.

"We found evidence someone matching her description was here until recently," Clark replied. "But the patient records have all been destroyed."

"I wonder..." Kate said, taking a hairbrush taken from Catherine Wells' bedroom from an evidence bag and letting Samson smell it. "Track," she commanded, and the big dog began to work his way methodically through the facility, but after twenty minutes, he returned to Kate's side and sat down: the signal that he'd found nothing matching the scent sample.

Kate heaved a sigh and shook her head. "Well, wherever she is now, she hasn't been here recently," she concluded. "Wherever Catherine Wells is now, if she is indeed still alive, she wasn't here when they evacuated the place."

Tim went immediately to the security office and began to analyze the facility's computer systems, most of which had been wiped clean. "They deleted pretty much everything, but I might be able to recover some data from the backup drives."

"How long will that take?" I asked.

"Hours, maybe longer," he replied. "I dunno. It's a sophisticated system."

Lieutenant Clark took over the search, while Kate and I went to the administrative offices where we found more evidence of a hasty evacuation: scattered papers, abandoned files, even a half-eaten lunch left on someone's desk.

"It looks like they left in a hurry," Kate observed with a wry smile. "I wonder who tipped them off."

The evidence from Mountain View raised more questions

than answers. We still didn't know for sure if Catherine Wells was alive or dead, but what we did know was that if she was indeed alive, then someone had been paying for her care. We also knew that the facility had been evacuated within hours of the arrests, but there was no recent trace of Catherine herself.

"Whoever's been protecting Catherine Wells," Kate said, "is still out there. And they're still protecting her."

Tim, who was riding in the back with Samson, looked up from analyzing the recovered financial data. "I think she is alive," he said, "and it looks like the payments came from someone with high-level access to police department accounts. That's a short list of people."

I shook my head at the complexity of it all. The question was whether Catherine's protector was an ally trying to keep a victim safe, or something more sinister. Frank's investigation had led him to that same question, and it had gotten him killed.

"If she is alive," Kate said, "she might be the key to solving the Riverside Strangler case and why Frank was killed."

"Or she might be more involved than we think," I replied. "Nine years is a long time to stay hidden. That level of secrecy suggests something more than just a victim."

As we drove back toward Chattanooga, I stared out at the Tennessee landscape and tried to make sense of what we'd discovered. The Mountain View facility had been evacuated within hours of the arrests, and someone with serious resources and inside knowledge had orchestrated Catherine Wells' protection for almost a decade.

"So what's our next move?" Kate asked, breaking the silence.

Tim looked up from his laptop. "I'll analyze whatever data I can recover from the facility's systems. There might be fragments they missed. But I'm not optimistic. I think they used BleachBit."

"I guess I'll coordinate with the chief about Reynolds' interrogation," Kate said. "If he's willing to talk, we might finally get some answers about what happened to Catherine Wells."

I watched the city skyline come into view as we descended Signal Mountain. Frank had spent ten years pursuing these same questions, following leads that ultimately led to his death. Now we had more pieces of the puzzle, but Catherine Wells herself remained as elusive as ever.

The question was whether we were getting closer to the truth or walking into the same trap that had killed my mentor. Either way, there was no turning back now.

16

THE ANONYMOUS MEETING

THURSDAY, AUGUST 25, 2024

I ARRIVED BACK AT MY OFFICE ON THURSDAY MORNING TO FIND Tim already deep into analyzing the data recovered from Mountain View, his workstation surrounded by the usual collection of coffee cups and energy drink cans. The morning light streaming in through the windows highlighted the intensity in his eyes as he worked to crack the facility's encrypted files.

I didn't bother to ask if he'd slept. It was a fight I was never going to win. Instead, I settled into the chair beside his desk, and said, "Good morning, Tim. Anything new?"

"Hey," he replied, gifting me with a quick glance. "I've been making progress, I guess," he replied. "They didn't use BleachBit as I thought, but they did use seriously tough deletion protocols, but they weren't quite thorough enough."

He leaned back in his chair, poked his glasses with his finger, then flipped the finger at his main display, which showed fragments of recovered data: partial financial records, incomplete patient files, and what appeared to be communication logs between the facility and external contacts.

"Did you find anything useful in that mess?" I asked, frowning.

"Yeah! Someone's been paying for long-term care at the facility for a little more than eight years," Tim said, adjusting his glasses. "The payments came through a series of shell accounts, and ended in September last year, but I was able to trace them back to their source."

I leaned closer to study the financial data. As usual, I couldn't make head nor tail of the garbled figures. "What am I looking at, Tim?"

"Specifically, accounts used for confidential operations and witness protection expenses."

I sat there for another ten minutes listening to a boring litany of financial misdirection I didn't understand until I was finally rescued by a call from Kate. "Harry, Reynolds is ready to make a deal."

"I want to be there," I snapped. "When?"

"This morning. Federal prosecutors are meeting with him at nine in the Federal Building, and they've agreed to let us participate, but only if we can provide information about local crimes."

I checked my watch. It was already eight-fifteen. "I'll be there in twenty minutes."

THE INTERVIEW WAS TO TAKE PLACE IN THE DOWNTOWN Federal Building, a stark, modern structure on Georgia Avenue. Kate met me in the parking lot at the rear of the building, along with Agent French and a briefcase full of case files.

"Reynolds has been talking since dawn," French said as we walked toward the entrance. "His lawyer is pushing hard for a plea agreement, and Reynolds seems genuinely terrified of spending the rest of his life in prison."

"What's he offering?" I asked.

"Complete cooperation with all federal and local investigations. Names, dates, financial records, operational details. He's willing to testify against his entire network in exchange for a reduced sentence."

Kate added, "The federal prosecutors want to hear what he knows about Frank's murder specifically. If Reynolds can provide information that leads to solving that case, it strengthens his case for a deal."

We passed through the multiple security checkpoints before reaching the interview room where Reynolds was waiting with his lawyer. The man who had once commanded respect and fear as Chattanooga's Police Commissioner looked diminished in his orange jumpsuit, his usual air of authority replaced by one of obvious desperation.

"Commissioner Reynolds," I said, taking a seat across from him.

"Former commissioner," he corrected grimly. "And I suppose I have you to thank for my current circumstances, Starke."

"You have only yourself to thank," Kate replied sharply.

Reynolds' lawyer, Charlene "Charlie" Osgood, a sharply-dressed woman in her fifties, leaned forward. "I don't know what the federal authorities have told you, but my client is prepared—"

"We know what he wants. Let's get on with it, shall we?" Kate said.

Osgood leaned back in her chair, folded her arms and stared stoically at Kate.

Agent French opened her file. "Let's begin with the protection services your network provided. Specifically, arrangements for people who needed new identities or medical treatment outside normal channels."

Reynolds nodded slowly. "We provided those services for clients who could afford them. Politicians avoiding scandals, witnesses who needed to disappear, even some criminals who wanted to start over with clean slates."

"What about the Catherine Wells case?" I asked.

At the mention of Catherine's name, Reynolds' expression shifted. He glanced at his lawyer, who nodded for him to continue.

"That was different," Reynolds said. "Most of our clients paid upfront for their services. But the Catherine Wells arrangement was ongoing, paid for by someone else over many years."

Kate leaned forward. "Who was paying?"

"Someone in local law enforcement. I never dealt with them directly. All communications went through intermediaries, and payments came through… a number of private accounts."

"How much money are we talking about?" French asked.

"Several hundreds of thousands over the years."

I studied Reynolds' face carefully. "Are you telling us Catherine Wells is alive?"

Reynolds hesitated, then said, "She was a year ago, but then she was removed from the facility and the payments stopped. What I'm telling you is that someone has been paying us to provide protective services for a person using that name. Whether she's actually Catherine Wells or someone else entirely, I couldn't say." He shook his head and folded his arms across his chest.

Osgood interjected, "My client never had direct contact with the individual. All arrangements and payments were made through intermediaries."

"He just said that," Kate said, wearily. "Let's stick to the point, shall we? What about the medical treatment? Where exactly was this person being treated?"

"Multiple facilities over the years," Reynolds replied. "The Mountain View Recovery Center was the most recent, but there were others. She was placed wherever the facilities provided the level of care and security the client required."

French made notes as Reynolds continued, "The protection arrangement was sophisticated. New identity documentation, regular medical monitoring, secure housing, even financial support. It was one of our most expensive operations."

"And you're saying someone in the Chattanooga Police Department was funding all of this?" I asked.

"Through private funding, yes," he replied.

Kate's phone buzzed with a text message. She glanced at it, then showed it to me: *Anonymous caller wants to meet. Says they have information about Catherine Wells. Tonight, 7 PM.*

Reynolds noticed our exchange, smiled, then said, "I think I should warn you. I don't know who was protecting Catherine Wells—and I say 'was,' because when the payments ended so did our association with her, Wells simply disappeared. Whoever it was protecting her has substantial resources and connections at their disposal, and they've already demonstrated they're willing to kill to keep their secrets safe."

"So what you're telling us is that whomever it was killed Frank?" I asked.

Reynolds shrugged. "Frank was getting close to exposing something that threatened us all. Whether it was Catherine's identity, her location, or the person protecting her, someone decided he was too dangerous to live."

And so it went on for two more hours until Agent French ended the interview. By then, Reynolds had provided detailed information about his network's operations, financial structures, and the scope of services they provided. For me, none of that mattered. It was the Catherine Wells case I was interested in, because I believed it was that case that had brought about my old friend's demise.

————

BACK AT MY OFFICE AT A LITTLE AFTER NOON, I FOUND THAT Tim had made additional progress analyzing the Mountain View data, and Jacque had some bee in her bonnet about our own case files that had not been properly closed. I told her that I couldn't do anything about it then and maybe not for several days and that she was to handle it herself or I'd put TJ on it. He was after all an ex-banker and well qualified to handle the problem.

She gave me one of her looks, but said nothing, turning away and slamming my office door behind her. It wasn't something she did often, but when she did, I knew I'd stepped over the line and that an apology from me would be required to set things straight again. *Geez, I need to get this damn case done and out of my head,* I though, angrily.

"Jacque!" I shouted, going to the door. "Wait."

"What is it," Harry?" she asked, testily, as she turned at her office door.

"I'm sorry," I said. "No excuses. That was uncalled for. I'll try not to let it happen again."

She nodded, "Apology accepted," she said with a half-smile. "I understand you're frustrated, but please try to keep it in check, okay?" And then she disappeared into her office and closed the door.

Me? I went back to the conference room where Tim was still working the data.

"I found the communication logs between the facility and someone at a police department email address," Tim announced as Kate and I reviewed Reynolds' statements. "The messages were sent through administrative accounts, but I'm working to identify which specific account was used."

"How long will that take?" Kate asked.

"I don't know," he replied, obviously frustrated. "Maybe a few hours. The department's email system has security protocols that make it difficult to trace individual users, but it's not impossible."

I nodded and turned to Kate. "What about the anonymous caller?" I asked.

"We set up the meeting for seven o'clock. If they have legitimate information about Catherine's protection arrangement, we need to hear it."

Morrison arrived a few moments later with updates from Chief Johnston and the ongoing investigation into Reynolds' network. She looked tired but determined as she settled into a seat in our conference room.

"Oh, and one more thing, Harry," Tim said. "I finally finished that research you asked me to do weeks ago about the Wells family jewelry discrepancy. You know, the insurance claim versus the police evidence?"

"And?" I asked.

"It looks like a garden-variety insurance fraud," Tim replied. "I compared the actual crime scene photos with the insurance claim documentation. The additional jewelry listed on the claim—the gold watch, pearl earrings, and initialed necklace—never existed at the crime scene. The Wells family inflated their claim by about thirty-two hundred dollars."

Morrison frowned. "That's completely separate from our corruption investigation?"

"Completely," Tim confirmed. "Howard and Margaret Wells filed a fraudulent insurance claim after their daughter's death, but it has nothing to do with Frank's murder or the corruption network. Just ordinary grief-driven greed, unfortunately."

I shook my head. "So Margaret's cryptic warning about asking the wrong questions wasn't about protecting her family's insurance fraud. She really was trying to point us toward the bigger conspiracy."

"What happens with the insurance fraud?" Kate asked.

"I reported it to the insurance company's fraud division," Tim said. "They'll pursue recovery of the fraudulent payout, but it's a civil matter now. The statute of limitations has probably run out on criminal charges anyway."

"Thanks, Tim," I said. It was disappointing in a way. The Wells family's suspicious behavior had seemed so significant, but it turned out to be unrelated to the main case.

Morrison looked thoughtful. "At least it shows Frank was methodical. He caught the insurance discrepancy even though it wasn't connected to what got him killed."

"Frank never missed details," I agreed. "Even the small frauds mattered to him."

"The chief is acting up," Morrison said. "Apparently the mayor's office is getting pressure from the media."

"What are you telling them?" I asked.

"The truth; that we're investigating all aspects of the case and will follow the evidence wherever it leads. But Harry, if someone in our department is involved in Frank's murder, the political fallout will be... Well, all hell will break loose. You can bet on it."

Kate brought Morrison up to speed on Reynolds' cooperation and the anonymous meeting request. Morrison listened carefully, taking notes and asking detailed questions about the protection arrangement.

"Reynolds' description of the funding is accurate," Morrison confirmed.

"Any idea who it might be that was making the payments?" I asked.

Morrison shook her head. "Private accounts. That's all I know. Could be anybody in the tri-state area."

THE AFTERNOON BROUGHT ADDITIONAL DEVELOPMENTS WHEN Agent French called with updates from the continuing interviews with Dr. Marsh.

"Marsh is providing detailed information about the medical treatment provided to Catherine Wells," French reported. "He confirms she survived severe injuries from the original attack and required extensive reconstructive surgery and ongoing psychological treatment."

"Is he willing to testify about her current condition or location?" Kate asked.

"That's where it gets complicated. Marsh says the patient was moved from Mountain View back in September of last year, but he doesn't know where, or even if she's still alive."

I put French on speaker so Morrison and Tim could hear. "Did Marsh identify who was coordinating the protection arrangement?"

"No, he says he dealt with intermediaries, but he does have records of communications and payment authorizations. We're analyzing those now, trying to identify the original source."

Morrison leaned closer to the phone. "Agent French, this is Captain Morrison. How long before you can identify the person who was making the payments?"

"Our forensic accountants are working on it, but it could take days, even weeks. The financial trail was deliberately obscured through multiple shell accounts and interme-diaries."

"I have Tim working on it, too," I said. "I'll let you know if he makes any progress.

After ending the call, we spent the rest of the afternoon preparing for the evening meeting with the anonymous caller.

"We'll use the same restaurant where Jason Mills was killed," Kate said. "and we'll have backup positioned throughout the area."

"Are you sure that's wise?" Morrison asked. "Using the same location where a witness was murdered sends a pretty specific message."

"That's exactly the message we want to send," I replied. "We're not backing down here, no matter what."

By six o'clock, Tim had identified several transactions that matched Reynolds' description of the Catherine Wells payments.

"The money trail is complex," he said, "but I'm seeing regular transfers from confidential accounts to external financial institutions," Tim reported. "The payments began about nine years ago and continued until last September."

"Can you identify who authorized the payments?" Kate asked.

"I'm still working on that," he replied, glancing up at me.

WE ARRIVED OUTSIDE THE FOUNDRY RESTAURANT AT A LITTLE after six-thirty, parked, and waited. At seven, Kate and I entered, and we seated ourselves in the same booth where Jason had been shot. I have to tell you, it was more than a little surreal.

At three minutes after seven, a woman in her sixties with gray hair and intelligent eyes that seemed familiar somehow entered the dining area from the rest room corridor. She wore a simple dress and carried herself with the bearing of someone accustomed to authority.

"Good evening, Mrs. Wells," I said, standing up.

"Mr. Starke?" Margaret Wells. "It's good to see you again. We need to talk."

"Mrs. Wells," Kate said, gesturing for her to sit down. "This is… unexpected."

Margaret Wells sat carefully, her hands trembling slightly as she placed a manila envelope on the table between us. "I've been following your investigation," she said, "and I realize it's time to tell you the truth about Catherine."

I nodded, then said, "That's… good news, Mrs. Wells. If it's all right with you, we'll record the interview, to protect you and us, you understand?"

She nodded, then began, "Catherine survived the attack on her, nearly nine years ago on February seventeen, 2016, but she was severely injured. The person who arranged her protection and ongoing medical care did so to keep her safe, not to hide criminal activity."

Margaret's revelation confirmed what Reynolds had told us, but raised new questions about who had been funding Catherine's protection and why they'd kept it secret for so long.

"Who arranged the protection?" Kate asked.

Margaret hesitated, then said, "Someone who understood that Catherine's survival made her a target. Someone who had access to resources and the ability to create new identities and secure medical treatment."

"Mrs. Wells," I said carefully, "who arranged Catherine's protection?" I asked, repeating Kate's question.

Margaret hesitated, her hands trembling as she gripped her coffee cup. "Someone in law enforcement. Someone who understood the danger Catherine faced and had access to resources."

"We need a name, Mrs. Wells," Kate pressed.

Margaret shook her head. "I'm sorry, I can't. Not yet. There are still people who could be hurt if this comes out the wrong way."

"Mrs. Wells, Frank Callahan died investigating this case," I said. "If you know who's been protecting Catherine, we need that information."

"I know," Margaret said quietly. "And I want Frank's killer caught, too. But Catherine's safety has to come first. She's been hidden for eight and a half years, and rushing to expose everything now could get her killed."

Kate leaned forward. "Then what more can you tell us, Mrs. Wells?"

"Catherine survived, and, as you know, she's been receiving medical care and protection. The person helping us has been doing it at great personal risk and expense. But Catherine's ready to testify if it means bringing justice for Frank and the other victims."

"Where is she now?" Kate asked.

"Safe. But she'll only come forward if we can guarantee her protection from the federal authorities, not the local police."

I leaned back in my seat and stared at her. I could tell from her attitude she wasn't going to tell us any more, but I tried. After asking her several more questions and receiving only noncommittal answers, I realized she'd shut down.

"Okay," I said with a sigh and a shake of the head, "we'll be in touch, Mrs. Wells."

"I'm sorry, I..." she trailed off, stood up abruptly, then turned and walked quickly out of the restaurant.

Kate and I remained seated. The meeting had provided *some* crucial information, but it also raised disturbing new questions. We now knew Catherine Wells was alive, but where she was and who was protecting her was still unknown.

"It's someone in law enforcement," Kate said as if reading my mind.

"But it narrows things down some," I replied. "Whoever it is..." I shook my head. "It takes serious commitment and resources. But why? Why would someone do that? Why go to so much trouble and cost for an attempted murder victim?"

I sighed, looked sideways at Kate and said, "I'm so damn frustrated I could bite through a sixpenny nail."

Kate smiled at me and said, "But you know better than most that police work is built on frustration and hard work, don't you, Harry?"

"Yeah, yeah, yeah," I muttered as I stood up and walked out into the darkening night.

Kate followed me and we said our goodnights and went home, knowing tomorrow would bring even more new challenges as we worked to unravel a decade-long secret that someone had been willing to murder Frank to protect. The truth was out there. I was certain of that, but getting to it... was not going to be easy.

17

FINDING CATHERINE

FRIDAY, AUGUST 26, 2024

I ARRIVED HOME THURSDAY NIGHT TO FIND AMANDA WAITING IN the living room, her laptop open and case files scattered across the coffee table. She looked up as I walked in, concern evident in her pale green eyes.

"Who was it? How did it go?" she asked, closing her laptop.

"It was Margaret Wells," I replied. "She confirmed Catherine's alive but wouldn't say where she is or who's protecting her," I said, settling beside her on the couch.

Amanda leaned against me, and I could feel some of the day's tension beginning to ease. "And you've no idea who it might be?" she asked.

"No, none. But I have Tim working on it, so maybe tomorrow. Maybe the financial trail will lead us to him... or her. It has to be someone willing to sacrifice their personal finances, but why would someone do that?"

"It sounds like family to me," Amanda observed.

I nodded, thinking about the patterns Agent French had described. "Or someone with a very personal reason for keeping Catherine safe," I muttered.

Jade appeared at the top of the stairs in her princess pajamas, rubbing her eyes. "Daddy? Why are you talking about work so late?"

"Come here, princess," I said, opening my arms. She ran down the stairs and climbed onto the couch between Amanda and me.

"Did you catch the bad man yet?" she asked, settling against my chest.

"Not yet, sweetheart, but soon," I replied, smoothing her hair. "Tomorrow might be the day."

"Good," she said with a yawn. "Then we can go fishing like you promised."

Amanda and I exchanged a look over Jade's head. I couldn't help it. I heaved a sigh and shook my head, knowing that tomorrow would likely bring about another dangerous confrontation.

"You bet," I said. "I'll make sure we have that fishing trip," I kissed Jade's forehead. "Very soon."

Amanda carried Jade back to bed while I sat quietly in the living room, thinking about Margaret Wells' words and the anonymous protector who, so it seemed, had sacrificed everything to keep her daughter safe. Deep in my gut, I knew we were close to solving the mystery, and that we'd soon know who killed Frank.

AFTER YET ANOTHER RESTLESS NIGHT AND A SIX-MILE EARLY morning run, I arrived somewhat refreshed at the office on

Friday morning around eight-thirty to find Tim practically vibrating with excitement.

"Harry, I found her," Tim announced, pushing his glasses up his nose. "I found Catherine Wells."

Kate appeared in the doorway with Samson at her side, having arrived just behind me. He ran to me and punched me in the side with his nose. I grinned down at him and fondled his ears.

"You did?" Kate said. "Where the hell is she?"

Tim pulled up a series of screens showing medical records, prescription databases, and insurance claims. "She's in Knoxville," he replied. Then to me he said, "I've been tracking prescription medications for someone matching Catherine's medical profile. Reconstructive surgery patients require specific medications for years after treatment."

"That's a lot of data to sort through," I said.

"Yeah, but I was able to narrow it down using the timeline from Margaret Wells and Dr. Marsh's medical records. Someone with Catherine's injury profile has been receiving prescriptions in the Knoxville area for the past eleven months."

Kate leaned over Tim's shoulder to study the data. "Knoxville makes sense. It's close enough for regular contact with her protector but far enough to maintain anonymity."

Tim clicked through several more screens. "The prescriptions are filled under the name Catherine Preston, but the medical profile matches exactly. Same birth date, same injury patterns, same ongoing treatment requirements."

"Do we have an address?" I asked.

"Well, yeah," he replied, "but here's where it gets interesting," he continued, pulling up property records. "Catherine Preston rents a small apartment near the University of

Tennessee campus. But the lease payments come from a bank account registered to someone else."

"Do we know who?" I asked.

"Not yet. I'm still working on it. The account holder used a post office box and provided minimal identification when opening the account."

My phone rang. It was Agent French.

"Harry, our forensic accountants made a breakthrough on the Mountain View payments. It's as we thought; someone in local law enforcement."

"Can you give me specifics?"

"Not over the phone. Can you meet me at the federal building in an hour"

After ending the call, I turned to Kate and Tim. "French has more information about Catherine's protector. Tim, I need Catherine Preston's address."

"I'm almost there," he replied, typing and glancing from screen to screen sporadically. "Give me a mom... Ah, here we go," he said, triumphantly, as he tapped the enter button to print out the page. "Apartment 2B, 847 Cumberland Avenue, Knoxville. It's an apartment building close to the Convention Center and within walking distance from the UT campus."

Kate studied the address. "We need to approach this carefully. If Catherine's been hidden for nine years, showing up unannounced could panic her."

"Or her protector," I added. "If they're monitoring her location, they'll know we're getting close."

———

AN HOUR LATER, AGENT FRENCH MET US AT THE FEDERAL

building with files containing the forensic accounting results. Her expression was grim as she led us to a conference room.

"The person funding Catherine's protection has been using personal bank accounts and private loans," French began. "The payments total over three hundred thousand dollars spread across nine years."

"That's a lot of money," Kate observed.

"Someone with serious financial resources and a powerful personal motivation," French continued. "The payments went to various shell companies and from there to the medical facilities, but they all trace back to a single funding source."

"Do you have a name?" I asked.

French shook her head. "No, the account holder used some pretty sophisticated methods to obscure their identity. We think, from the personal financial arrangements, that there has to be some sort of family involvement."

"Family?" Kate asked. "Really?"

"We think whoever it is, it's someone protecting a family member. Either that or there must be some sort of close personal connection."

I studied the financial data. "It doesn't make any sense," I muttered. "Someone is keeping Catherine Wells hidden. But again, the question is who and why? I think if we had the why, we'd have the answers we need."

"There's something else," French said, pulling out additional documents. "The financial activity shows increased stress in recent months. Large cash payments, signs that the funding arrangement was becoming difficult to maintain."

Kate leaned forward, frowning. "What's the timeline?"

"The stress indicators begin about six months ago and intensify around the time Frank was murdered. Whatever was threatening the protection arrangement, it was serious enough to force some pretty desperate financial measures."

I thought about that. If it began around the time Frank was murdered, it seemed to me that Frank must have been on the cusp of exposing Catherine's protector, who had no choice but to shut him up, permanently.

"We need to get to Catherine," I said. "Before this person who's protecting her realizes we're closing in."

———————

THE DRIVE TO KNOXVILLE, STRAIGHT UP I-75, TOOK ABOUT ninety minutes. Kate and I and Samson rode together while the federal agents followed in unmarked vehicles. The closer we got to Catherine's address, the more questions arose in my mind about her protector's identity and motives.

"If someone killed Frank to protect Catherine," I said to Kate as we crossed the Knoxville city limits sign, "they're probably monitoring her location."

"Which means they might already know we're coming," she replied. "We need to move fast and hope Catherine cooperates."

We found Catherine's apartment building on Cumberland Avenue, a modest three-story, rectangular, brick-built structure. French's agents established a perimeter while Kate and I approached the main entrance.

Apartment 2B was on the second floor, accessible through an external staircase. I could see lights on inside and movement behind the curtains.

Kate knocked gently on the door. "Catherine Preston?" she said. "Open up. We're with the Chattanooga Police Department.

The movement behind the curtains stopped. And, after a long pause, a woman's voice called out, "I don't know anyone by that name."

"Catherine, we know who you really are," I said. "Please open the door."

After a minute, the door opened just a crack and a voice said, "Who are you, and what do you want?"

I introduced myself and Kate, and again asked her to open the door.

"We're investigating Frank Callahan's murder," I said, "and we think you might have information that could help."

There was another long pause, then the sound of a chain being unhooked and the door opened to reveal an attractive young woman I knew to be in her early thirties. She had long dark hair, a full figure, and what I can only describe as cautious brown eyes. It was also easy to see that reconstructive surgery had altered her features, but I could still see a resemblance to the photographs from the original case files.

"You're Catherine Wells, aren't you?" Kate asked gently.

The woman nodded slowly. "I haven't used that name in nine years. How did you find me?"

"May we come in?" I asked.

Catherine hesitated for a moment, then stepped back to let us enter. The apartment was small but comfortable, with medical equipment in one corner and art supplies scattered throughout the living area.

"I knew someone would find me eventually," she said, settling into a chair near the window. "I just didn't think it would be the police."

I sat at the table while Kate turned one of the dining chairs to face her and sat down. Samson settled down on the floor nearby, watching Catherine with interest.

"How are you doing, Catherine?" I asked. "You've been through a lot these past nine years, haven't you?"

"I'm okay," she replied, twisting her fingers together in her lap. "But it's been, hard, yes."

I nodded, then said, "Catherine, we need to ask you about the night you were attacked on the Riverwalk. Do you remember what happened?"

Her hands trembled as she spoke. "Of course I do. I remember everything. I was jogging along the path when someone grabbed me from behind. I fought back, but he was stronger. He had a wire or cable that he put around my neck."

"Did you see him?" I asked.

"Yes, she replied. "When I broke free for a moment, I saw his face clearly. I knew him."

Kate leaned forward. "Who was it, Catherine?"

Catherine hesitated, her eyes darting between Kate and me. "Someone I'd seen before. A man with a history of violence who I knew was dangerous." Her hands trembled more noticeably. "I can't say any more than that. My... friend made me promise never to identify him. They said it would put me in even more danger if I did."

"But you could identify him if you needed to?" I asked.

"Yes. I'll never forget his face. But I need to talk to my friend first before I say anything else."

Samson suddenly raised his head, his ears perking up at a sound outside. Kate glanced at him, then stood up and moved closer to the window.

"How did you manage to get away?" I asked.

"I kicked him in the... well, you know. He went down and I kicked him again in the same place, hard. But by then my..." She trailed off and put her hand to her face.

"What happened after the attack?" Kate asked, keeping one eye on Samson.

"I managed to get to the road, you know. I'd lost my phone somewhere. It was never found. Anyway, I flagged down a car and the man—he was so nice—called the police and an ambulance and I was taken to the hospital. My injuries were... really bad. My neck was ripped and my face..." Her voice was trembling. "The doctors said I nearly died. But someone arranged for my death to be faked and for me to receive treatment at a private facility just outside Chattanooga."

And again, I couldn't help but wonder why.

"Who was it, Catherine? Who arranged all that for you?" I asked.

"I can't tell you. I can only tell you that it was someone who understood that my survival made me a target. They convinced me that my attacker had connections to dangerous people who would kill me if they knew I was alive."

"And this person didn't tell you their name?" Kate asked.

Catherine shook her head. "No, for the first few years all our contact was through intermediaries. I only met my friend after the person who attacked me died in a car accident five years ago."

Samson stood up and moved toward the door, his tail swishing from side to side, a low growl issuing from the back of his throat. "Samson, heel." The big dog backed slowly away from the door, his eyes never leaving it.

Kate grasped his collar while I went to the door, my hand on my weapon, and opened it. I stepped carefully out into the corridor, weapon at the ready, but there was no one there. I holstered the gun, stepped back inside, and closed the door. Then I looked at Kate and shrugged.

"And this person has been paying for your care all these years?" Kate said, as if nothing had happened.

Me? I sat down again, wondering what the hell Sammy had heard. He'd heard something. I was sure of that. The dog was infallible.

"Everything." Wells replied. "My medical treatment, housing, living expenses, even art supplies so I could continue painting. I don't know how they managed it, but they did."

Catherine walked to a desk and took a cell phone from the drawer. "I should call them. They need to know you've found me."

Kate and I exchanged glances. Catherine was about to contact her mysterious friend.

"She's been like family to me for nine years," Catherine said, dialing a number. "Whatever you think about the situation, she saved my life when no one else would."

So, her friend is a female, I thought. *That's something new.*

She waited as the phone rang, then said, "Hey, it's Catherine. The police are here asking about Frank Callahan. I think they know about David. You need to come now."

Catherine listened for a moment, then said, "Yes, please hurry. I'm scared."

After ending the call, Catherine turned back to us. "They're already on their way," she said. "They'll be here in twenty minutes."

Twenty minutes? I thought. *That means they're already inside the Knoxville city limits. They must have known, but how? That leak again?*

"Catherine," Kate said carefully, "we have evidence that Frank Callahan was murdered to prevent him from discovering you're still alive. Do you know anything about that?"

Catherine's face went white. "That's impossible. My friend

would never hurt anyone. They've spent nine years sacrificing everything to keep me safe."

"From who?" I asked. "And who's David?"

"David is… You'll have to wait. From… people. I don't know." She was becoming agitated, and that was something we didn't need.

But the complexity of the situation was becoming clear. Someone had convinced Catherine that her ongoing safety was necessary even after this David's death, creating justification for the continued secrecy.

My phone buzzed with a text from Tim: "Monitoring police communications. They know you found her."

Twenty-five minutes later, we heard footsteps on the external staircase. Catherine rushed to the window, then opened the door before anyone could knock.

"Lisa! Thank God you're here. These officers are asking about Frank Callahan. Tell them you didn't kill him."

Captain Lisa Morrison entered the apartment and stood for a moment, as if she was assessing the situation: Kate and I were positioned on either side of the door, and Federal agents were visible through the windows, Catherine was looking back and forth between us, a look of confusion and fear on her face.

And then, Morrison's composure cracked slightly as she realized her carefully constructed deception was finally crumbling.

"Hello, Lisa," I said quietly. "We've been waiting for you." Oh, yeah, I was shocked to see her, but not totally surprised . I mean, it had to have been someone with the rank and audacity to pull off a ten year long deception such as this one, didn't it?

I looked at Kate. Her mouth was open and her face was… I

could see she was feeling both stunned and betrayed. Morrison had been our trusted colleague throughout the investigation, helping coordinate resources.

"Lisa? What the hell?" She almost shrieked. "What in God's name...?" She trailed off, reaching for her restraints.

"Catherine, are you all right?" Morrison asked, her first concern still for the woman she'd protected for nine years. "Did they threaten you or try to force information from you?"

"I told them nothing. I let David's name slip, but not yours. I told them how you saved me," Catherine replied. "But they think you killed Frank. That's crazy, right?"

Morrison looked at Catherine with genuine affection, then at Kate and me with resignation. "I suppose it was inevitable, really. I knew you would eventually piece it together, and that it was just a matter of time before you did."

"Lisa Morrison," Kate said, her voice heavy, "you're under arrest for the murder of Frank Callahan."

Catherine stepped between Morrison and Kate. "No! You don't understand. Lisa protected me for nine years. She gave up everything to keep me safe. She's not a killer!"

"Catherine," Morrison said gently, "it's time for the truth. All of it."

And it was. The investigation that began with a retired detective's murder had led us to this moment of revelation, where the line between protector and killer had become impossibly blurred. Lisa Morrison's arrest finally brought justice for Frank, but it would also shatter Catherine's world and expose a decade of secrets.

My friend Frank's pursuit of truth had ultimately succeeded, but at a cost far higher than anyone could have imagined.

18

MORRISON'S CONFESSION

FRIDAY, AUGUST 26, 2024

THE RIDE BACK TO CHATTANOOGA IN THE FEDERAL TRANSPORT vehicle was unlike anything I'd experienced in all my years of law enforcement. Kate sat beside me in the back seat, her face a mask of composure that I knew was costing her considerable effort. Across from us, Morrison sat in handcuffs.

Catherine had chosen to ride in a separate vehicle with Agent French, unable to process the revelation that her protector was also Frank's killer. The image of her confusion and pain as we'd left the apartment I knew would stay with me for a long time.

"You know, I always wondered if this day would come," Morrison said, breaking the silence that had lasted for the first thirty minutes of the drive. "Ten years is a long time to keep a secret."

Kate turned to look at her former colleague. "Lisa, you

have the right to remain silent. Your lawyer should be present for any—"

"I've already waived my rights," Morrison interrupted. "Agent French has it all recorded. At this point, keeping quiet won't help anyone, least of all Catherine."

I studied Morrison's face in the dim light. "Why don't you start from the beginning? Help us understand what the hell happened and how it got started."

Morrison leaned back against her seat, the handcuffs clinking softly. "It started with my sister Jennifer. She was my twin, Harry. She was seven minutes older than me and she never let me forget it."

Kate's expression softened slightly. "Jennifer Morrison was the first Riverside Strangler victim."

"Jennifer Morrison was my brother David's first victim," Morrison corrected. "There was no Riverside Strangler. There was just a sick, twisted young man who killed his own sister and then tried to cover it up by killing nine more inno-cent women."

The revelation was almost beyond belief, but Morrison continued quietly, "David had been showing signs of violence for years. Mental health issues that my parents refused to acknowledge. He'd hurt animals as a child, gotten into fights, shown all the warning signs that everyone ignored because he could be very charming... when he wanted to be."

"What happened the night Jennifer died?" I asked.

Morrison's composure cracked slightly. "They'd had an argument. Jennifer had discovered that David was stealing money from our parents, and she was threatening to tell them. She said she was going to tell them everything and make sure he got the help he needed."

Kate leaned forward. "So he killed her to keep her quiet."

"He followed her to the Riverwalk where she went jogging. He used a cable from his construction job to strangle her. But when I got the call as the responding detective, David was already there, playing the grieving brother."

The vehicle hit a pothole, jarring us momentarily. Morrison used the interruption to gather herself before continuing.

"I knew immediately something was wrong. David's story didn't match the evidence, and his emotional reactions felt... performative. But he was my brother, and Jennifer was dead, and I couldn't bring myself to believe he'd actually killed her."

"When did you realize the truth?" Kate asked.

"Three days later, when the second victim was found. Lisa Haldon. She was twenty-two, a waitress. She was found strangled in the riverside park. David had an alibi for that night—he'd been with me, having dinner at my apartment. But something about his behavior during the investigation bothered me."

Morrison paused, staring out the window at the passing Tennessee countryside. "So I started watching him more carefully, following him. And I caught him stalking the third potential victim, planning his attack."

"Catherine Wells," I said.

"No, Sarah Mitchell was his third victim," she corrected me. "I missed that one. Catherine was supposed to be victim number four, but she was stronger than David expected. When she fought back and escaped, he panicked. He came to me, covered in scratches, claiming he'd been mugged. That's when I knew for certain."

Kate's professional mask was slipping, replaced by genuine curiosity about Morrison's impossible situation. "What did you do?"

"I made the worst decision of my life," Morrison replied. "I chose to protect my brother instead of arresting him. I told myself I could control him, get him help, prevent more deaths, but I was wrong."

"But the killings continued," I pointed out.

Morrison nodded grimly. "David said he had to continue killing to make Jennifer's death look like the work of a serial killer. I loved my brother. I just couldn't bring myself to arrest him."

"So you helped cover up the other murders," I said. "You let him kill another six innocent women. What the hell were you thinking?"

"I really don't know," she replied, looking genuinely confused. "It was as if I... I don't know, Harry," she shook her head as if she couldn't believe it herself. "I altered evidence, misdirected investigations, made sure that leads pointing toward David were never properly pursued. I used my position in the department to protect a serial killer." Morrison's voice was heavy with self-loathing.

Kate asked the question I was thinking. "I still don't get it, Lisa, why didn't you stop him? Why didn't you arrest him after the first murder?"

"Because he was my brother, and I was a coward," Morrison replied simply. "Every time I tried to confront him, he'd threaten to either kill himself or implicate me as an accomplice. I kept telling myself each one was the last, and that I'd find a way to get him help without destroying our family. But..." she heaved a sigh and stared down at the floor.

The federal transport driver adjusted his mirrors, probably listening to every word. It would all be documented, recorded, used in court proceedings that would destroy what remained of her life.

"So tell us about Catherine," I said.

Morrison looked up at me. There were tears in her eyes. She wiped them away with the back of her hands. "When Catherine survived David's attack," she said, "I knew she could identify him. I knew she'd seen his face. "

"So you convinced the medical staff to fake her death?" Kate asked.

"I had connections with Dr. Marsh through some earlier cases. He was already involved with Reynolds, providing medical services for people who needed to disappear. So I approached him about Catherine's situation."

Kate leaned back, frowning. "You used Reynolds' network to protect Catherine from your own brother."

"It was the only way to keep her safe. I convinced David she was dead, and everyone else believed the official reports, and I got Catherine the medical treatment she needed."

"And you funded it all yourself," I said.

Morrison nodded. "It took every penny I had, plus loans I'll be paying off for the rest of my life. Catherine's medical care, housing, living expenses. It cost me my marriage, my savings, my financial future. But she was alive, and that was worth everything to me. It was my way of atoning for what I'd allowed my brother to do... I suppose."

The vehicle began slowing as we approached Chattanooga's city limits. Morrison's confession was nearing its end, but there was one more thing I needed to know.

"What about Frank?" I asked quietly.

Morrison's composure finally broke completely. Tears started flowing down her cheeks as she struggled to speak. "Frank was the best detective I ever worked with. Methodical, persistent, absolutely dedicated. But it was those qualities that made him dangerous."

"He was getting close to discovering Catherine was alive," Kate said.

"Frank had always suspected something was wrong with the Riverside Strangler investigation," she replied. "When he retired, he became obsessed with proving his theories. And, eventually, his research led him to discover that Catherine was alive, and from there..."

"He would have identified David as the killer and you as the person covering it up," I finished.

Morrison nodded through her tears. "I tried everything else first. I monitored his investigation through my access to department resources. I even had Reynolds' people try to discourage him with subtle intimidation. But Frank wouldn't stop."

Kate's voice was barely above a whisper. "So you killed him."

"I went to his house to beg him to stop his investigation. I offered him money, information about other cases, anything I could think of. But Frank was Frank. He was absolutely committed to the truth."

"What happened that night?"

Morrison wiped her eyes on her shoulder. "Frank showed me his evidence board, all the connections he'd made. He was maybe twenty-four hours away from proving Catherine was alive. He said he was going to call you, Harry, and ask for your help in locating her."

I thought our conversation was about to end, but Morrison continued.

"I asked him one more time to drop the investigation. When he refused, I... I lost control. There was a letter opener on his desk. I grabbed it and..." She couldn't finish the sentence.

Kate spoke for her. "You stabbed him."

"I arranged the crime scene photos around his body to make it look connected to the Riverside Strangler case. I thought it would misdirect the investigation toward the old murders instead of Catherine's survival."

The vehicle came to a complete stop. Federal agents were approaching to escort Morrison into the building for formal processing.

"One more question," I said. "David died five years ago. Why continue the cover-up after he was gone?"

Morrison looked at me with exhausted eyes. "Because by then, I was guilty of covering up ten murders and killing Frank. Exposing the truth would have meant life in prison and destroying Catherine's life all over again. I convinced myself I was still protecting her, but really I was protecting myself."

As the transport vehicle slowed for a red light, I found myself staring out the window at the passing storefronts, a coffee shop, a gift shop, an undertaker, my mind still processing Morrison's confession. The systematic corruption, the cover-up, Frank's methodical investigation. It all churned through my thoughts. *An undertaker—*

Then it hit me. Frank's backup evidence. The dead-man switches that never triggered. The insurance policies Tim couldn't find.

"Kate," I said suddenly, sitting forward in my seat. "I know where Frank hid his backup files."

She looked at me with tired eyes. "Harry, we've been through this. Tim searched everywhere—"

"Not everywhere," I interrupted, pulling out my phone. "Frank's wife, Margaret. She died eight years ago. Breast cancer. Frank visited her grave every Sunday without fail, and on their anniversary, their first date, her birthday. He'd bring fresh flowers and sit there for hours."

Morrison looked up from her handcuffs, suddenly interested despite her exhaustion.

"The grave marker," I continued, dialing Tim's number. "Margaret always loved gardening. Frank had this large square granite vase installed as part of her headstone. He said it was so she'd always have fresh flowers."

Tim answered on the second ring. "Harry? How did the—"

"Tim, I need you to meet me at Chattanooga National Cemetery as soon as possible. Bring tools; you're going to need them."

"What? Why?"

"Frank's backup evidence. I think it's hidden in Margaret's grave marker."

There was silence on the other end, then Tim's excited voice: "The dead-man switch. Harry, if Frank hid thumb drives there, they'd be weatherproof, secure, and somewhere only someone who really knew him would think to look."

"Exactly. I still have… I'll call you when I'm ready. Stand by your phone." I hung up.

Morrison spoke for the first time since her confession ended. "Frank talked about his wife sometimes during department meetings. He said visiting her grave helped him think through difficult cases."

Kate looked at Morrison, then at me. "If Frank's evidence is there…"

"It changes everything," I finished. "We'll have documentation to corroborate every part of her confession and strengthen the federal cases against Reynolds and the corruption network."

The transport doors opened, and federal agents prepared

to escort Morrison into the building. As she stood up, she turned back to Kate and me.

"Kate, I want you to know that every piece of help I provided during your investigation was genuine. I was trying to solve Frank's murder while preventing you from discovering my role in it. I know that doesn't make sense, but I wanted Frank's killer caught, even if it was me."

Kate's response was cold. "Lisa, you manipulated our investigation from the beginning. Every piece of cooperation was designed to control what we discovered."

"You're right," Morrison agreed. "But my care for Catherine was real. My friendship with Frank was real. My respect for you was real. I just tried to compartmentalize my crimes from my genuine feelings, and it destroyed everything."

As federal agents led Morrison into the building, Kate and I remained in the transport vehicle for a moment, processing what we'd heard.

"Ten years," Kate said finally. "She maintained this deception for ten years while working beside me every day."

"Frank always said the most dangerous criminals are the ones who understand the system from the inside," I replied.

Agent French appeared at the transport door. "We need to process Catherine's statement and coordinate with local prosecutors about Morrison's charges. This is going to be a complex case to prosecute."

As we walked together into the federal building, I couldn't help but remember that old adage, that the truth is stranger than fiction. And that this case had more than proved the point. I still couldn't get my head around how Morrison, a senior police office, had allowed her brother to continue to kill. *I guess the bonds between families really do run deep,* I thought as the doors closed behind us. *And in this case, they turned a loving sister into a severely conflicted killer.*

Morrison's confession was... a revelation; something I'd never forget. We finally knew who killed Frank, and for some unknown reason, the answer wasn't as satisfying as I thought it would be. His dogged pursuit of the truth had exposed not just a killer, but a decade of secrets that had corrupted law enforcement and destroyed countless lives, and it had gotten him killed.

Two hours later, as the afternoon sun cast long shadows between the rows of white headstones, Kate and I met Tim at Chattanooga National Cemetery. Margaret Callahan's grave was in the older section, marked by a simple granite headstone with a large square vase that had weathered eight years of Tennessee seasons.

"This feels wrong somehow," Kate said quietly, looking down at the peaceful grave site.

"Frank would understand," I replied, kneeling beside the vase. "He'd want his evidence to see the light of day."

Tim had brought a trowel, a small pry bar and work gloves. The vase was heavier than it looked, but we managed to tip it carefully onto its side. Underneath, carved into the granite base, was a small rectangular depression—clearly not original to the stonework.

"Frank modified his wife's grave marker," Tim observed. "He knew this was the one place he could hide something that no one else would disturb."

Tim took out a pocket knife and chipped away at the depression. Inside was a waterproof metal box, sealed tight against moisture and time. My hands shook slightly as I opened it to reveal four thumb drives, each labeled in Frank's careful handwriting: "Riverside Evidence," "Financial Corruption," "Sullivan Files," and "Insurance Policy."

Kate picked up the drive labeled "Insurance Policy" and turned it over in her hands. "This contains it all, doesn't it?"

"I'd say so," I said. "If I know Frank it will name names, provide dates, financial records, evidence of case tampering. Frank's complete investigation into the corruption network."

Tim, seated cross-legged on the grass, was already connecting his laptop to portable power. "If these files contain what I think they do, we'll have enough evidence to prosecute not just Morrison and Reynolds, but everyone connected to this network across all three states."

As Tim began accessing the files, the scope of Frank's investigation became clear. Hundreds of pages of documented evidence, recorded conversations, surveillance photos, and financial records that painted a complete picture of systematic corruption spanning over a decade.

"My God," Kate whispered, reading over Tim's shoulder. "Frank documented everything. Every bribe, every altered case file, every witness who was intimidated or paid off."

The "Sullivan Files" drive contained copies of all the communications between Frank and the undercover FBI agent, including Sullivan's final report identifying the key players in the corruption network and his planned arrest timeline.

"This proves Sullivan was murdered," Tim said, highlighting several entries. "His investigation was within days of exposing the entire operation when he died."

The "Financial Corruption" drive revealed the money trail that Reynolds and his associates had been using to launder bribes and pay for services. Shell companies, offshore accounts, and a sophisticated system for moving money that had been operating for years.

But it was the "Riverside Evidence" drive that contained the most shocking revelations. Frank had documented every aspect of Morrison's cover-up, including communications that proved she'd known about the additional victims her brother planned to kill.

"This changes the prosecution's case completely," Kate said. "Morrison had advance knowledge of future murders and did nothing to prevent them."

As we carefully resealed the grave site and prepared to leave, I placed my hand on Margaret Callahan's headstone.

"Your husband was one hell of a detective," I said quietly.

19

AFTERMATH

I arrived home that Friday night to find Amanda on the phone in the kitchen, frantically taking notes while Jade was eating cookies and milk at the table. Amanda was frowning as she listened and scribbled.

"You're sure about this?" she asked, looking up at me and holding up a finger. "When was the arrest made? And you're certain it was Captain Morrison? Lisa Morrison from CPD?"

Oh shit! I thought. Here we go.

I shook my head at her. Jade looked up, her mug of milk in both hands, and smiled.

"Daddy! Mommy got a big phone call about work!"

"I can see that, princess," I said, settling down beside her at the table.

Amanda continued her conversation for at least ten minutes more. "I need confirmation of the charges. Murder?

What murder? Frank Callahan?" Her voice rose with excitement and shock. "I'll need to verify this, but if what you're telling me is accurate... Yes... Yes... Of course I do... I've got to go. I'll get back to you."

She ended the call and immediately dialed another number, her fingers moving rapidly across her phone's screen.

"What's going on?" I asked, though I already knew.

"Someone called the newsroom twenty minutes ago. Apparently, Lisa Morrison has been arrested," Amanda said, holding the phone to her ear. "My source says she was arrested in Knoxville for Frank's murder. Is that true?"

I nodded, unable to hide my exhaustion from the day's events. "We arrested her this afternoon. She confessed during transport."

"Oh... my God, Harry. Lisa Morrison? Really? That's... That's... You were there, weren't you?"

I hesitated then scrunched up my face and said, "Well, yes, but it's... it's... complicated."

Amanda's second call connected. "Jack? It's Amanda. I know it's late, but we need to talk about some breaking news. Lisa Morrison was arrested for Frank Callahan's murder this afternoon, and I need to get on this story immediately."

She listened for a moment, then her expression changed to frustration. "What do you mean Charlie's already working on it? I've been covering this case from the beginning... No, I don't think it's a conflict of interest... Fine, we'll discuss it first thing tomorrow morning."

Amanda ended the call and slammed her phone onto the counter. "That bastard Charlie Grove got the same call and convinced Jack Sharp to let him handle the story because of your involvement."

"Maybe that's for the best," I said. "It's a particularly nasty one, Amanda, and it's been consuming our lives for weeks. I think you should leave it to Charlie."

"Absolutely not," Amanda replied sharply. "I've been building this story for months, developing sources, tracking the corruption angles. Grove just wants to swoop in and take the credit for all my hard work. It's not happening, Harry!"

Jade looked at us, frowning. "Is Mommy mad about work again?"

"Mommy's frustrated, sweetheart," I said. "But don't you worry; we'll figure it out."

After putting Jade to bed, Amanda spent the rest of the evening reviewing her coverage of the case and preparing arguments for tomorrow's meeting with Jack Sharp. I was sure the news of Morrison's arrest was going to go national. It was exactly the kind of story that could define a journalist's career, and losing it to Charlie Grove's political maneuvering was unacceptable to her.

Saturday Morning, August 27, 2024

The following morning, I woke up to find Amanda gone.

I heaved a sigh, rolled out of bed and went downstairs to find her fully dressed and in our home office. It was only five-thirty and she was reviewing her notes and preparing for Channel 7's morning broadcast. She'd confirmed the basic facts of Morrison's arrest through her sources while being careful not to reveal any information I'd also provided during our conversations of the night before, though I was sure she'd find a way to embellish what she already had from her official sources.

I poured myself a cup of coffee, and then joined her. "How

are you handling the conflict-of-interest issue?" I asked, as I sat down beside her desk, cradling the hot coffee in both hands.

"By being completely professional," Amanda replied, adjusting her notes. "I'm reporting only verified facts from official sources, and I'm focusing on the broader implications rather than specific details about your investigation. Ooh, I must go. I have a meeting with Sharp before I go on the air. Maria will be here at seven-thirty. Can you manage by yourself until then? You can let Jade sleep in."

I gave her a wry look, then smiled and said, "Go on, get out of here."

At eight o'clock, I watched Amanda deliver her report live from the Channel 7 newsroom. And I smiled, as I always did, at the stark change from loving mother to hard-nose professional she managed to achieve. It was like she was two totally different people. And, as I always did, I had that flashback to the time, long before we were married, when she did that on-air hatchet job on me, and my smile widened to a grin as I watched her navigate the complex story.

"This is Amanda Starke reporting for Channel 7 News. In a stunning development, Chattanooga Police Captain Lisa Morrison was arrested yesterday in connection with the murder of retired detective Frank Callahan. Morrison, a twenty-four-year veteran of the department, had been assisting in the investigation of Callahan's death before her arrest."

Amanda's delivery was measured and professional, providing context without sensationalizing the story. "The arrest raises serious questions about corruption within the Chattanooga Police Department and follows recent federal operations that resulted in the arrest of Police Commissioner Robert J. Reynolds and other officials across the Southeast."

She continued, "Morrison's arrest is particularly shocking given her role in coordinating departmental cooperation with federal investigators. Sources close to the investigation describe a complex case involving decade-old crimes and systematic evidence tampering, though specific details remain sealed by federal prosecutors."

Amanda concluded her report by noting that Morrison would face federal charges and that the investigation was ongoing. Her coverage was thorough, factual, and appropriately cautious about details that hadn't been officially confirmed.

"Not bad," I said when she returned home an hour later. "You managed to cover the story without compromising the investigation or revealing inside information. Good for you! What happened with Sharp?"

"Sharp made his decision," she said, settling beside me on the couch. "I get to keep the story, but with conditions."

"What kind of conditions?" I asked.

"All my reports have to go through him before broadcast, and I have to work with Charlie to ensure we're covering all the angles." And she didn't look at all happy about that. "Sharp also said if there's even a hint that my personal connections influenced my reporting, Charlie takes over immediately."

"At least you won the assignment battle," I said.

"Barely. Charlie kept pushing the conflict-of-interest angle, but Sharp didn't go for it." She paused, then added, "Working with that smug little bastard is going to be a nightmare."

She was obviously upset, so I took her in my arms and pulled her close. I felt her take a deep breath as she laid her head on my shoulder, and I felt her tension gradually ease. "You get to keep the story," I said. "Your coverage has been too good for Sharp to sideline you now."

"I hope you're right. But Grove has connections with the mayor's office that I don't have. He might be able to pressure Sharp into reassigning the story."

We spent the next hour discussing the complexities of reporting on a story where Amanda had both professional and personal stakes.

LATER THAT MORNING, AT JUST AFTER ELEVEN, KATE CALLED requesting my presence at the federal building for Reynolds' formal debriefing. The former police commissioner had been cooperating with federal prosecutors, but his attitude toward the process was becoming problematic.

I found Kate and Agent French in a conference room reviewing Reynolds' preliminary statements. Through the observation window, I could see Reynolds sitting at a table with his lawyer, looking far more confident than someone facing multiple federal charges should appear.

"Morning, Harry." French said. "You had a good evening, I hope."

"I did," I said. "Kate." I nodded to her.

"Harry," she replied. "Nice job Amanda did this morning. Tell her congratulations from me."

I nodded. "I will."

I looked again through the glass at Reynolds and said, "What's with him?"

"He's being difficult," French said. "He seems to think his

cooperation entitles him to special treatment and a minimal sentence."

Kate looked frustrated. "He's providing useful information about Morrison's use of his network, but his arrogance is making it hard for the prosecutors to work with him."

"What's he saying about Morrison?" I asked.

French opened a file containing transcripts of Reynolds' statements. "He confirms that Morrison approached his network about nine years ago, requesting protection services for someone with a sensitive background. He claims he never knew the client's real identity or the specific reasons for her protection."

"But he was charging substantial fees for the service," Kate added.

"Exactly. Reynolds made significant money from Morrison's desperation and at the same time maintaining plausible deniability about the underlying crimes."

I watched as Reynolds gestured dismissively at something his lawyer was telling him. Even in federal custody facing serious charges, he carried himself with the arrogance of someone who was accustomed to being the most powerful person in the room.

"The problem is," French continued, "that Reynolds' information is crucial to the prosecution of Morrison's use of his criminal network to cover up her brother's crimes. We need his testimony, but his attitude could undermine his credibility with a jury."

Kate stood and moved to the window. "Reynolds thinks he's still in control, still able to negotiate from a position of strength. Someone needs to remind him that he's facing life in prison."

"Let me talk to him," I said. "I always got along with him.

He might be more cooperative if I can make him understand how his arrogance is hurting his case."

French nodded. "Good enough. Give it a try. You can't make it any worse."

Two minutes later, I was seated across from Reynolds in the same interview room where we'd questioned him about Catherine Wells just days earlier. His orange jumpsuit and handcuffs hadn't diminished his commanding presence, but the look in his eyes was strained.

"Starke," Reynolds said with a thin smile. "I assume you're here to discuss my case."

"I'm here because you're acting like an idiot, Bob," I replied. "The federal prosecutors are offering you a chance to reduce your sentence significantly, and you're treating them like they work for you."

Reynolds' smile faded. "I'm providing valuable information about criminal activities that I was never directly involved in. My network provided services to clients, including Detective Morrison, but we never asked about the underlying reasons for those services."

"That's bullshit, and you know it," I said. "You were running a criminal organization that corrupted law enforcement across three states. Morrison used your services to cover up serial murders, and you profited from it."

"Morrison's personal motivations were her own business," he replied. "We provided protection to many clients with various backgrounds and needs."

I leaned forward. "Let me explain something to you, Bob. Right now, the federal prosecutors are deciding whether to recommend twenty-five years or life without parole or something less. Your cooperation could be the difference between you seeing freedom again or dying in prison."

For the first time, Reynolds' arrogance cracked slightly. "My lawyer says the cooperation agreement—"

"Your lawyer is telling you what you want to hear," I interrupted him. "But the prosecutors don't have to recommend anything. If they decide you're more trouble than you're worth, they'll prosecute you to the fullest extent of the law."

Reynolds was quiet for a moment, considering my words. "What do they want from me?"

"Honesty, Bob. Complete honesty about your network's operations, detailed information about Morrison's use of your services, and testimony that helps convict everyone involved in Frank's murder and the cover-up of the serial killings."

"And if I provide all of that?"

"Then you might get out of prison before you're eighty years old. But only if you drop the arrogant act and start treating this process with the seriousness it deserves."

Reynolds studied my face, trying to determine if I was bluffing. "Morrison killed a retired detective to protect her brother's crimes," he muttered. "My network simply provided services that she requested and paid for."

"Louder, Bob."

He glared across the table at me then repeated the statement.

"Which makes you an accessory to murder and conspiracy to cover up serial killings. The federal government doesn't distinguish between the person pulling the trigger and the person providing the gun, you know that."

After thirty minutes of direct conversation, Reynolds seemed at last to understand the gravity of his situation, and that his cooperation would be essential for prosecuting Morrison and dismantling what remained of his criminal network, but only if he approached the process with the appropriate humility.

———————

LATER THAT AFTERNOON, I MET CATHERINE AT THE FEDERAL building where she was preparing for her role as a prosecution witness. The revelation that Morrison was both her protector and Frank's killer had devastated her physically and emotionally, and she was struggling to process the complexity of her situation.

She looked exhausted as she sat in the interview room with Agent French and a victim's advocate. The past twenty-four hours had shattered her perception of the person who'd saved her life and the circumstances that had kept her hidden for nearly a decade.

"How are you holding up?" I asked, settling into a chair beside her.

"I don't know," she replied. "For nine years, I thought Lisa was my hero who sacrificed everything to keep me safe. Now I find out she killed Frank and..." She trailed off and dabbed her eyes with a tissue.

The victim's advocate, a woman in her forties named Sarah Patterson, leaned forward. "Catherine, it's important to remember that both things can be true. Morrison did protect you and save your life, even as she committed serious crimes."

"But how do I testify against someone who gave up everything to help me?" she asked. "Lisa spent hundreds of thousands of dollars, ruined her marriage, and... And... she gave up everything for me."

Agent French opened her briefcase and took out a file containing photographs of the Riverside Strangler victims.

"Catherine, these women deserve justice too. Morrison's protection of you doesn't excuse her from her criminal activities. She knew exactly what she was doing."

Catherine studied the photographs with tears in her eyes. "I know. I just... I wish there was some other way. I want to help her, like she helped me."

"There is," I said. "You have to be honest about both aspects of what she did. You can acknowledge what she did for you, and at the same time, demand justice for Frank and the other victims."

"The prosecution understands the complexity of your relationship with Morrison," French added. "Your testimony will be more powerful because it comes from someone who genuinely cares about her."

Catherine nodded slowly. "I'll testify. Frank does deserve justice, and so do the families of David's victims. They deserve to know the truth. But I want the court to understand that Lisa Morrison isn't just a killer. She saved my life and gave me a new one."

I RETURNED HOME LATE THAT AFTERNOON TO FIND AMANDA reviewing her notes. The Morrison story had become the biggest investigative piece of her career, and the potential conflict with Charlie Grove was adding unnecessary stress to an already complex situation.

"Any word from Sharp?" I asked, settling beside her on the couch.

"Nothing since this morning," she replied. "But knowing him, this thing is not over yet. Charlie's like a dog with a bone. He's not going to give up, especially now we're supposed to be working together. I've been going through every story, every interview, every piece of analysis to prove that my reporting has been objective."

"It has been," I said. "You know it has. You've been tougher on the investigation than most reporters would have been."

"I know, but Grove is arguing that my access to inside information through you gave me an unfair advantage. He's claiming that Channel 7's coverage should be handled by someone without personal connections to the case."

There was nothing I could say to that because, in a way, though I hated to admit it, Grove was right. Amanda did have access throughout the investigation that no one else did. I didn't mention that to her, of course. She would have been devastated, and knowing her, she would have immediately turned the story over to Grove. He was a weasel and didn't deserve it.

"Look," I said carefully, "your reporting has been professional and accurate. Sharp knows that. If he didn't trust your judgment, he wouldn't have let you keep the story, even with conditions."

Amanda set down her notes and looked at me. "But what if Grove's right? What if my connection to you has compromised my objectivity? What if I've been so focused on supporting your investigation that I've missed important angles?"

"Have you?" I asked.

She was quiet for a moment, then shook her head. "No. I've been harder on the department than Grove has. I've asked the tough questions and reported facts that made you and Kate uncomfortable. That's why Sharp kept me on the story."

"Then trust him," I said. "Grove is playing politics. You're doing journalism. Sharp knows the difference."

Amanda nodded slowly, some of the tension easing from her shoulders. "You're right. I just need to keep doing what I've been doing and let my work speak for itself."

"Exactly," I replied. "Besides, Morrison's trial is going to be a media circus. You've got months of coverage ahead of you, and Grove will eventually make a mistake that reminds Sharp why he gave you the assignment in the first place."

She smiled for the first time that evening. "Thanks, Harry. I needed that."

20

BUILDING CASES AND DEPARTMENTAL FALLOUT

SUNDAY, AUGUST 28, 2024

SUNDAY MORNING BROUGHT AN UNEXPECTED CALL FROM CHIEF Johnston requesting an emergency meeting at the police department. The Morrison arrest had triggered a cascade of political and administrative consequences that required immediate attention.

I arrived at headquarters to find Johnston's office filled with people I hadn't expected to see on a weekend: Mayor Patricia Hawkins, City Attorney Michael Foster, and Internal Affairs Captain Robert Hayes. The atmosphere was tense, which is putting it mildly.

"Harry," Johnston said as I entered. "Thank you for coming. We need to discuss the implications of Captain Morrison's arrest. It affects a number of ongoing and past cases, as well as departmental integrity."

Mayor Hawkins, a sharp woman in her fifties who'd built her political career on government accountability, got straight to the point. "Mr. Starke, your investigation has exposed a level of corruption that could affect dozens of criminal cases over the past decade. We need to understand the full scope of the…" she hesitated, then continued, "potential evidence tampering."

Captain Hayes opened a thick file folder. "Internal Affairs is beginning a comprehensive review of every case Morrison touched during her tenure. Preliminary analysis suggests she may have influenced investigations far beyond the Riverside Strangler case."

I heaved a visible sigh. "How many cases are we talking about?" I asked.

"Potentially hundreds," Hayes replied grimly. "Morrison worked in various capacities for over twenty years. If she was systematically altering evidence or misdirecting investigations, the legal ramifications could be staggering."

Hayes pulled out several specific case files to illustrate what he was suggesting. "Take the Rodriguez murder case from 2019," he said. "Morrison was the supervising detective. Key witness testimony was altered in the reports, and crucial evidence from the crime scene went missing from the evidence locker."

"What was the outcome?" Foster asked.

"The charges were dismissed due to insufficient evidence. The defendant walked free, and the victim's family was devastated. Now, having looked into it more deeply, we find the evidence wasn't lost at all; it was deliberately misplaced."

Mayor Hawkins leaned forward. "Are there more cases like this?"

"Dozens, that we know of so far," Hayes continued, opening another file. "The Patterson rape case from 2020. Morrison supervised that investigation and somehow the

DNA evidence was contaminated in the lab. The chain of custody records shows irregularities that weren't caught at the time."

I studied the file Hayes showed me. It was true. Morrison did have access to the DNA evidence and could easily have orchestrated the contamination. "This doesn't prove anything," I said.

"It does when you consider she had administrative authority to modify lab protocols and evidence handling procedures. The contamination appears to be deliberate when you know what to look for."

Hayes opened a third file. "Then there's this one, the Williams drug trafficking case. Morrison was involved in the warrant applications and evidence review. Surveillance photos that would have proven the defendant's guilt mysteriously became too blurry to use in court."

"How many convictions could be overturned?" Foster asked, obviously trying to calculate the legal ramifications.

"We're estimating between forty and sixty cases where Morrison's interference significantly affected the outcomes. And that's just from the preliminary review of her most recent five years."

City Attorney Foster leaned forward. "We're looking at potential grounds for appeals on numerous convictions, civil lawsuits from wrongfully convicted defendants, and massive liability exposure for the city."

Johnston rubbed his temples as he looked at me. "The mayor wants a complete assessment of Morrison's activities and recommendations for preventing similar corruption in the future."

"What about the federal investigation?" I asked. "Agent

French mentioned ongoing operations related to Reynolds' network."

"That's another complication," Mayor Hawkins replied. "Federal investigators are requesting access to our personnel files, case records, and administrative systems. We're cooperating fully, but the political implications..." She trailed off shaking her head.

Hayes pulled out additional documents. "We've identified several cases where Morrison's involvement correlates with unusual outcomes. Dismissed charges, lost evidence, witnesses who recanted testimony. It's a pattern of systematic interference, Harry."

"Do any of them involve other officers?" Johnston asked.

"Not as yet, but we're only at the beginning of the investigation. Morrison was skilled at working within the system without raising obvious red flags."

Foster reviewed his legal notes. "The district attorney's office is preparing for a wave of appeals and potential retrials. Defense attorneys are already filing motions based on Morrison's arrest."

Mayor Hawkins turned to me. "Mr. Starke, given your role in exposing this corruption, we'd like you to consult on the internal investigation. Your insights into Morrison's methods could be a big help."

I considered the request. The extent of Morrison's potential corruption was overwhelming, and untangling a decade of manipulated investigations would require enormous resources.

"I'll help where I can," I said. "But this is going to take months, maybe years to fully resolve."

"We understand," Johnston replied. "But we need to start

immediately. Public confidence in the department depends on demonstrating that we're taking this seriously."

"And this time you're going to pay me?" I said.

Johnston looked at me, nodded, and said, "Of course. We'll pay your usual rates and expenses."

"Very well," I said. "When and where do we start?"

"You start now," Johnston replied. "You'll work closely with Captain Hayes and report to me."

———

LATER THAT AFTERNOON, I MET KATE AT THE FEDERAL BUILDING where she was working with the prosecutors about Morrison's case and the broader implications for law enforcement. She looked exhausted.

"How bad is it?" I asked as we sat down at the conference room table.

"Worse than we initially thought," Kate replied. "Internal Affairs found evidence that Morrison accessed and potentially altered files in dozens of major cases over the past five years alone."

She took out her phone, which had been buzzing constantly. "I've been fielding calls all morning from officers worried about their cases, media wanting statements, and city officials demanding updates. Morale in the department is at an all-time low."

"How are the officers handling the news about Morrison?" I asked.

"Mixed reactions. Some are shocked and angry. Others are worried that their own cases will be scrutinized. A few veteran detectives admitted they'd always thought something was off about some of Morrison's investigations, but never spoke up."

Kate's phone rang again. She glanced at it and declined the call. "That's the fourth reporter in the past hour. The story's going national, and everyone wants to know how a police captain could corrupt investigations for a decade without detection."

"What are you telling them?"

"The truth; that we're conducting a thorough investigation and will hold everyone accountable. But Harry, the damage to public trust is going to take years to repair. People are already calling for federal oversight of the department."

She turned to look at me. "What about you?" she asked. "I understand the mayor asked for your assistance."

I nodded. "I was wondering if you'd heard. Yes, I'll be working with Captain Hayes."

"So, the wheel turns," she said with a half-smile. "Harry Starke, one-time cop turned PI is now heading up Internal Affairs."

I wasn't sure I liked that, but it was essentially true.

I was about to make a smart remark when Agent French appeared in the doorway. "Kate, I hate to interrupt, but we have a problem. Three defense attorneys have already filed motions for immediate release of their clients based on Morrison's arrest. They're claiming prosecutorial misconduct and demanding dismissal of all charges."

Kate rubbed her temples. "Which cases?"

"The Henderson assault case, the Williams drug trafficking case, and the Martinez murder case. All three had Morrison's involvement in evidence processing or witness interviews."

"Can we fight the motions?" Kate asked.

"We're trying, but the attorneys have a strong argument.

Morrison's corruption creates reasonable doubt about the integrity of any case she touched."

Kate sighed, shook her head in frustration, then said, "You'd better come in and show us what you have."

French joined us at the table with updates from the federal investigation. "There's even more bad news, I'm afraid," she said. "Reynolds' cooperation is providing information about other law enforcement officials who used his network's services. Morrison wasn't the only one."

"How many others?" I asked.

"Six! Maybe as many as eight high-ranking officers across the three states."

Kate shook her head. "The damage to public trust is going to be enormous."

"You think?" French asked. "Some of the affected cases involved violent crimes. Murders, sexual assaults, major drug operations. Morrison's interference may have allowed some dangerous criminals to escape justice altogether."

"What about prosecuting the other corrupt officers?" I asked.

French shrugged. "We're trying to build cases, but it's complicated. Reynolds' testimony is helping, but his credibility issues make it... challenging. We need additional evidence to corroborate his claims."

Kate reviewed her notes. "So far, we've identified three specific cases where Morrison's interference clearly affected the outcome. All of the suspects involved have connections to Reynolds or his network."

"Can those cases be reopened?" I asked.

"That's already happening," French replied. "But some of the suspects have died or disappeared, and that makes prosecution difficult even with new evidence."

I sat back in my chair and closed my eyes for a minute. The extent of what Morrison had done was staggering: more than a decade of evidence tampering had created a web of compromised cases that would take years to untangle, and her protection of herbrother, David Morrison, was just one aspect of a much larger criminal enterprise.

I opened my eyes again, leaned forward and put my elbows on the polished tabletop, and I realized I had some serious thinking to do. Now that I was officially part of the internal investigation, I'd have direct access to all the case files Kate and Hayes were reviewing, along with the authority to compel cooperation from officers who might otherwise be reluctant to discuss Morrison or her methods. It was a lot, and it was a situation I'd not been in before. In fact, like many other officers, I'd hated the name, Internal Affairs. Now I was conducting an internal affairs investigation. As Kate had said, 'How the wheel has turned.'

The irony wasn't lost on me. I'd spent years as a patrol officer and detective viewing Internal Affairs as the enemy— the cops who investigated cops, the ones who could end careers with a single report. We called them "the rat squad" behind their backs, and most of us avoided them like the plague. Now here I was, about to become one of them.

But this was different, I told myself. This wasn't about petty policy violations or questionable use-of-force incidents. This was about systematic corruption that had allowed murderers to walk free and denied justice to countless victims' families. Morrison hadn't just bent a few rules, she'd perverted the entire system from the inside.

I thought about Frank, methodically building his case in retirement, following leads that no one else would pursue. He'd died because he'd gotten too close to the truth, but his death had ultimately exposed a level of corruption that might have continued for years if left unchecked.

"Harry?" Kate's voice brought me back to the present. "You okay?"

"I was just thinking about what we're up against," I replied. "Morrison fooled everyone for over a decade. How many other officers like her are out there? How deep does this really go?"

French leaned forward. "That's exactly why we need someone like you heading up this investigation. Someone who understands the system but isn't beholden to it. Someone who can ask the hard questions without worrying about departmental politics."

"The hard questions," I repeated. Like how many innocent people were sitting in prison because of Morrison's manipulations? How many guilty people were walking free? How many families had been denied closure because a corrupt cop decided their loved one's case was inconvenient?

I stood up from the conference table. "I need to talk to Jacque, and I need to talk to my wife."

The internal investigation would consume months, maybe years of my life. It would mean working closely with federal prosecutors, testifying in court cases, and potentially making enemies of colleagues who might see me as a traitor to the badge. More importantly, it would mean less time at home with Amanda and Jade during what was already a stressful period for our family.

And then there was Jacque, my business partner. She needed to know what this commitment would mean for our business. We had existing clients, ongoing cases, and financial obligations that couldn't be ignored. Taking on a massive internal affairs investigation would essentially put me on retainer with the city for the foreseeable future, which might be good for our bottom line but could complicate our other work.

And Amanda: she deserved to know what I was walking into before I made any commitments. She'd already sacrificed enough for my cases, endured death threats, protective custody, and the constant worry that came with being married to someone who made enemies for a living. She'd even killed for me. Now I was about to take on a role that would make me a target for every corrupt cop who thought I might expose their secrets.

"I need to make a couple of calls," I told Kate and French. "Can you give me fifteen minutes?"

Kate nodded. "We'll be here when you're ready."

I stepped out into the hallway and took out my phone. *First Jacque, then Amanda*, I thought.

SUNDAY EVENING, AFTER I'D HAD A LONG TELEPHONE conversation with Jacque, I returned home to find Amanda working on a comprehensive investigative piece about the broader implications of the Morrison case. She'd spent the day interviewing legal experts, victims' advocates, and law enforcement officials about the potential consequences of the police corruption.

"How's the story developing?" I asked, settling beside her in our home office.

"It's bigger than I initially realized," Amanda replied, gesturing to her research materials scattered across the desk. "As I'm sure you know, Morrison's arrest is just the beginning. The federal investigation involves multiple agencies, dozens of potentially affected cases, and widespread corruption."

Amanda showed me her interview notes. "I spoke with Professor Missy Harper from the University of Tennessee Law School. She says this could be one of the largest police corruption scandals in Tennessee history. The legal precedents alone could reshape how internal investigations are conducted."

That could have been my lead, but instead, I said, "What about the victims' families?"

"That's the heartbreaking part," Amanda said, pulling up another set of notes. "I interviewed Maria Rodriguez, whose son's murder case was dismissed in 2019. She never understood why. Now she's learning it was because Morrison deliberately compromised the investigation, and she's devastated."

Amanda continued reading from her interview. "Maria told me, 'I thought the police just weren't competent enough to catch my son's killer. I never imagined they were actually helping him.' She's planning to sue the city."

"How many families are in similar situations?" I asked.

"According to the victims' advocate I spoke with, they don't yet know, but it's a lot. They're organizing a support group for families affected by Morrison's corruption. The psychological impact is enormous. Harry, these people lost faith in the justice system."

She opened her laptop to show me additional research. "I also interviewed Detective Mike Thompson, who worked under Morrison for three years. He said he always thought she was an excellent supervisor, but looking back on it, he now realizes she steered him away from evidence or suggested alternative theories when investigations were getting too close to the truth."

"Is he willing to go on record?"

"He's scared about his career," she replied, "but yes. He

said, 'If good cops don't speak up about bad cops, we're all bad cops.' Thompson's providing examples of cases where Morrison subtly redirected investigations."

Jade appeared in the doorway in her pajamas. "Daddy, are you still working?"

"Yes, but we won't be long," I replied. "Go and watch TV for a few minutes more, okay?"

"Okay," Jade said, then, "Can we have pancakes for breakfast tomorrow?"

"Of course," I replied. "All detectives need pancakes."

Some twenty minutes later, after putting Jade to bed, Amanda and I settled down in the living room, me with a glass of Laphroaig and her with a full glass of red wine. It was time to relax, and I still hadn't told her about my new assignment.

I turned off the TV and we sat together on the couch, enjoying the moment of silence. But it didn't last for long. We couldn't have been there but a few minutes when I could tell Amanda sensed I had something on my mind. She turned to face me.

"There's something else, isn't there?" she asked quietly. "Talk to me, Harry."

I took a deep breath. "The mayor and Chief Johnston want me to head up the internal investigation into Morrison's corruption. It would mean working with Captain Hayes to review potentially hundreds of cases over the next year, maybe longer."

Amanda was quiet for a moment. "That's a big commitment."

"It is. And it means I'd essentially be investigating my former colleagues. Not exactly a way to make or keep friends in the department."

"But it's important work," she said. "And someone has to do it. Those victims' families deserve to know the truth."

"It would change everything about how we operate the business. Long hours, court testimony, probably threats from people who don't want their secrets exposed."

"Threats?" she said. "What kind of threats should we expect? Are we talking about anonymous phone calls or something more serious like what happened with Jason Mills?"

I shrugged, looked her in the eye, and said, "I don't know."

"Okay, so will you have any kind of protection detail, or are you walking into this without backup?"

"That hasn't been discussed, but I would assume something will be arranged."

Amanda reached for my hand. "What do you want to do, Harry?"

I shook my head, heaved a sigh and looked into her beautiful green eyes.

"You already said yes, didn't you?" she asked quietly.

I nodded slowly. "I had to," I said. "I owed it to Frank. He died trying to expose this corruption. If I don't finish what he started, who will?"

"Then we'll figure out how to make it work," she said simply. "We always do."

For once during the past several months, I slept easy that night. But that's not to say I didn't dream, and I woke with images of Lisa Morrison and Catherine Wells still floating around in the back of my mind. But it wasn't until I finally rolled out of bed that I realized it was Monday morning and the start of a new phase in my life.

Monday, August 29, 2024

Monday morning brought additional developments as federal prosecutors announced formal charges against Morrison and expanded their investigation into Reynolds' network. The media coverage was intense, with Amanda working alongside Charlie Grove to provide comprehensive coverage of the rapidly unfolding scandal.

At ten AM, I received a call from Tim. His technical analysis had revealed some of the sophisticated methods Morrison used to alter evidence and monitor investigations.

"Morrison was incredibly careful about covering her tracks," Tim reported. "She used her administrative access to modify records gradually, making changes that wouldn't trigger automatic alerts or raise suspicions."

Tim's technical expertise was proving crucial for understanding the scope of Morrison's digital manipulation, and his findings would now become part of the official internal investigation record I was compiling for Chief Johnston.

"She had three primary methods," he continued. "First, she would modify database entries during normal business hours when system activity was high, making her access look routine. Second, she used her supervisory access to alter automated timestamps on evidence logs. She could make it look like evidence was processed at different times than it actually was, creating false chains of custody. And third, she created false backup versions of critical files, so that when investigators accessed the database, they'd see Morrison's altered version, but the original files were hidden in archived folders she controlled. If anyone questioned discrepancies, she could claim database corruption or system errors."

"What else do you have, Tim?" I asked, knowing full well that there would be more.

"Morrison also monitored database access logs to see who was viewing which files. If someone started investigating a case too thoroughly, she'd know immediately and could take preemptive action."

"Like contacting Reynolds' network to intimidate witnesses?" I said.

"Exactly. She had a sophisticated early warning system that let her stay ahead of any investigation that threatened her. The database logs show she accessed the system remotely hundreds of times."

"I need you to document everything, Tim, and get it to me. Then I need you to stop. I'm not going to be around much for a while and Jacque will need you more than I do."

"But, Harry—"

"No, Tim," I said, cutting him off. "No arguments, please."

"But how will you—"

Again, I cut him off. "How will I get along without you? I won't, but I'll have full access to Jack North—"

"Oh yeah," Tim snapped, obviously upset. "And how d'you think that's going to work for you?"

At that, I couldn't help but smile to myself.

"Goodbye for now, Tim. Take care of Jacque, TJ and Heather for me. Talk to you soon."

And with that, I hung up.

21

MORRISON'S TRIAL

Monday, November 11, 2024

THE HAMILTON COUNTY CRIMINAL JUSTICE COMPLEX BUZZED with media activity as Morrison's trial began on a crisp November morning. I arrived early, carrying the file folders that had become my constant companions over the past months of intensive investigation with Captain Hayes. Our probe had uncovered even more evidence of Morrison's systematic evidence tampering, creating additional ammunition for the federal prosecutors.

Amanda stood among the crowd of reporters outside the courthouse with her cameraman while Charlie Grove positioned himself for the best angle. Despite their professional rivalry, they'd worked pretty well together to cover the pretrial developments, though I could see the tension in Amanda's posture as Grove attempted to claim the prime interview spots.

"Harry," Agent French said as I climbed the courthouse steps. "How's it going?"

"Hayes and I have identified seventy-three cases where Morrison's interference affected outcomes," I replied. "Some are worse than others, but the pattern is clear."

"Any new revelations that could affect the trial?" she asked as we entered the small conference room that had been set aside for us.

"Some," I replied, as I took a file folder marked Rodriguez R 6/2020. "We found proof that Morrison deliberately destroyed DNA evidence in this one." I set it down on the table in front of her.

She glanced quickly through it, then closed the file, handed it back to me, and said, "We should get on with it. We don't want to keep the judge waiting."

Inside the courthouse, the atmosphere was electric with anticipation. Morrison sat at the defense table with her attorneys, looking smaller somehow in her civilian clothes. The orange jumpsuit had been replaced with a conservative navy suit, but I could see, even from a distance, her expression was the one of resignation I'd seen during her confession. She was sitting back in her seat, unmoving, her arms folded, her eyes fixed on the bench.

It wasn't five minutes later that Judge Patricia Williams appeared, seemingly out of nowhere, and called the court to order. After a brief statement and an admonishment to the court that she would, as she put, 'not stand for any shenanigans,' jury selection began. The process took the rest of the morning and then some with the defense attorneys challenging only three potential jurors who expressed strong opinions about police. But it went way more quickly than I expected. The process had been completed a little before one PM and the court broke for a late lunch.

During the lunch recess, I met with Captain Hayes in the courthouse cafeteria to review our latest findings.

"Detective Mike Thompson finally agreed to testify," Hayes said, tiredly. "He's agreed to provide specific examples of how Morrison redirected his investigations."

"What about Detective Sarah Martinez?" I asked.

He shook his head. "Eh… She's more reluctant," he said. "Martinez worked closely with Morrison for three years and she feels betrayed. It's not that she's overly fond of Morrision, it's more that she's worried she'll look incompetent for not realizing what was going on."

"I can't say I blame her," I said. "She should have caught on. I mean, over three years…" I trailed off. There was no need to say more. Hayes knew what I was talking about.

I reviewed Thompson's statement as I ate my sandwich, listening while Hayes continued updating me on the officer interviews.

"Thompson says Morrison was subtle but persistent. She'd suggest alternative theories, question evidence that pointed toward certain suspects, or reassign cases when investigations got too close to dangerous territory."

"That matches what we're seeing in the case files," I said. "Morrison obviously knew what she was doing."

The court reconvened at two-thirty, and James Mitchell for the prosecution delivered his opening statement to a packed courtroom. Mitchell was a veteran prosecutor in his mid-fifties, a friend of my father's, and known for his methodical approach to complex cases.

"Ladies and gentlemen of the jury," he began, "this case is about the ultimate betrayal of public trust. Police Captain Lisa

Morrison swore an oath to protect and serve the people of Chattanooga. Instead, she used her position to cover up serial murders, corrupt criminal investigations, and ultimately kill a retired detective who threatened to expose her crimes."

Mitchell outlined the prosecution's case systematically: Morrison's brother David was the Riverside Strangler, Morrison covered up his crimes for years, she used criminal networks to hide Catherine Wells, and she murdered Frank when his investigation threatened her.

"You will hear testimony from Catherine Wells, the sole survivor of the Riverside Strangler attacks. Ms. Wells will tell you how Captain Morrison saved her life by faking her death and providing protection. But you will also hear how that same protection came at the cost of six more victims for a total of ten. Six more victims who died because Morrison allowed the killer to remain free."

Morrison's defense attorney, Sarah Hendricks, presented a different narrative during her opening statement. Hendricks was a skilled criminal defense lawyer who specialized in law enforcement cases.

"Captain Morrison faced an impossible choice," Hendricks argued. "Yes! When she discovered her brother was a killer, she could have arrested him. She could also have let Catherine Wells die. Or she could try to find another way to stop the killing while protecting the life of an innocent victim. She chose to save a life."

Hendricks acknowledged Morrison's crimes while arguing for understanding of her motivations. "Lisa Morrison is not a monster. She's a dedicated police officer who made terrible decisions while trying to protect someone who couldn't protect herself. Yes, she killed Frank Callahan, and that was wrong. Of course it was. But she did it to prevent the exposure of a woman who had already suffered unimaginable trauma."

It was a weak argument, but it was all she had. The extent of Lisa Morrison's criminal activity was undeniable.

The first witness was Catherine Wells, and the courtroom fell silent as she took the stand. Catherine looked composed but fragile as Mitchell guided her through her testimony.

"Ms. Wells, can you tell the jury what happened on the night of February 17th, 2016?"

Catherine's voice was steady as she described her attack, her survival, and her decade of hiding. "David Morrison tried to kill me, but I fought back and escaped. When Detective Morrison found out I could identify her brother, she arranged for my death to be faked so I could receive medical treatment and stay hidden. She gave me a new identity and a new life."

"Did you know at the time that David Morrison was Detective Morrison's brother?"

"No. I only learned that when she was arrested. For nine years, I thought my protector was just a dedicated police officer who wanted to keep me safe."

Mitchell showed Catherine photographs of the other Riverside Strangler victims. "Ms. Wells, you were David Morrison's fourth victim. How do you feel knowing that six other women died while David Morrison remained free?"

Catherine wiped tears from her eyes. "I'm grateful to be alive, but I'm devastated that those young women lost their lives. David was never arrested. But if I'd known..." She trailed off, dabbing her eyes with a tissue.

By the time Mitchell finished with her it was almost five o'clock and Judge Williams called it a day. Court would resume at nine the following morning.

The following morning, defense attorney Hendricks

cross-examined Catherine gently, emphasizing Morrison's protection and sacrifice.

"Ms. Wells, Captain Morrison spent hundreds of thousands of dollars to keep you safe, didn't she?"

"Yes. She gave up her marriage, her savings, everything to protect me."

"And without her protection, you believe you would have been killed?"

"Absolutely. David was still alive for five more years after my attack. He would have found me and finished what he started."

"No more questions," Hendricks said, and sat down.

By then it was almost noon. Judge Williams dismissed the witness and broke for lunch.

The afternoon brought testimony from Reynolds, who strutted to the witness stand with his characteristic arrogance despite his orange jumpsuit. His cooperation had been valuable, but his attitude remained problematic.

Mitchell first spent a few moments establishing Reynolds' credentials both as a police commissioner and the head of the criminal network. Then:

"Mr. Reynolds, did Captain Morrison approach your organization for assistance?"

"She did. About nine years ago, she requested our services for what she claimed was someone with a sensitive background. We provided those services professionally and discreetly."

"How much did Captain Morrison pay for these services?"

"Over nine years, approximately four hundred thousand dollars. She was one of our best customers."

"Did you know the person being protected was supposedly dead?"

Reynolds shrugged. "We didn't ask questions about our clients' backgrounds. Morrison needed our services, and we provided them."

Defense attorney Hendricks attacked Reynolds' credibility during cross-examination.

"Mr. Reynolds, you're currently facing life in prison for running a criminal organization, aren't you?"

"I'm cooperating with federal authorities," he replied carefully.

"And in exchange for that cooperation, you're hoping for a reduced sentence?"

"My cooperation is based on my commitment to justice," Reynolds replied smugly.

"Justice? You profited from hiding someone who was supposed to be dead while helping cover up serial murders."

"I provided services that Morrison requested. I didn't know about her personal motivations, or that her brother was a serial killer. Our clients demanded confidentiality, and that's what they got."

The next two days brought more testimony from federal agents and technical experts who outlined the scope of Reynolds' criminal network. By the time Judge Williams recessed court for the day late Thursday afternoon, the prosecution had painted a clear picture of systematic corruption that extended far beyond Morrison's individual crimes.

That evening, I returned home exhausted from the day's proceedings and my ongoing investigation with Hayes. Amanda was reviewing her trial coverage while Jade worked on homework at the kitchen table.

"How did Morrison look during Catherine's testimony?" Amanda asked.

"She was quiet, composed. Stoic, I think is the word that

would describe her best. She didn't look around, conversing only with her attorneys," I replied. "I think she genuinely cares about Catherine. You were in court. What did you think?"

"I watched her during Catherine's testimony," Amanda said as she set down her pen and turned to face me. "When Catherine described the attack on her, Morrison closed her eyes. Not like someone who was bored or disconnected, but like she was reliving it herself. And when Catherine talked about being grateful for Lisa's protection, Morrison actually wiped away a tear."

She paused, considering her words carefully. "As a journalist, I'm supposed to stay objective. I know that, but there's something tragic about watching someone who genuinely saved a life get sentenced for murder. The complexity of it... I keep thinking about how she could be both Catherine's savior and Frank's killer."

Amanda picked up her notes again. "What struck me most was when Catherine looked directly at Morrison during her testimony. Morrison nodded at her, just slightly, like she was giving her permission to tell the truth. Even about the murders she'd covered up. That's not the behavior of someone who's purely evil. Is it?"

I didn't answer that. Instead, I took a sip of whiskey and waited.

She shook her head. "I've covered plenty of criminal trials, Harry, but I've never seen anything quite like this one. Usually, it's clear who the victim is and who the perpetrator is. This case... Morrison destroyed countless lives, but she also saved Catherine's life at enormous personal cost. How do you reconcile that?"

"I can't," I replied.

"Why not? You have a masters in criminal psychology."

I smiled ruefully. "Criminal psychology helps explain behavior, but it doesn't resolve moral paradoxes. Some questions don't have clean answers, Amanda. Morrison's one of those cases where the contradictions are so fundamental that trying to reconcile them misses the point entirely."

"Nice save, Harry," she said with a wry smile. "What about Reynolds?"

"Arrogant as always. His testimony helps establish Morrison's use of criminal networks, but his attitude could backfire with the jury."

Amanda and I spent the rest of the evening discussing the trial's emotional complexity. Morrison's genuine love for Catherine complicated the prosecution's narrative while not excusing her crimes. She was going to have a seriously compelling story for the morning broadcast.

On Friday, the court heard testimony from Detective Mike Thompson, who provided evidence about Morrison's systematic manipulation of investigations.

"Detective Thompson," Mitchell began, "how long did you work under Captain Morrison's supervision?"

"Three years, from 2020 to 2023."

"Did you notice anything unusual about her supervisory style?"

Thompson looked uncomfortable but answered honestly. "Morrison was a good boss, very hands-on. She'd review all our cases personally and often suggest alternative approaches to investigations."

"Can you give the jury a specific example?"

"The Williams drug case in 2021. I had surveillance photos that clearly showed the defendant making drug transactions. Morrison reviewed the photos and said they were too blurry to be useful evidence. She had the lab enhance them, but they came back even more blurry."

"And what happened to the Williams drug case?"

"The charges were dropped due to insufficient evidence. I thought it was just bad luck with the photo quality. Now I realize Morrison must have arranged for the photos to be deliberately degraded."

"Objection," Hendricks barked. "Calls for speculation, Your Honor."

"Sustained," the judge responded. "The jury will disregard Detective Thompson's statement."

Mitchell quickly moved to redirect Thompson's testimony toward factual observations rather than speculation, but the damage was done. Thompson's credibility had been brought into question.

Judge Williams called for the lunch recess at twelve-thirty, and Hayes and I used the break to interview Detective Sarah Martinez, who had finally agreed to provide a statement about Morrison's activities.

"Sarah, we need you to be completely honest about your experiences working with Morrison," Hayes said as we settled in a courthouse conference room.

Martinez looked nervous but determined. She was a woman in her early thirties with dark hair pulled back in a professional bun, and her hands shook slightly as she opened a notebook filled with her own observations.

"I've been thinking about this for weeks," she began. "There were things Morrison did that seemed strange at the time, but I trusted her judgment. She was my mentor, you know? When I made detective, she took me under her wing."

"Tell us about your working relationship," I said.

"Morrison was... protective. Almost motherly. She'd

review every case I worked, offer guidance, suggest different approaches. At first, I thought it was because I was new. But even after two years, she was still micromanaging my investigations."

Hayes leaned forward. "Can you give us specific examples?"

Martinez consulted her notes. "The Patterson rape case in 2020 was the first one that really bothered me. We had DNA evidence that strongly implicated Marcus Patterson. Solid case, easy conviction. But Morrison questioned the chain of custody procedures."

"What did she do?" I asked.

"She insisted we retest the evidence. Said she wanted to be absolutely certain before we destroyed someone's life. I thought she was being thorough, but when the retesting came back contaminated…" Martinez shook her head. "Morrison seemed almost relieved. She said it proved we needed to be more careful with evidence handling."

I made notes as Martinez continued. "Looking back, there were at least six cases where Morrison found procedural problems that forced us to either drop charges or accept plea bargains for lesser crimes. She always had reasonable explanations."

"What kind of explanations?" Hayes asked.

"Protecting the department's reputation. Avoiding civil liability. Making sure we followed proper protocols. She'd say things like, 'It's better to let one guilty person go free than to convict an innocent one on flawed evidence.'"

Hayes frowned. "Did you ever question her decisions?"

"Once. The Henderson assault case in 2021. We had three witnesses who positively identified the defendant, but Morrison kept finding reasons to delay filing charges. When I pushed back, she got... not angry, exactly. Disappointed. She said I was being impulsive, that good detectives think through all the consequences before acting."

Martinez paused, gathering her thoughts. "She had this way of making you feel like questioning her meant you were questioning your own competence. She'd been on the force for twenty years, had commendations, solved dozens of major cases. Who was I to doubt her judgment?"

"Tell us about her supervisory style," I said.

"She was hands-on. She would review witness statements before I filed them, sometimes suggesting minor changes in wording. 'For clarity,' she'd say. She'd examine physical evidence personally, even when it wasn't necessary. And she always insisted on being present during interviews with key witnesses."

"Did that seem unusual?"

"At the time, I thought she was teaching me proper procedure. But now..." Martinez looked uncomfortable. "Now I realize she was controlling the narrative. Making sure witnesses said exactly what she needed them to say, nothing more."

Hayes consulted his notes. "What about her relationship with other departments? The lab, the DA's office?"

"Morrison had connections everywhere. If we needed expedited lab results, she knew who to call. If we needed cooperation from federal agencies, she had contacts. I thought she was well-respected. Turns out she was probably calling in favors."

"You can't say that in court," I said. "It's speculation."

"Did you ever suspect she was corrupt?" Hayes asked.

Martinez hesitated. "There were moments..... Late one night, I came back to the office for a file I'd forgotten.

Morrison was there, working on a computer that wasn't hers. When she saw me, she seemed startled. Said she was helping another detective with database searches. But the look on her face..."

"Go on," Hayes said.

"She looked guilty. Like a kid caught with her hand in the cookie jar. She was perfectly friendly, made some joke about working too late, but I could tell she was rattled."

I leaned back in my chair. "Sarah, do you honestly think Captain Morrison deliberately sabotaged investigations?"

Martinez met my eyes directly. "Yes. I hate to admit it because it makes me look like a fool, but yes. She used her position and my trust in her to ensure certain cases never resulted in convictions, and I was too naive to see it."

"How does that make you feel?" I asked.

"Angry. Betrayed. But mostly guilty." Martinez's voice cracked slightly. "I should have spoken up years ago."

Hayes closed his notebook. "Sarah, your testimony could be crucial for understanding how Morrison operated. Are you prepared to testify in court?"

Martinez nodded firmly. "Yes. I owe it to the victims. And to Frank Callahan."

After Martinez presented her testimony without interruption from the defense, Mitchell sat down and looked expectantly at Hendricks.

"No questions, Your Honor," Hendricks said without looking up from her notes.

"The prosecution rests, Your Honor," Mitchell said, rising to his feet then sitting down again.

"That being so," Judge Williams said, "we'll recess until Monday morning."

The Monday morning session began and ended with

Morrison's testimony, which had been the most anticipated moment of the trial. Hendricks called her to the stand and she was sworn in. She sat down, took a deep breath and straightened her back. But it was obvious to me that she was in a fragile emotional state as Hendricks began her questioning.

"Captain Morrison, did you kill Frank Callahan?"

"Yes, I did."

Hendricks nodded. "Let's start at the beginning. When did you first suspect your brother David was involved in your sister Jennifer's murder?"

Morrison's hands trembled slightly as she gripped the witness stand rail. "Almost immediately. David's reaction at the crime scene felt... wrong. Too controlled, too rehearsed. But I told myself I was being paranoid. He was my brother."

"What changed your mind?"

"Three days later, when Lisa Haldon was found. David had been with me that night, having dinner. He seemed almost relieved when I told him about the second murder, like it proved his innocence. That's when I knew."

Hendricks moved closer to the witness stand. "What did you do with that knowledge?"

"I followed him." Morrison's voice grew quieter. "For weeks, I watched my own brother stalk potential victims. I saw him choose them, study their routines. I kept telling myself I could stop him without destroying our family."

"But you didn't stop him."

Morrison closed her eyes. "No. When I confronted David after he attacked Catherine Wells, he broke down completely. He was sobbing, begging me not to turn him in. He said if I arrested him, Catherine would die anyway from her injuries, and our parents would lose two of their children. He promised he'd stop killing if I helped him cover up what he'd done."

"Did you believe him?"

"I wanted to." Morrison wiped her eyes. "For about two weeks, I thought maybe it was over. Then Sarah Mitchell was found strangled by the river. David told me he had to continue killing to make Jennifer's death look like the work of a serial killer, or the police would figure out the family connection."

Hendricks paused, to let her words settle over the courtroom. "How many more times did your brother promise to stop?"

"After every murder." Morrison's composure finally cracked. "Every single time, he swore it would be the last one. And every time, I believed him because I couldn't face the alternative. I was trapped in this delusion that I could control him, that I could save Catherine while somehow limiting the damage he caused."

"When did you realize you couldn't control him?"

"When he told me about his plans for victim number seven. Rebecca Martinez. He described her in such detail: where she worked, when she jogged, how he was going to approach her. That's when I understood he wasn't going to stop. He was going to keep killing until someone caught him or killed him."

"What did you do?"

"I tried to turn him in." Morrison looked directly at the jury. "I drove to the police station three different times, sat in the parking lot with a written confession in my hand. But every time, I thought about Catherine dying in that private medical facility, about our parents. I was a coward."

Hendricks' voice softened slightly. "Captain Morrison, why did you kill Frank Callahan?"

Morrison's voice trembled as she answered. "Frank was methodical, relentless. He'd figured out Catherine was alive, and he was maybe twenty-four hours away from proving it. When he showed me his evidence board that night, I saw my entire house of cards collapsing. Not just Catherine's safety, but the exposure of everything: David's crimes, my cover-up, the corruption I'd enabled."

"So you went to his house intending to kill him?"

"No. I went to beg him to stop. I tried everything to persuade him, but he wouldn't listen. Frank was Frank." Morrison broke down completely. "When he refused to back down, I snapped. I grabbed the letter opener from his desk and... I stabbed him with it."

"Do you regret protecting Catherine Wells?"

"No. She deserved to live. But I regret every decision I made after saving her. I should have arrested David immediately and trusted the system to protect Catherine properly. Instead, I became part of the very corruption I'd sworn to fight."

"Captain Morrison, in those moments when you were deciding whether to arrest your brother, what was going through your mind?"

"Terror. Complete terror. I was afraid Catherine would die, afraid David would kill himself, afraid of destroying my parents. I convinced myself I could find a middle path that would save everyone. It was naive and selfish and wrong."

"But you did save Catherine's life."

"At the cost of six other women's lives." Morrison looked at the photographs of the victims displayed on the prosecution table. "I tell myself I was trying to minimize harm, but the truth is I prioritized one life over others because I felt personally responsible for Catherine. That's not justice – that's playing God."

Defense attorney Hendricks used Morrison's testimony to humanize her while acknowledging her crimes.

Closing arguments began on Wednesday afternoon. Prosecutor Mitchell emphasized Morrison's systematic corruption and Frank's murder while acknowledging the complexity of her motivations.

"Captain Morrison's love for Catherine Wells doesn't excuse the other nine murders her brother committed, or Frank Callahan's death. Justice demands accountability, even when the defendant's motivations are understandable."

Defense attorney Hendricks argued for mercy while accepting Morrison's guilt.

"Lisa Morrison saved Catherine Wells' life and spent everything she had to protect an innocent victim. Yes, she made terrible choices, but they came from love and desperation, not evil intent."

The jury deliberated for only eight hours before returning a verdict: guilty on all counts, including the first-degree murder of Frank Callahan, accessory before and after the fact for covering up the nine serial murders.

Judge Williams scheduled sentencing for Friday, December 13, not a good omen. Morrison's conviction marked the end of a decade-long era of deception and corruption, but not mine and Hayes' investigation. That would continue, but Morrison's trial had established a somewhat fragile foundation for rebuilding public trust.

Catherine Wells had finally emerged from hiding to tell

her story, Morrison would face the consequences of her crimes, and Frank's legacy would be the truth he died trying to expose.

22

JUSTICE AND REDEMPTION

FRIDAY, DECEMBER 13, 2024

THE SENTENCING HEARING FOR LISA MORRISON TOOK PLACE ON a gray December morning that seemed to match the somber mood in the Hamilton County Criminal Justice Complex. I arrived early, carrying the final report from Captain Hayes and my internal investigation. It was a document that would influence Morrison's fate and reshape how the Chattanooga Police Department conducted business.

Amanda sat in the press section with Charlie Grove, their professional rivalry temporarily set aside as they prepared to cover the conclusion of the biggest story of their careers. The past weeks had seen their collaboration evolve from mutual antagonism to grudging respect, though I could still see the competitive tension in Amanda's posture.

Judge Williams entered the courtroom with her usual commanding presence, and the packed gallery fell silent.

Morrison sat at the defense table looking smaller than I'd ever seen her.

"Ms. Morrison," Judge Williams began, "before I impose sentence, do you wish to make a statement to the court?"

Morrison stood slowly, her voice barely above a whisper as she addressed the court. "Your Honor, I want to apologize to Frank Callahan's family, to the families of my brother's victims, and to the people of Chattanooga who trusted me to uphold the law."

She paused for a second, looked down, then up again and continued, "I know my actions were inexcusable. I covered up serial murders, corrupted dozens of investigations, and killed a good man who was only trying to do his job. I tell myself I was protecting an innocent victim, but the truth is I was protecting myself and my family's reputation."

Morrison turned to face Catherine Wells, who sat in the front row with tears streaming down her face. "Catherine, I want you to know that protecting you was the only good thing I did during this entire nightmare. You deserved to live, and I'm grateful I could give you that chance. That's all, Your Honor." And with that, she sat down again and her attorney took her hand and squeezed it.

Judge Williams consulted her notes before addressing the courtroom. "The court has reviewed pre-sentence report, victim impact statements, and the comprehensive internal investigation conducted by Captain Hayes and Mr. Starke. The scope of corruption in this case is unprecedented in Tennessee law enforcement history."

She continued, "Ms. Morrison, your systematic evidence tampering affected seventy-three criminal cases over eight years. Nine families were denied justice for their murdered daughters. Frank Callahan died because he refused to abandon his pursuit of truth. These crimes strike at the foundation of our justice system."

Judge Williams paused, "However, the court also recognizes the complexity of your motivations. Your protection of Catherine Wells represents both the best and worst aspects of human nature: love and sacrifice corrupted by fear and self-preservation."

The courtroom was absolutely silent as Judge Williams pronounced sentence. "Lisa Morrison, you are hereby sentenced to life in prison without the possibility of parole for the first-degree murder of Frank Callahan. Additionally, you will serve concurrent sentences of twenty-five years for each count of..." and she continued to list each of the twenty-two counts on the charge sheet. By the time she'd finished, it was clear that Lisa Morrison would never again see the light of day outside the prison walls.

Morrison remained standing, showing no emotion as the sentence was read. Catherine Wells sobbed quietly while Morrison's parents, who had attended every day of the trial, held each other in the back row.

"Furthermore," Judge Williams continued, "the court recommends that the Tennessee Bureau of Investigation conduct a comprehensive review of all cases touched by your corruption, and that the federal government provide oversight of police reform measures in Chattanooga."

As court officers led Morrison away in handcuffs, she stopped at the gate separating the gallery from the defendant's table. She looked back at Catherine Wells and mouthed the words "stay safe" before disappearing through the secure door.

AFTER THE SENTENCING, I MET WITH CHIEF JOHNSTON, Captain Hayes, and Mayor Hawkins in the courthouse conference room to discuss the implementation of the reform measures we'd developed during our investigation.

"The final count is eighty-seven cases affected by Morrison's tampering," Hayes reported. "Forty-three convictions will likely be overturned, twelve dismissed cases will be reopened, and thirty-two cases require complete reinvestigation."

Mayor Hawkins rubbed her temples as she processed the numbers. "What's the timeline for addressing all of these cases?"

"Eighteen months minimum," I replied. "We'll need additional prosecutors, investigators, and victim advocates. The city should also prepare for substantial civil liability as wrongfully convicted defendants file lawsuits."

Chief Johnston leaned back in his chair. "What about preventing future corruption?"

Hayes opened his reform recommendations. "Mandatory rotation of supervisory assignments, independent oversight of evidence handling, random audits of case files, and psychological evaluation of officers with access to sensitive investigations."

"We're also recommending body cameras for all detective work, not just patrol," I added. "Morrison was able to manipulate investigations because too much happened behind closed doors."

Mayor Hawkins reviewed our budget projections. "This is going to cost millions, but we don't have a choice. Public trust in law enforcement is at an all-time low."

"The federal government will provide some funding," Johnston said. "Agent French confirmed that Chattanooga qualifies for justice reform grants based on the scope of corruption we've exposed."

Hayes closed his files. "The important thing is that we've identified systemic weaknesses and developed comprehensive solutions. Morrison's crimes were possible because our internal controls were insufficient."

Chief Johnston gathered the scattered files from the conference table. "This investigation has been costly in every sense," he said. "Financially, politically, and personally. But it was necessary. Morrison's corruption could have continued for years if Frank hadn't been willing to go the distance."

Mayor Hawkins nodded grimly. "The federal oversight requirements alone will cost the city millions, but the alternative was worse. We can't allow systematic corruption to undermine public safety."

"What's our timeline for implementing the new procedures?" Hayes asked.

"Six months for the critical changes," Johnston replied. "New evidence handling protocols, mandatory rotation of supervisory assignments, independent oversight systems."

I stood to leave.

"This case has changed all of us," the mayor said quietly. "None of us will look at internal investigations the same way again."

Hayes packed his briefcase. "The new systems won't eliminate corruption entirely, but they'll make it much harder to sustain. We have a long road ahead, Harry."

He was right about that!

LATER THAT AFTERNOON, I MET CATHERINE WELLS AT Coolidge Park, near the area where her nightmare had begun almost nine years earlier. She'd requested the meeting to discuss her plans for moving forward now that Morrison's trial was over.

Catherine looked healthier than when I'd first found her in Knoxville, but I could see the emotional toll of the past months in her careful movements and watchful eyes.

"I wanted to thank you," she said as we walked along Riverfront Parkway. "Frank deserved justice, and you made sure he got it."

"Thanks," I said. "Frank deserved more."

She paused at a bench overlooking the water. "I keep thinking about the other victims' families. They lived for years thinking their daughters' killer had escaped justice, never knowing he was already dead. Did you know I testified at three of the victim impact hearings. Meeting those families was the hardest thing I've ever done. They were gracious and understanding, but I could see the pain in their eyes."

She sat down on the bench and I sat beside her. "So, Catherine, what are your plans now?"

"I'm staying in Knoxville for the time being. The university has offered me a position in their art therapy program, working with trauma survivors. I think maybe I can help people who've experienced what I went through."

"No one has been through what you've been through," I said.

She turned her head to look at me and smiled. Then she pulled out a small canvas from her bag: it was a painting of the Tennessee River at sunset, peaceful and beautiful. "I painted this last week. For years, I could only create dark images, scenes of fear and violence. But now I'm starting to see beauty again."

"That's good. That's healing," I said.

"I want you to have it," she said, looking me in the eye. "I've also established a foundation to provide support for families of crime victims. Lisa gifted me a substantial amount of money. It was everything she had left after paying for my protection. I'm using it to help other people navigate the justice system."

The irony wasn't lost on me. Morrison's final act was to ensure that Catherine could continue helping others. I thanked her for the painting and told her I'd hang it in my office.

"Have you visited her?" I asked.

Catherine shook her head. "I've written her letters, but I'm not ready to see her yet. Maybe someday... soon. Despite everything, she saved my life, and that means something."

As evening approached, we walked back toward downtown Chattanooga. The city lights reflected off the river, creating the same peaceful scene that had drawn Jennifer Morrison out for her final jog so many years ago.

"Catherine, do you think you'll ever feel completely safe?" And having spoken it, I immediately realized what a stupid question it was. But she answered it with a smile. But first, she considered it carefully.

"I don't know if anyone could feel completely safe after what I've experienced. But I'm not hiding anymore. I'm using my real name, living openly, building relationships. That's a kind of safety I never thought I'd have again."

A little later, after I'd seen her safely to her car, we said goodbye and I watched her drive away. *What a sweet kid*, I thought. *I hope she does well and that one day I'll see her again.*

And then I thought about Lisa Morrison. *I need to see her, too, but not yet. It's too soon... Way too soon.*

I ARRIVED HOME THAT NIGHT TO FIND AMANDA IN THE KITCHEN with Jade, helping her with a school project about community heroes. They'd spread poster board and art supplies across the table, creating a colorful tribute to police officers, firefighters, and teachers.

"Daddy!" Jade announced. "We're making a poster about people who help other people!"

"That's wonderful," I said. "What kind of helpers are you including?"

"Police officers who catch bad people, firefighters who save houses, and teachers who help kids learn things."

Amanda smiled at me over Jade's head. "We've been talking about how most people who work in law enforcement are good people trying to help their communities."

"That's right," I said, settling at the table. "Sometimes bad people get into good jobs, but that doesn't mean all the good people are bad."

Jade looked up from her coloring. "Mommy, is Kate a good police officer?"

"She is," Amanda replied. "Kate is one of the best."

Jade looked up at me and said, "And you help her catch the really bad people, don't you, Daddy?"

I laughed. "Something like that."

Amanda and I exchanged glances. We'd been careful to shield Jade from the worst details of the Morrison case, but children pick up more than parents realize.

After putting Jade to bed, Amanda and I went out onto the

patio and sat on the retaining wall overlooking the city. It was a cool, clear December evening, and the city twenty-five hundred feet below was a blaze of twinkling lights, the great river meandering northward toward the cooling towers of the Sequoya nuclear plant on the far horizon. I never ceased to wonder at it all.

"How do you feel now that it's finally over?" Amanda asked.

"Relieved, but not satisfied," I replied. "Morrison's going to prison, Catherine's safe, and we've implemented reforms to prevent future corruption. But Frank is still dead, and nine other families lived for years without justice."

"You did everything you could, Harry. Frank would be proud of you."

"You know, I can't help but think about Morrison. She always seems to be on my mind. What a complex, twisted mind she has. She genuinely loved Catherine and sacrificed everything to protect her. But she also allowed nine women to die and then killed Frank to cover it up. How do you reconcile those contradictions?"

Amanda leaned against me. "I think some people are capable of both tremendous love and terrible evil, sometimes simultaneously. Morrison's protection of Catherine was real, but so were her crimes."

"The families of David Morrison's victims will never get their daughters back," I said. "Frank's family will never get him back. Reform measures and prison sentences won't undo that damage."

"No, but they will prevent future damage," she said.

We sat quietly for a while, watching the city lights twinkle in the valley below.

"Any word on your assignment?" Amanda asked.

"Chief Johnston wants me to stay on. There are still cases to review and officers to interview. Hayes thinks we'll be working on this for at least another year."

"And after that?" she asked.

I shrugged. "Back to my agency, I suppose. Though after exposing police corruption at this level, I'm not sure how comfortable local law enforcement will be working with me."

Amanda laughed. "Harry Starke, the private investigator who's too effective for his own good."

"Something like that," I replied with a smile.

SATURDAY MORNING BROUGHT A CALL FROM KATE REQUESTING my presence at the police department for a special ceremony. When I arrived, I found the main conference room filled with officers, federal agents, and city officials.

Chief Johnston stood at the podium with a framed certificate and what appeared to be an award plaque.

"Ladies and gentlemen," Johnston began, "we're here today to recognize the exceptional work of Mr. Harry Starke in exposing the corruption that has damaged our department and endangered our community."

Kate smiled at me from the front row while Captain Hayes nodded approvingly. Even some officers who'd initially resented my involvement had come to respect the thoroughness of our investigation.

"Mr. Starke's investigation led to the arrest and conviction of a corrupt police captain, the dismantling of a regional criminal network, and the implementation of reform measures that will protect our community for years to come."

Johnston looked at me and nodded for me to come

forward. I frowned, looked around, but saw only smiling faces, so I reluctantly stepped forward.

Johnston presented me with the award: "For Outstanding Service in the Pursuit of Justice." It was a nice gesture, but I didn't feel right in accepting it.

"More importantly," Johnston continued, "Mr. Starke honored the memory of one of our own, Detective Frank Callahan."

At that, everyone stood and clapped. Me, I leaned forward toward the mike and said, "Thank you. I really appreciate it. Frank was my friend and mentor. I'm accepting this on his behalf. Thank you."

After the ceremony, Kate and I walked out to the parking lot together. Samson padded alongside, wearing his badge and harness.

"So what's next for you?" Kate asked.

"Hayes wants me to continue with the internal investigation. After that, probably back to insurance fraud and cheating spouses."

"Somehow I doubt you'll be satisfied with routine cases after this."

I shrugged. "I was a cop for more than eleven years, Kate. Add another eighteen months of this investigation, it will be thirteen. I'll be glad to get back to my team and what I do best."

Kate smiled. "Frank said that the best investigators are driven by curiosity rather than glory. You've got plenty of curiosity left."

LATER THAT AFTERNOON, I DROVE TO CHATTANOOGA NATIONAL Cemetery where Frank had been buried with full honors three months earlier. His grave was marked by a simple headstone that read "Detective Frank Callahan He Never Gave Up."

I placed a small American flag beside the headstone and sat on the nearby bench. The cemetery was quiet except for the distant hum of traffic and the occasional rustle of leaves in the old oak trees that provided shade for the rows of white markers.

"We got them, Frank," I said quietly. "Morrison's in prison for life, Catherine's building a new life helping other trauma survivors, and every one of your corruption suspicions turned out to be right. Seventy-three cases, Frank. Seventy-three families who deserved better than what they got from the system."

The afternoon sun cast long shadows across the cemetery grounds, and I found myself remembering our conversations over the years. Frank's methodical approach to evidence, his refusal to accept convenient explanations, his insistence that victims deserved the truth no matter how long it took to find it.

A gentle breeze rustled the trees around the cemetery, and somewhere in the distance I could hear the sound of a train whistle as freight cars rolled through the valley.

I sat there alone for almost an hour, thinking about the past three months and all that had happened. And, even today, thinking back on it, I still can't fully grasp the enormity of it.

"I keep thinking about that evidence board in your office. All those red strings connecting the dots that everyone else missed. You were something else, Frank. I love you, man!"

As I prepared to leave, I thought about the phone call that

had started everything. Kate's voice telling me Frank was dead, murdered while working on the case that had consumed his retirement.

"Rest in peace, my old friend," I said, finally.

ONE YEAR LATER, ALMOST TO THE DAY, AT EIGHT-THIRTY ON A Monday morning, I walked into my offices and knocked on Jacque's door frame. She looked up from her computer, her mouth opened in surprise and then snapped shut. She gulped, stood up and said, "Oh... my God. Will you look at what the cat dragged in?" She came around the desk, threw her arms around my neck and kissed me on the cheek. "You back to stay?" she asked. "We need all the help we can get. Will you just look at dat?" She gestured to the healthy stack of new client files.

"Yep," I replied. "I'm back. Where is everybody?"

"Let's go see," she said.

We found Tim hunched over his computer as usual. He was working on a routine insurance fraud case rather than tracking corrupt police officers. The familiar sight brought a smile to my face—normalcy had finally returned to our operations.

"Harry," he yelled when he saw me. "You're back." And he jumped to his feet.

TJ emerged from the break room with his morning coffee, looking more relaxed than I'd seen him in months. "No shit?" he said. "Finally. You back, or what?"

"I'm back. Where's Heather?"

"She's wrapping up a surveillance case in Knoxville," he replied. "She should be back this afternoon. Nothing's more exciting than a cheating spouse and a bunch of hidden assets," he said with a grin.

"Okay," I said, "lock it up, Jacque. I'm taking you all out to breakfast. Cracker Barrel okay?"

As we gathered our things and headed for the door, I felt something I hadn't experienced in months: contentment. The internal investigation had been necessary work, important work, but it had also been a weight on my shoulders that I hadn't fully realized until it was gone.

"Boss," Tim said as we walked toward the elevator, "it's good to have you back. The office hasn't been the same without you."

"Neither have I," I admitted. "But maybe that's not such a bad thing."

At the Cracker Barrel, over plates of eggs and country ham, Jacque filled me in on the cases they'd been handling. TJ regaled us with stories from a particularly nasty and complicated divorce case, and Tim complained good-naturedly about having to work actual business hours without the adrenaline rush of chasing corrupt cops.

"So what's next?" Jacque asked as we finished our meal.

"Next is back to what we do best," I said. "Private investigation work that doesn't involve federal agents, corrupt police officers, or people trying to kill us."

"Boring," TJ said with a mock sigh.

"I'll take boring," I replied.

Driving back to the office, I thought about Amanda and Jade, who were both thriving. Amanda's Peabody Award sat proudly on our mantelpiece, and Jade had finally gotten that promised fishing trip; several of them, in fact. We'd become a normal family again, with normal problems and normal weekend plans.

Frank's photograph still sits on the credenza behind my desk. I truly loved that man. I still do. He fundamentally changed my life in ways I'm still discovering.

The wheel had indeed turned, just as Kate had predicted. And for the first time in a long while, I was exactly where I wanted to be.

Thank you for reading *Who Killed Frank?* the twenty-sixth book in the Harry Starke Novels. I hope you enjoyed it, if you did please help others find Blair Howards books by leaving a few words about it in the form of a review.

The next book in this series is in the works.

If you would like to read more from Blair Howard please look to the next page for his full list of work.

Short Stories and Novellas

Buried Secrets(Harry Starke)

The Painted Lady(Kate Gazzara)

Stand Alone

Hunter's Moon(Kate & Harry)

Series

The Harry Starke Genesis Series

9 Books in Series as of 2025

The Harry Starke Series

26 Books in Series as of October 2025

The Lt. Kate Gazzara Murder Files

22 Books in Series as of October 2025

Randall And Carver Mysteries

4 Books in Series as of October 2025

The Peacemaker Series

3 Books in Series as of October 2025

The O'Sullivan Chronicles: Civil War Series

5 Books in Series as of October 2025

Science Fiction From Blair C. Howard

The Sovereign Star Series

7 Books in Series as of October 2025

also available in German

Blair Howard is the international best-selling author of more than seventy novels that span the worlds of gritty detective fiction, espionage thrillers, sweeping historicals, and hard-science military space opera. A Royal Air Force veteran and former journalist, he draws upon a rich background of service and storytelling to breathe life into unforgettable characters such as ex-cop turned private eye Harry Starke, and the fiercely determined homicide detective Lt. Kate Gazzara, who breaks her own trail as the head of a serious-crimes unit.

Under his sci-fi pen name Blair C. Howard, he expands his reach into the cosmos with the Sovereign Stars saga—an epic journey born from his lifelong love of the heavens, and the Predecessors hard science fiction trilogy. Whether unraveling a brutal crime scene or commanding starships in interstellar conflict, his stories are propelled by relentless pacing, vivid realism, and a watchful eye for justice.

Visit www.blairhowardbooks.com.
Email: BlairHoward@BlairHowardBooks.com

You can also find Blair Howard on Social Media

*9 7 9 8 9 9 8 8 0 2 4 7 8 *